Almost Home
The
New Paltz
Novel

Almost Home: The New Paltz Novel

by Frank Marcopolos

Copyright © 2011 by Frank Joseph Marcopolos

Cover design and photography by and copyright 2015,
    Frank J. Marcopolos

Book design by Invisible Order

Frank J. Marcopolos

Visit my website at http://www.FrankMarcopolos.com

Printed in the United States of America

Published April 2015

ISBN (Print): 978-0-9862428-4-7

Almost Home

The New Paltz Novel

By Frank Marcopolos

Critical acclaim for the stories of Frank Marcopolos

"There's plenty here that Updike and Cheever fans will like, even if they've never given postmodernism a second glance."

— **Kirkus Reviews**

"Almost Home *by Frank Marcopolos is a fun and fast-paced novel about the seedy side of student life on a college campus in upstate New York — a netherworld, like any college town, where young adults create lives for themselves, yet are too young to realize the consequences of their actions.*

Almost Home *keeps you in its thrall. The language rings true — and reads seamlessly within each character's alternating chapters. The vivid atmosphere settled me in a sleepy burg where the cultural and social center was the college. The powerful and vivid atmosphere, much the same as when I was in college, although much more hypnotic and alluring, goes further. It seduces one to remain on the cusp of adulthood forever. In* Almost Home *that powerful temptation seems possible — at the price of selling one's soul."*

— **Kathleen Maher**
Author of *Diary of a Heretic*

"Once my brain had time to fill in all the gaps, I would say that Marcopolos can certainly weave a tale. In this story's case, the end justifies the means. Yes, the process of figuring out what was going on made for a rough read. But after everything ties together you can't help but think that it was a really good story."

— **Alain Gomez**
Author of the *Space Hotel* series

"Marcopolos' descriptions snap back and forth between playful and gritty, and the narratives in each short piece are well-paced. One unfurls to reveal a woman who seems lovely and exciting at first, but who, as the story continues, has definite chips in her veneer; another reveals the pathos of the secret-agent-turned voyeur, who, like his expensive watch, was once awe-inspiring and manly, but is now beat up and dirty."

— **Tracy Lawson**
Author of *Counteract*

"These are rich quick-paced stories where not a lot happens, but still manage to be page-turning because of Marcopolos' clean, spirited prose. Complex, even profound, stories leave the reader with more questions than answers, which is part of the book's appeal. Marcopolos is an eloquent and provocative writer. These are strong stories that work very well."

— **Self-Publishing Review**

"It does hold together, it's a wonderful read, but I give up on trying to coherently explain it."

— **Ann Sterzinger**
Author of *NVSQVAM (Nowhere)*

For Bill

1

Prinziatta

"Everything is a fight. You want comfort, go see your moth..." Queen Elizabeth's words evaporated.

Xena the Warrior Princess was running toward me. She pulled up right in front of me. Her brown eyes — Japanimation large and bright — dominated her otherwise small-featured face. They burned with the spark of challenge, an unmistakable flame mixed with mischief and cunning sport that said, "I challenge you to *win* me, to *steal* me from another man, and to *love* me like madness. I challen, no, I double-dog *dare* you to."

Breaths heavy, *she* said, "Are you... a brother?" She tugged up a leather bracelet on her right upper arm. Her apple-curve cheeks glowed with pink-tinged chaos.

Nervous anxiety, skittish and strung-out, bubbled up my gut. Our eyes bolt-locked onto each other's. I thought, *my God.* In a paternal tone, higher-pitched than would have preferred, but still befitting my Jesus of Nazareth costume, I managed to say, "We are all brothers and sisters in the eyes of God, my child."

Xena pulled loose brown bang-strands away from her forehead. They swung right back. She looked down, then back up. Her tawny eyes still gleamed with that mysterious flame of joyful adventure. "Uhh, no," she said. A smile tugged at the sides of her mouth. "I meant, are you a Sammy brother? There's an emergency meeting in the kitchen about a passed-out stripper and I'm rounding people up."

Disappointment struck me as I realized that this encounter was more random than I had thought. I gently smoothed out some dirt with my right, sandal-bound, foot. "Oh, uhh. Then, no. I'm not."

"Okay then. See ya!" She turned to go, but her eyes—still lit by that alluring, dangerous fire—stayed locked on mine a little too long. She bumped into some other dude, laughed, then continued on her way toward the house.

Queen Elizabeth, known as Shannon Hestian on non-Halloween nights, said, "Stop ogling, dude. She's not even the hottest Xena at this party." She poured yellow beer from her orange cup through her red lips.

The spell broke. It felt like being jerked awake from a wet dream. "Huh? Who is that girl? No, I'm good. I'm good."

The queen laughed. "Yeah?"

"She didn't do that with anyone else," I said. "Did she?"

"I think she lives in our dorm, actually. Jennifer, I think. Jennifer...Burger, or Bernice...something like that. Something with a B, I dunno. I've seen her up on the second floor. You sure you're good? You seem a little...loopy, chief."

"I'm good. I'm good, man. Oh, I mean...Your Majesty. Jennifer, huh? Jennifer Somethingwithabee?" I scanned the big Sammy House backyard. Bunches of co-eds on the mud and grass patches swayed to the music booming from big speakers on the house's wrap-around porch. "But she didn't do that with anyone else, though," I said.

"Yeah? And?" Shannon said.

"Y'know, when I used the bathroom in the basement, I *thought* I saw one of the girls from Rolando's in there, hanging out with the stoner guys on the couch," I said. "And she was there, too. But I didn't know who she was, this Jennifer Somethingwithabee."

"And how would you know a girl from Rolando's, exactly?"

"So I like looking at hot chicks dancing without their clothes on. So, sue me."

"Yah," said Shannon.

My mind insisted on returning to a point that seemed small yet colossal. I said, "And the thing is, she did *not* do that with any of the other guys out here."

"Yeah, okay. Can you stop saying that, please?" Shannon said. Her light blue eyes flipped upward and back. "'Kay, so, what's on that little mind of yours?"

"I dunno," I said. "Something. Somethingwithabee, maybe. Hey, let's go find out."

"Find out what?"

"Hey, let's go find out about this girl," I said. "This girl, I dunno, she feels different."

"Excuse me?"

"She feels like a Pedro Martinez curveball," I said. "There are lotsa pretty girls, and they're like a Pedro fastball, y'know? Powerful, yeah, and can blow right past you, make you swing for the fences and fail. But then this girl, she's more like a Pedro curveball. She's unexpected, soft, swerving, arcful, and artful.

The way she moves, it's poetry. It's unusually beautiful. A Pedro curveball."

"You're starting to worry me, Enz," Shannon said. "You got all that from a five-second encounter?"

An electric energy seized me, a super-charged need to take immediate action. I smiled. I took in a deep, gathering breath, trying to cobble together my fractured nerve. I could feel the rise and smoke of the amped emotions mixing in me. I enjoyed it. I craved it. I got off on it. "That's all I need, shorty. Follow me," I said. "If you wanna have some fun, that is. Your Majesty."

"No," said Shannon. She grabbed my forearm, arresting my progress. "Enzo, whatever's going through your head, and I can see it in your eyes, whatever it is, you got something going on up there. I am telling you, it's a bad idea. These guys don't... you don't wanna mess with these guys, dude."

"Don't be such a wuss, man," I said. "Relax. This is me. I got this." I flashed the most convincing smile I could muster at her.

Shannon grabbed my white tunic's collar. She pulled me in tight, looking up straight into my eyes. "Enzo," she said. "I am warning you. If you interfere with frat-house business, you will regret it. Do not do anything stupid just because some cute girl gave you a look. Promise me."

"Okay, I promise," I said. "You win."

"Good," said Shannon. She let go of my lapels. "Didn't mean to get rough on ya, buddy, but you were gonna do something really stupid."

"See ya later, non-believer," I said. "Had my fingers crossed!" I jogged toward the Sammy frat house.

A plan had congealed in my endrunkened mind. After about eight beers, my bravado started to outweigh my cautiousness, and risky, dangerous ideas like this one made perfectly good sense. The Duke LaCrosse "rape" case flashed through my mind. Then came that fixer guy from *Pulp Fiction*.

"Hey!" I heard Queen Elizabeth holler after me, but it sounded way off in the distance, like a fading memory.

A crowd of nervous-looking kids surrounded the doorway connecting the back porch to the Sammy-house kitchen. Some were looking inside, others were just buzzing to each other with concerned looks on their faces. Jennifer Somethingwithabee was leaning in, looking over people on the outermost ring of the crowd.

I approached her, and placed my hand on the small of her back.

She half-turned toward me.

In a deep, resonant voice I whispered, "The funny thing is...when you meet a total stranger...if you let the moment slip, nothing new will *ever* come into your life." I let the words linger for a moment, then removed my hand from her back. Our eyes never disconnected.

I backed up a half-step. I said, loud to the crowd, "Make a hole! Make a hole! Make it wiiiide! Comin' through!" The crowd parted. I lifted my chest, threw my head back, and sauntered right through and into the house, playing it Bogart all the way.

In the kitchen, a small ring of frat boys dressed up like various NFL and NBA players surrounded a barely dressed, light-skinned, pretty black girl, lying on the linoleum. They were just sort of milling around the body, in groups of two or three, arguing with flailing hands and expletives flying through the air.

Jennifer ran into the kitchen. She whispered into one of the NFL players' ears.

I winked at her, then walked over to the stripper, feeling

the hard stares on me from all the Sammy boys the whole way. I kneeled down next to her. I placed my right index finger on the side of her neck. I looked up and, in the most authoritative voice I could muster, announced: "Okay, people! She still has a pulse. This is good, because it means that she's not dead yet. Was she drunk, or doing any kinda drugs?"

Jennifer the Warrior Princess flitted over. She knelt down next to me. In an *E.R.*-type performance-voice, she said, "She must have ingested several forms of dangerous substances, Doc. Alcohol, marijuana, cocaine, heroin. Who *knows* what else? What should we do now, Doctor? Prep her for a stomach-pumping?"

"Well, look," I said, more to the room than the Warrior Princess. "What we need to do now is call an ambulance, call Nine-One-One, and get the E.M.T.'s here *now*. If she turns up dead, you guys are toast. So, you basically have to hope like hell she turns out okay. But if you don't get the E.M.T.'s here now, you'll be completely *fucked*." A giant smile spread across my face as I finished my prepared script. I looked at Jennifer Some-thingwithabee, Xena, with stern reassurance in my eyes, to let her know I had the entire situation under control. Somewhere in the dark mileage of the night, I heard the distant wail of an ambulance siren. I looked up.

A little guy in a Benito Mussolini costume stepped out from the crowd. He dripped with the authoritative confidence of someone who was proud of his high rank. He looked like he enjoyed executing the fullest extent of his despotic power daily, just because he could. "Who the hell are you?" he said to me. "Who the hell is this?" he said to the brethren.

My confidence transformed into a confrontational anger boiling like lava beneath the surface. Keep cool, I told myself.

Keep cool, but stay ready to attack. I stood. "I'm Enzo," I said. "Enzo Prinziatta." I stabbed out my handshake hand.

He ignored it. "Well, *I'm* Barry Budski, President Budski, actually, and I run shit around here. I dunno who you think you are, and what you think you're doing…"

"I'm just trying to help, dude," I said.

"And you," he said to Xena. "Get the hell up. Don't be encouraging this guy. Whoever he is."

Xena, short-fingered hands on thighs, stood up, slow, with a sheepish, embarrassed look all over her face.

"Look," I said.

"No, *you* look," Budski returned fire before I could make any kind of argument, before I could win the room, before I could win Jennifer Somethingwithabee. "Thanks but no thanks. We got this shit handled. We already called 9-1-1. How dumb do you think we are?"

"This *is* a frat house," I said. "What else could I assume?"

"Jimmy, Tommy, Leonard, get this ass-clown outta here," Mussolini said.

Three dudes emerged from the crowd and grabbed me.

"We don't have time for this shit," Mussolini said. "Make sure not to rough him up too bad. Disposal. And get ridda this, too. Chardine had it on. Make sure you bury it good." Mussolini tossed a white Sigma Alpha Mu T-shirt at them.

One of them snatched it. They shoved me toward the door. The ambulance sirens wailed louder.

"*Disposal*, you heard me?" Mussolini said.

I turned and spotted Jennifer leaning on Barry Mussolini, with one arm draped around his shoulders, amid a semi-circle of brothers. She smiled at something he said, whisper-kissed something in his ear, then laughed an easy, inebriated laugh, like she was the most secure girl on Earth.

My gut bottomed out. "Fuck," I whispered. As a Hail Mary, I said, "Hey, you might want to, uhh, take this a little more seriously. That girl could be in serious trouble, dude."

"She'll be fine," Barry said. "Probably just passed out drunk. Happens all the time. Like I said, we got our scandals handled, *Señor Jesu Christo*. Guys? Take care of him already?"

The three frat goons pushed, yanked, and pulled me out of the house, past all the merry partiers, out through a chain-link gate, and into an enclosed area where a bunch of garbage cans overflowed with rotting frat trash.

Guessing at their pugilistic intentions, I said, "C'mon, guys, no harm done here, right?"

"Hey, you heard the Prez," one of them said. "He said take it easy on ya."

"Exactly," I said, relaxing a bit. "So there's no need to—"

The three of them grabbed different parts of me. They chucked me into the rubber garbage cans.

As I hit the concrete, I felt shivery fear mix with the physical pain running down my left side. Disposal, Mussolini had said. Maybe that meant these cretins were going to bury me.

I hauled myself off the ground. Smirking, the three goons approached me. I threw a right cross at the fat one's head, but he flinched and turned. It landed on his shoulder. Then they were on me. I shielded myself as best I could, and got in a random punch and kick or two, but still. It was a beat-down.

When they finished beating me, the fat one ripped the gold #42 pendant off the chain around my neck. He laughed.

"Hey, price o' gold these days, man!" the tall one said. He flipped the white Sammy T-shirt toward the rubber trash cans. Then they walked off, laughing.

I laid still as stone, bleeding in the garbage. I touched my face to survey the bloody damage. It didn't seem so bad. I grabbed the T-shirt. I held it against some of my cuts, to help stop the blood flow.

Then my thoughts returned to what I had lost. "Not the pendant," I muttered. "Not the fucking pendant. Damn it!" I pounded the ground with the bottom of my fist. It didn't hurt bad enough.

Budski

That was not at all cool, I thought. Some guy trying to get all heroic on my turf, in *my* kitchen? Um, no. I looked at Jenny. When she caught my stare, I brushed some imaginary dirt off my shoulder and smiled, Jay-Z cool.

She smiled her *Maxim*-girl smile back at me.

"Okay guys, listen up," I said to the brotherhood and the girlfriends assembled in the kitchen. "We need to get our act together here. Who has pics or video of Chardine here on their cells?"

Three reluctant hands went up.

"All right, lemme have 'em."

"What are you gonna do with 'em?" Johnny McMahen said.

"You'll get 'em back, trust me," I said. "Just wanna swipe all the pics off."

They handed the phones up. I shook my head. Even in my

own house with my own guys who wouldn't have a pot to piss in if it wasn't for me, everything was a God-damned negotiation.

"Okay, now. You three guys stay here, and when the paramedics arrive, you let 'em know what happened. Which is that she came in, started dancing, and then passed out. Nobody gave her shit. Nobody touched her. Nobody did anything. Got it?"

"Gotcha boss," Ed Stanley said.

"Okay, Bobby and Marcus, need you to go close down the kegs outside, and start herding people out. Just say the party's over because... a storm's coming or something."

"No prob," said Marcus. They hurried out.

"Okay, everyone else up to my room. Jenny, you come with. But no other girlfriends. All the other girlfriends go home. We'll get with you later and give you information. After we sort this all out. Don't talk to anyone about this until I come talk to you. Okay, let's go."

Don't die, I thought. Just. Don't. Die. Please, God. Don't let her die. Please. Anything less and I won't have to involve him. Just. Don't. Die.

Everyone assembled up in my room, squeezing into the space.

I felt a pang of anxiety forming at the prospect of doing public speaking even in this small way, in front of my own bros. I tried a new technique I had read about recently: I forced myself to become happy about the anxiety. I blew out an exhale. It didn't seem to be helping. "Uhh," I said. "Okay. Now, we've gotta be smart about the situation we have downstairs. So, lemme ask one more time. Any other cell phones with video or pics on them of the stripper?"

"Yeah, I do," Kent Clarke said. "I snapped, like, I dunno, five or six maybe."

"All right, lemme see, Man-Super," I said.

Man-Super fiddled with the phone, then passed it up.

I examined the pics. Nothing seemed exculpatory. I thought about deleting them, then decided against it. "I'm gonna hold your phone for the night, Man-Super, same as the other three. Okay?"

"Yeah, fine, whatever you want, Barry," he said.

"So, now," I said. "Anyone give her anything? Anything at all. Drinks, drugs, prescription drugs? Aspirin for a headache. Anything."

"Wait. Who was this girl anyway?" Man-Super said. "I mean, did we just call up Dial-A-Stripper and get this chick or what?"

"Not that it matters much, but no, rook. We got a long-standing deal with Rolando's where they send us a girl or two whenever we have a blowout, and we make sure our guys frequent their business every week. So, to get to the root of your question, we did not compensate this girl for her time. Which is good. As far as narrative goes, she came over here of her own free will to party, as girls tend to do, and just started doing what comes natural to a stripper."

"Which is?" Juan Arroz said.

"Take her clothes off and dance to Def Leppard tunes," I said.

"Right!" Juan said. A ripple of laughter vibrated through the room.

"So, did anybody give her something? That's gonna be important, if this thing goes bad," I said.

Silence for a few seconds. My room was a large space, but the guys were still all crammed in to fit in there. I probably should have used a different room with more space, but I just instinctively directed everyone up here for some reason. I'd have to think about why I made that decision in a moment of crisis and try to make a correction for similar situations in the future.

Finally, Roger Freldo, a junior with a full beard and a "Don't Fear the Reefer" hoodie said, "Uhh, I mighta smoked her out, dude."

Roger was our resident pothead. I wasn't thrilled about having a resident pothead in the house, but there wasn't much I could do about it. It was a part of frat-house culture, a part of the college culture. For now, anyway. Still, it made me nervous, mainly because of the unnecessary risk it exposed us to. "Weed?" I said.

"Well, *my* weed," he said, smiling with a goofy, gleaming pride.

"Oh shit," I said. "What's mixed in?"

"Hah, nothing, really," he said. "A little Sally-D, a sprinkle of heron, that's it. Totally mellow-ass high, and nothing that'd kill you, that's for sure. She took, like, three tokes, most. No way that could knock anybody out," he said.

"Yeah, but what if she did a bunch of other stuff before she got here?" I said. "You start combining shit, and there's a multiplier effect."

Roger shrugged. "Then it ain't our fault. What she did on her own time's on her."

"Agreed," I said, "but we have to look at this from all angles, including public relations. That's what worries me. But hopefully she'll be all right, and it won't even be an issue."

"Fuckin' lightweight," Roger said. "No good deed, know what I'm sayin'? Or no good *weed*, I should say. Shit."

The guys laughed again, a nervous kind of laughter.

Jenny leaned in toward me. She whispered into my ear, "We might have another issue. With that kid you kicked out. I'll tell you later."

"Okay," I said. "We'll handle that next."

"It's no big deal, but I just wanted to let you know."

"Thanks, babe," I said. "Good lookin' out." I kissed her robust cheek.

"Get a room!" one of the guys said.

I heard footstomps bum-leaping the stairs. A feeling hit me—this wasn't right, wasn't going to turn out right. Something was going to come up aces and eights.

Nick Jackson ran into the room, out of breath with the look of death on his blanched face.

"Boss?" he said.

"Yeah?"

"We got issues."

"Yeah?"

"That stripper downstairs?"

"Yeah?"

"She's, uhh. She's, like, dead, dude."

I considered the news for a moment. My spirits deflated. "*And* we got a non-Greek witness that we just sent out for disposal," I said. "Shit. Shitshitshit."

There was just no way around it now, no way to avoid it. I was definitely going to have to call my dad.

When everyone cleared out and I could shed the tough-guy persona, I got down on one knee and said a prayer for Chardine. I also prayed for divine forgiveness for the fact that I couldn't protect her, couldn't save her. In my house, it all came back to me, I knew. So, I felt responsible. And that was one heavy-ass weight to carry.

Prinziatta

I slowly, gently, maneuvered my way into a standing position. I heard footsteps pounding toward me. I prayed it was not the second wave of the beat-down spree. The footsteps stopped as a shadow fell beside me.

"Oh my God, are you okay?" Shannon Hestian said. "Enzo, are you all right?"

I looked up. Her face was full of motherly concern. "Yeah, I'm fine," I said. My voice-tone, groggy and unstable, contradicted my words. "No problem."

"You don't *look* fine," she said. "Here lemme see." She held my face in her hands, surveyed the damage. "You need to go to the E.R. right now. Get checked out. Make sure everything's really okay. Come on, I'll get us a ride." She turned to go.

"No, stop. I'll just rub some dirt on it," I said. "Not a problem."

"Don't be ridiculous," she said. "I'm taking you to the E.R. right now. And then we're gonna file a report with the police against those thugs." She grabbed my wrist and yanked me toward Eastern Street.

"No, seriously, stop it, Shan," I said. "File a report? You gotta be kidding me. I'll be fine. I need to get back to my room, wash up. Just lie down. Maybe see where Semzy and the guys are at. I think they said they're goin' to P&G's."

"Don't be crazy," she said. "You'll do no such thing. You need someone to look after you, not pound some beers. You're hurt. You need the right kind of attention."

"Thanks, but no thanks," I said. I jerked my arm out of her grasp. "I'm fine, Shan. Really. I'll go back to my room and just chill. Leave me alone. I don't want you to take care of me. Lemme just get back to my room. I'll see ya later." I started walking the other way, toward campus.

"You're gonna need someone to look after you, Enzo!" she said, fading in the distance. "You will!" It sounded more like grandmotherly advice than an argument to let her take me to the emergency room.

I felt bad because she was just trying to help, but Shannon was a smotherer, and I wasn't in the mood for smothering.

I stopped for a second. My head pounded, more from humiliation than the blows, most likely. I palmed the now-bloody Sammy T-shirt like a softball, held it against my pounding head, and rested in the New Paltz street-lamp light, darkness, and shadow. When the pounding subsided, I jammed the T-shirt into my Jesus-robe pocket. My left side still pulsed with a dull ache, but it felt manageable.

Some doofus yelled out from across the street, "Hey, Jesus! Looks like Pilate got the best of ya!"

"Don't worry," I yelled back. "I forgive your asshole-ness, my child!" I got going again, and picked up the pace.

Back in my dorm suite, I cleaned myself up, calmed myself

down. Changed into a sweatshirt and jeans. I'd had enough of
being the Son of God for one day. I chucked the bloody Sammy
T-shirt under my twin bed. "Fuckin' Sammy," I said.

I looked over at Fred, my flame-tailed tetra. He swiveled
his swim, carefree and happy as always. I walked over to his
tank and sprinkled in some food. "Gotta keep your strength up,
buddy," I said. "Hard morning tomorrow." I was training him to
be an attack fish.

The school had a policy against students keeping pets in the
dorms, attack fish included. But I *had* to bring Fred. I owned
a bunch of cool-looking tetras, different kinds, in a big tank at
home, but I snuck my first and favorite, Fred, and a little three-
gallon tank into my room on moving day. I kept a beach towel
nearby for whenever I needed him to get stealthy for Resident
Assistant check-ins. I don't know why I liked tetras so much.
They're beautiful creatures, certainly, but beyond that, they just
had a calming effect on me. Maybe it was the way they moved,
smooth and burden-free, in the water. I don't know.

I called home on the landline. Got the answering machine.
I called my mom's cell. Got her friggin' voicemail. "Hi mom," I
said. "Guess you're out dancing or whatever. Just wanted to let
you know...well. I just wanted to say I love you and I miss you.
I'm having fun, too, but I just wanted to let you know that.
Nothing urgent. Call me when you get a chance. Don't stay out
too late, now."

In the era of cougars and MILFs, my widowed mother had
found her dancing shoes and a different flirt-target almost every
night. She said it made her feel young again. Made her *feel* for
the first time since my dad passed. All it made me feel was sick.

I texted Semzy. The guys, my boys, my teammates, my true
bros, were downing beers at P&G's, he replied. After lying down
for a while and feeling much better, I headed out, ready to bury

my anger and humiliation with beer. The kind of in-your-face embarrassment I had just endured would require at least five beers per hour, I figured. Even at that rate, the wound of shame would still be pretty hard to heal.

I walked into the bar and saw Semzy and starting short-stop Jared Besto sitting at a table in the corner to the right of the entrance. A tray of fifty-cent beers in clear plastic cups, like amber waves of pain-salve, spread out before them on the table. The Drive-By Truckers played overhead.

I threw myself down, grabbed a plastic cup, and poured. "You will *not* believe what just happened to me," I said. I told them the story.

They laughed, falling over each other in hysterics. Jared almost disappeared within Semzy's massive retro Red Wings jersey, with Semzy slapping Jared's yellow graphic Polo. It felt good to have such close, compassionate friends.

"Fuckin' loser," said Jared. "Never fuck with the frats. That's, like, Campus Etiquette One-Oh-One, dude."

"Hey, at least I tried *some*thing," I said. "You losers woulda just stood there babbling with Hot Shannon. Least I tried. Damn."

"Wait, wait," Jared said. "You were with Hot Shannon, and you went after some *other* chick?"

"Yeah," I said. "Shannon's just my friend."

"You never told me that, dude," Jared said. He quickly ran a hand through his curly hair. It immediately reverted back into place, like brown shrubbery.

"Don't you get enough pussy as it is?" I said.

"Ain't no such thing as enough pussy, brother," he said. "And I am telling you that *that* girl's way too fine for me to forget that you told me you're friends with her."

"Jesus Christ, man," I said, my voice rising with frustrated anger. "For the last time, I'm good friends with Hot Shannon!"

I watched Semzy's and Jared's faces contort into embarrassed expressions of warning and caution.

Then I heard Shannon's voice behind me: "Uhh, you call me *Hot* Shannon, Enzo?"

A pang of embarrassed disgust arose from my gut. My face warmed. This was turning out to be the Worst. Night. Eva. I turned to Her Hotness and said, "Yeah, well. There's a lotta Shannons runnin' around. It's hard to keep track of all o' ya."

She smiled with self-satisfaction. "Yeah, okay," she said. "You need your rest. And *even*tually you'll realize you need someone, maybe even someone hot, taking good care of you. Don't stay out too late, Enzo." She turned and bounced back to her friends on the other side of the bar. They were sitting with the school's biggest sports star, a breast-stroke champion named Phillip Donpiseo, whom everyone called, "Flipper the Swimmer."

Was she following me? When did she get there? It was confusing. What the hell? I needed more beer to get some clarity on the issue.

"G.," Semzy said.

"God save the Queen!" said Jared.

"What?" I said. I downed a whole cup of beer. I picked another off the tray, but I kept it in front of me. I rotated the cup a quarter-turn.

Semzy said, "She so wants to be yo' li'l wifey." Facially, Lakewood "Semzy" Semend looked like Buck O'Neil, the great negro-leagues player, with that wise and reassuring quality his face held. His body most closely resembled a Mack truck.

"Nah, you're crazy, dude," I said. "She's like my annoying little sister or something." I turned the cup another quarter-turn.

"You're nuts, dude," Jared said. "You're soooo introducing me to her, in like five minutes, dude."

"Yo, listen up, though. Some shit popped off before. You need to hear this," Semzy said.

I turned the cup another quarter-turn. "Yeah?" I said. I drank a sip of the piss-beer. It wasn't really helping me feel any less shameful. I turned the cup another quarter-turn.

"Oh yeah, that's right," Jared said. "Coach was just in here. He said that guy, that Budski kid you were talking about, the Sammy bigshot or whatever. He's, like, trying out for the team tomorrow. Coach's been trying to get him to come down for like a year now."

"You *can't* be serious," I said. I quarter-turned the cup.

"I is," said Semzy.

I slapped the table. "That's great, just great," I said. "So now I gotta get along with this guy? Unbefuckinglievable. Fuck!"

"Ain' no thing, man," Semzy said.

"Wait," I said. "What is he? A sophomore?"

"Yeah," said Jared. "I think so."

"That doesn't make any sense," I said.

"Why not?" said Jared.

"Well, he seemed like he was running the frat house." I said. "I mean, he flat-out told me that he was in charge of the place. How's a sophomore running a frat house? That's crazy."

"Don't know," said Semzy. "Don't care. Maybe the boy was frontin.'"

Jared shrugged. "Guess we'll find out at some point. If the kid decides to play."

"I guess," I said. I gulped down the rest of my cup, poured, gulped, poured. "Hey, Semz," I said. "I'm gonna throw tomorrow, right?"

"Yeah," he said. "Coach said."

"Good," I said. "I'm gonna knock this kid on his pompous ass."

"Don't be stupid," Semzy said. "No reason to start beefin' over this shit now. Let it go, dawg. You don't want no war with Sammy. Nah. Best let it be. You fucked up, they made you pay, call it even. You still alive. Shit, you came out on top in the deal, even." He and Jared laughed.

"Yeah," I said. "You're right. Let it be. Of course. Of course. You're right."

But of course I could not, and would not, let it *be*.

Budski

The Director of Greek Affairs was definitely not thrilled about the situation. I knew this because when I walked into his office the day after the stripper incident he said, "Barry, I'll be honest with you. I am definitely not thrilled about the situation." He pulled a bottle of The Glenlivet from the bottom drawer of his desk and shook it at me. "You mind?"

"Nah, go 'head," I said. "It's happy hour. You're entitled. None for me though, Professor."

"Splendid." He poured himself a short glass and placed it on his sturdy oak desk. He looked like the very stereotype of a college professor — glasses, tweed, elbow patches, the whole deal. He knew he fit the stereotype, he had told me at a party once, but he thought his awareness of it made the look "ironic," and thereby post-modernly cool. Purely delusional, but the intel had helped me appeal to his "Prof-Vanity" on more than one occasion. "Know thy enemy," my dad had told me about a million times.

I felt my gears grinding. I knew what I had to do, but knowing it didn't make me hate the dance any less. "But about what you said about our situation here, I can appreciate what you're saying, Professor Gembull," I said. I became aware of the repulsion I felt, and made a mental note to try and control my body language. The "tells." To keep everything copacetic. I wondered whether he knew exactly how transparent he was being. He probably thought he was being pretty clever. Suave as hell. Gloriously ironical. And *that's* how he'd tell the story to his wife, to his mistress, to whomever he was trying to impress at the little Prof-Parties. The pontificating prick.

"You know that up until now I've done everything in my power to help you guys out, and protect you as much as possible, whenever possible," the Professor said.

"And we certainly do appreciate that as well," I said.

"So, it brings me a great amount of sadness, this situation we have here," Professor Gembull said. "A great amount of sadness. Because, due to the nature of the incident, and just the plain undeniable facts we have to deal with here, I'm not so sure there's very much I can do this time."

"I understand," I said. "Whatever you can do, even if it's only give us a little extra time to get our affairs in order, that would certainly be appreciated."

"Where was the House Mother during all this mess? Ol' whatsername?"

"Mrs. Tilden," I said.

"Yeah, Tilly. Where was she?" he said. He sipped his scotch whisky.

I shrugged. "She's an employee of the house, so for blowouts and things like that we advise her to spend the night elsewhere. That way, in case of some stupid incident, she has plausible deniability."

"Good legal position," Professor Gembull said. "But not best practices, you know." He took another drink of his scotch whisky.

The clinking ice appealed to me. I needed to cool down my internal furnace. Keep the churning under control. I shrugged with my right shoulder. The right side of my mouth curled up into an expression of, "Oh well."

"Okay," said Professor Gembull. "Let's see where this goes. You have my cell number. Call me any time if you need to chat. But I'm still not sure on this one, Barry."

A final pang of hatred struck a cord in my gut. I stood up. I slid a stuffed manila envelope across his desk. "Okay," I said. "Here's something to, perhaps, enable you to free up some of your time to make some calls, talk to some people, or whatever."

"Very gracious of you, Barry," he said. "As you know, my time is quite valuable."

That internal inferno blazed away, but I just smiled, tight-lipped, and said, "Indeed it is. Indeed it is."

"Hey, whaddaya think of this Tucker Max character maybe coming to campus?" he said.

"I think it'd be cool," I said. "I'm a fan. Gonna bring a lotta heat, probably."

"Precisely," the Professor said. "Which is why Administration wants to do it. You can't *buy* publicity like that."

I smiled, eyes included. "Exactly," I said. "Have a pleasant evening, Professor." I turned and walked out of the office. Behind me, I heard him swig down more of his drink. Damn good racket, I thought. That concluded my campus obligations.

My gut turned again, thinking of what was next: meeting with my dad. I had yet to find a coping technique in a book or from real-world experience that could help me deal with that specific anxiety. And it was the one for which I was most in need of assistance.

I drove over to Main Street, and parked the Scion in the lot behind the bar/restaurant. I looked at my reflection in the rear-view mirror. I thought: okay, now. I took care of everything that needed to be handled on campus. I took care of all the potential evidence. I greased any potentially squeaky wheels. And I'm handling the "Eat Me" girls tomorrow. That should cover it. That's every angle taken care of. My gut said something else entirely, but I told it to quiet the hell down.

I trudged into the place and there he was. Campus Legend, Alumnus Benefactor, and My Dad: Bartholomew Budski, Senior, in a navy blue Armani suit, sitting at a campus dive bar with a dark beer in his hand. The bar had only a few other patrons scattered about. It didn't really get packed until much later.

I felt the surge of anxiety, and tried to keep it under control. I took a few deep breaths, told myself not to worry, that I had everything covered. I walked in and sat down next to him. I felt my leg start to bounce up and down. I tried to get it to stop. "Hello, Father," I said. "Stella, Bobby," I said to the bartender.

"Hello, Son," said my dad. "The number's three."

"What number is three?" Always something. It was always something. He just couldn't be normal. I wish he could just be normal for once.

"The number of business meetings I had to cancel or postpone so I could come up here and handle this for you." He drank down some of his dark beer.

"It's also nice to see your oldest son, isn't it?"

"Of course, Bartholomew," he said. "But not when I am unexpectedly pulled away from important business matters."

"It's not like I planned this," I said.

"Well, maybe you *should* do more planning," he said. "Failing to plan is planning to fail." The man was full of lessons. Always had been since I was a kid. Everything was a cold, hard "life lesson," emotionless as chalk sticks.

"Okay, yeah," I said. "I know." I gulped down some of my Stella. "Listen, I just finished up with administration personnel. I hit everyone who needed a talking-to."

"And?"

"And...it went pretty well. I think that considering the fact that you're going to pay a visit tomorrow and reassure them personally....well, they're okay with it. As long as they're not gonna have any trouble with the girl's family. They're mostly concerned about bad P.R."

"And you personally destroyed any pictures, or anything potentially damaging, I assume," he said.

"Of course," I said. "That's the first thing I did."

"Good," said my dad. "How are you going to secure the stories of the witnesses?"

"Secure them?" I said.

"Yes. You had a lot of guests at this party, I assume. How can you make sure no one's gonna talk?" he said, with a lawyerly agitation in his voice.

I drank down some beer. I half-shrugged, and mumbled, "M-mmm d-know." It sounded a lot like, "I dunno know."

"*Espe*cially the girls," he said, "who might feel some sort of sororital kinship to the stripper?"

"Well, I did speak to the brothers, and they're no problem. And we told the girls not to say anything until we, until *I*, talked to them," I said. "I figured that was a pretty good way to go."

He said, "And have you done so?"

I said, "Not yet."

"Okay, the way I see it, you got two major problems here, Barry," my dad said.

My heart dropped. I knew what was coming. I could see the anger—a dirty mix of paternal disappointment and business-partner frustration—billboarded all over his Jack Welsh-like face. "Uh-huh," I said.

"One, you got a bunch of girls sitting around gossiping, with no real reason to keep their damn mouths shut other than because of your say-so. How solid do you think that is? You need to march up to that sorority house right after this, and make a deal, a sweet deal, that secures their cooperation, got it?"

My whole body clenched, hard. I drank my Stella. "Yes, sir," I said.

"And, two, that's the first thing you shoulda done, even before you went to the administration. Now you've had hours where a bunch of Chatty Cathies are running around shooting their damn mouths off because *you* didn't lock down their coordination by incentivizing their silence. Do you understand me, Barry?" His high-pitched voice didn't make the advice any easier to swallow. It was like trying to heed dire instructions from an Elmo doll.

"Yes, sir." I closed my eyes for a moment, inhaled the negative emotions through my nose, and then exhaled them through my mouth. It was a new visualization technique I had been reading about. Didn't seem to work right then. "I'll take care of it. I... I got it."

"Speaking of girls, how's that girl of yours? What's her name again? Wendy?"

"No. It's Jenny, Dad," I said. "For the millionth time. Jenny Drama's fine. She'll be fine."

"Jenny Drama?" he said, as if her name were Gonorrhea McSyphilis.

"Little nickname I have for her," I said. "Like Johnny Drama on *Entourage?*"

"Whatever, listen," he said. "You have to keep her in line, son. Discipline."

"I know, Dad."

"Girl like that, she's bound to get off track partying and socializing, all that stuff. You know she's an extreme extrovert. Away from home, free, for the first time in her life, all that stuff. She's like a social butterfly on speed. Is she going on auditions? Sending pictures to modeling agencies and whatnot?"

My gut rumbled again. I drank more beer. "Ummm," I said. "You know, it's weird, she wants to be an actress, she's a theater major and everything, but then she gets, like, lazy and stuff. I dunno."

"Lazy? How in hell are you calling yourself her manager if you're not even managing to get her into that kind of shit, Barry?" he said. "And I'm certainly not making any connections for you unless I know she's serious about this. I can't call on favors from people, and then have her flaking out. That's an embarrassment I can't have. Wasting people's time is just not acceptable."

"I, uhh," I said. "I hear ya."

"See, this is what I'm saying," he said. "You have to manage her *now*, so any success she has, *you're* responsible for it. If you wait, it'll be too late. Discipline, Barry. You can't afford to have someone else discover her, quote-unquote. Then it's, like, 'Thanks, Barry, see ya never.' You understand?"

"Yes, sir," I said. I poured the rest of the Stella down my throat. "Bobby, another beer?"

"How much did her, uhh *things*, cost again?" Dad said. He made a gesture with his hands that made it clear he was referring to her implants.

"'Leven thou."

He whistled, to say, "Wooowwww." He said, "And when do I start seeing some R.O.I.? What's it been? Like eight, nine months now?"

"Yeah, 'bout that," I said. "I'm working on it."

"Yes, but—" He cut himself short.

I could almost see him halting his true emotion, right there on his pinkened face. I felt a twinge in my gut. I felt like I was going to be sick.

"Okay, son," he said. "Just stay on her. No one gets anything for free. You start giving out gifts, everyone's got their hand out. You'll never have time for anything else. Like I said, time is a currency. Spend it wisely."

"Right-o."

"Just stay on top of her's all I'm saying," he said.

I felt ashamed, embarrassed. I hated it, maybe, but the man happened to be right. I had to quit fucking around and get my act together. Difficult as it was, getting the house up and running wasn't the endgame. It was only the first step. "I'm sorry. I'll do more to try to stay on top of her," I said. "I will. I will."

"How's the house doing otherwise?" he said.

"On track," I said. "Coming along."

"Profitable yet?"

"Dad, you know we have a five-year plan in place," I said. "Be patient. Years four and five should be black."

"Okay," he said. He chucked a couple of peanuts from the bar bowl into his mouth and looked up at the T.V.

That right there pissed me off more than anything. When I knew he had more to say, but just cut himself off with something terse, like "okay." Fucking okay. He did that kind of shit all the time and it drove me mad. I'm not even sure why. It just pissed me off.

"Just remember. Sometimes you just have to grab your balls and take action, Son," he said. "Great, you got the frat up and running. That's great, but it's done now. Now it's time to keep moving the plan forward. There's a time for finesse and there's a time for aggressive action. Get it?"

"Yes, sir," I said. "I promise." I knew then exactly what I had to do. Get both Jenny Drama and that Enzo Fucking Prinziatta in line. A.S.A.P.

Dad said, "Now, what about sports, Son? Where do we stand with that?"

"Baseball," I said. "I'm playing baseball this year."

"Good," said Dad. "You need to be getting as many athletes into the house as possible. The higher profile the better. They're the celebrities on any campus."

"I know, Dad, I know," I said. "You've said."

"Any big-time guys on the baseball team?"

"Couple guys, yeah. Some of the guys told me about this Prinziatta kid. Was a big deal in high school, then he hurt his arm. Had Tommy John, still rehabbing it. If he ever gets to even eight-five percent of what he was, he could jump to D-1. Maybe even get drafted, some people say."

"So there's your prime recruit," he said.

"Yeah," I said. "There's a small problem with that, but I'll find a way to work around it. Then there's the catcher, this 'Semzy' kid, the guys call him. All-Conference. He'll be tougher, though. Definitely a never-joiner."

"So, what is he looking to get out of his college experience? What's the man's passion?"

"Psych major," I said. "I heard he wants to get his Master's and Ph.D., and then establish a practice in the neighborhood he grew up in, in Queens. One of the bad 'hoods, Queensbridge? Something like that."

"Sounds like you've got your info-feeder network in place. That's good. Interesting," said Dad. "Okay, so, what benefits can you offer him? What is he? White, black, Latino?"

"African-American."

"Even better," Dad said. "We need more minority representation, too. So, maybe mention that we have a number of psychiatric professionals over at national that he could tap into their expertise for where the best place to go for his post-grad degrees are, how to establish his practice, stuff like that. Especially considering he wants to set up shop in a low-income area, how can he survive financially, this sort of thing."

"Right," I said. "Yeah, definitely."

"Seems like this might be a good angle you could use with the flex-purpose structure," he said.

"Yeah," I said. "Maybe."

"What's the social purpose, exactly?" he said. "Something about wells in Africa somewhere? Clean water for everyone, or some such?"

"Yeah," I lied.

"Well," he said. "That may appeal to him, then. Since he's African-American."

"True," I said.

"And never forget Feel, Felt, Found," Dad said. "I know I harp on it, but the success rate speaks for itself."

"I know, Dad, I know it," I said. "I'm gonna make a full-court press for those two guys."

"Sounds good. Anything else we need to discuss?"

"I don't think so," I said. I felt drained, like a grey-spotted and black-grit bathtub.

"Okay," said Dad. He finished his beer. "Make sure to get up to the Sigma Delta Tau house immediately and secure those bulimic bitches. Tighten up your ship." He stood up, and marched out of the bar. Just like that.

My eyes watered a bit. Trying to hide it, I dropped my forehead on my folded arms on the bar. "Pull it together, chief," I told myself. "Let's go."

I heard Bobby the bartender say, "You pickin' up his tab, too, or what?"

Prinziatta

"Okay, so we're gonna split it up like this," Coach Hicks said to all of the potential members of the 2007 New Paltz Hawks baseball team. "Upper-classmen against lower. Separate the men from the boys, here. Remember, I'm not sure right now how many guys I'm gonna carry in the spring. So, that means everyone should give it their all because you never know. I don't wanna see anyone doggin' it out there. Play hard, but play clean, boys. Coach Skybrando and I will sit your ass on the bench for any dirty stuff. We're all team-mates here, so *compete*, but we don't need anybody gettin' hurt, not during the first fall-ball intra-squad game. Got it?"

Ripples of mumbled compliance emanated from the guys. I tugged on my cap and looked up at the gloom-pregnant sky.

Coach said, "Okay, you already got the line-ups, so, Uppers you're in the field, Lowers you're up first. Let's go."

I ran out on the field, and into my position at first base. In the third inning, I noticed Jennifer, whom I found out was surnamed "Burnette," not "Somethingwithabee," climbing up into the stands behind their bench—to watch Budski, I gathered, since there weren't any other Sammy guys on the team. By the time the fifth inning rolled around, the score was tied, 2-2, and Coach brought me in to pitch. I noticed Shannon in the third base stands, behind our bench.

The first batter was a big kid, a freshman named Jimmy Brennan who, by the way he had played so far in this game, looked like he'd be starting at third base for us in the spring. I threw him a get-it-over fastball to start the at-bat and he promptly crushed it over the leftfield fence. After he connected, he stood at the plate admiring the shot for what seemed like four years. Then he took five years to get around the bases.

Coach Skybrando, umping behind the plate, threw me a new ball.

I snatched it out of the air with my glove.

Semzy ran out toward the mound. Budski was the next hitter.

"Don't do it," Semzy said.

I glared at him like he just insulted my mother. I felt betrayed, back-stabbed by the guy I most trusted. "You're kidding," I said.

"Don't do it, dawg," he said again. "Ain't worth it. Not for no intra-squad game, son."

I couldn't believe what I was hearing. It only made me dig in harder. A rising, steel-hewn-solid indignation caught in my throat. With a skewed lip and hard, narrowed eyes, I said, "Not worth it?"

"Yeah yo," said Semzy. "You just projectin' anyway." Sweat glistened off his lengthy face. His eyes were pleading with me.

I peered over at the stands behind their bench to catch an eyeful of Jennifer Burnette, dressed all in white, laughing at something. The vision brought the humiliation of what just happened—and what had happened at the Sammy house—flooding back. "I guess the integrity of the game ain't worth shit then, huh?" I said, coming back to Semzy.

"Dawg, c'mon," my catcher said. He flicked sweat off his forehead with his mask. "Just get your work in. We'll hit P&G's after, knock back some beers. Psychologically, you just projectin' yo' insecurity onto him. That's all this is, man."

"Fuck you and your Psych-Major psycho-babble," I said.

"It's truth, dawg," he said. "This ain't about no integrity of no game."

My resolve cement-hardened. "Sorry you feel that way, Semzy," I said. "You saw Brennan, standing there like he did something, and Cadillacking it around the bases. He deserves it, they deserve it. Everyone on this team needs to know how to play this game. And *not* play this game. Some freshman dumbass starts disrespecting teams, it's you or me's gonna get beaned. *That's* the truth."

"Fine. Wait 'til his dumb ass come 'round, then," Semzy said. "Let *him* get got then."

From the batter's box Budski yelled, "Hey, let's go out there! We don't got all day!" The Lowers bench laughed and began throwing out random taunts.

"*Hell's* no," I said. "They gotta learn. One of 'em screws up, it's on all of us."

"*Learn*ing," Semzy said. "It's all about learning, now? That how it is?"

"Yeah, man," I said. "That's exactly how it is."

"And this got nothin' to do with that shorty sittin' up there, lookin' all pearly white and shit?"

"Just go back there and catch my shit," I said. "Damn. Like you know somethin'."

"Why you gotta be this way?" His eyes registered his resignation. He knew that when I really wanted to do something, a freight train couldn't stop me. "Huh?"

The dangerous emo-cocktail of indignation and humiliated anger mixed and swirled in me. Lips mashed, I went to flip my #42 pendant out from beneath my orange jersey. Of course, it wasn't there. "We let this shit slide now," I said, "it gets outta hand sometime during the season, and then it's all of us on the line."

"Yo, kill the drama, biotch," he said.

"Hey," I said. "It's your ass on the line, and mine, and the rest of the guys out here."

"We ain't in Vietnam or some shit, man. Relax. Just get your work in," Semzy said. "Okay, look. Let's not make it more than it is. One pitch, got it? Not at the head." He jammed the catcher's mask back over his face, turned, and trotted back to his position.

I smiled like a base-runner who just juked a pitcher into balking. I looked up at Jennifer again, and flashed her a big, confident grin.

"Hey! Keep your eyes on the field, Prinziatta!" Budski yelled.

I turned to him. I made a kissing gesture at him.

His cheeks flooded red. "Yeah, yeah!" he said.

I laughed. I adjusted my cap and brushed dirt off the rubber with my cleat. I drew in a deep breath. Chaos City, here we come.

Budski dirt-adjusted the batter's box with a steel-plate look on his square-chinned face. He dug into his right-handed stance. From sixty-feet-six-inches away, I could feel, and almost smell, his smoldering determination.

The Lowers bench came alive as I settled onto the rubber.

"Chick-en Shit! Scared to Pitch!" they chanted, cheerled by Brennan, the Cadillacker. "Chick-en Shit! Scared to Pitch! Chick-en Shit! Scared to Pitch!"

Skybrando index-pointed at me from behind Semzy. Time in. Time to get fired up.

Semzy dropped the sign. Fastball. In. I loved this guy. Even in an intra-squad game, he knew how to make it look right. He was the man.

I brought my left leg back, and torqued my body over the rubber. Right before my right hand released the ball, I yanked my focus off Semzy's mitt, and shot a cross-haired look at Budski's eyes. I then fired, grunting to emphasize the point even more. The ball flew right under his chin.

Budski's head ducked away, his left shoulder jerking up, protective. Then he spun backward, lost his balance, and splayed out on the dirt. His aluminum bat rattled—klink-klanklinkinkinkinkink—down onto hard-packed dirt.

The Lowers bench went into hyperdrive, their voices a cacophonous jamble of barked obscenities and taunting epithets.

Budski jumped up off the dirt. His eyes were hardened into battle-mode. Pointing at me, he yelled, "That's horseshit, dude! Bush league!"

Skybrando ran out in front of him; he put his hands on Budski's heaving chest.

I heard Coach Hicks scream from behind me, "Easy, Prinzy, easy!"

The adrenaline amping me pushed a giant smile onto my face. Turning toward their bench, I yelled at Brennan, "Respect the game, bitch!" I turned and stomped to the back of the mound with their hostile noise at my back growing louder. I picked up the resin bag and turned around, still smiling a maniac's smile. I launched the resin bag toward Brennan and the Lowers' bench. They all reacted like it was a grenade. I laughed.

Coach Skybrando turned toward Coach Hicks and said, "You wanna talk to this guy? Somebody better get a hold of him."

Hicks held out his hands to say, "He's all right, he's all right." "Nice and easy, Enzo, nice and easy. Finish it up, now!" he yelled to me.

Our shortstop and captain, Jared Besto, ran up from behind me. He placed his hand on my back and said in a WTF? tone, "Dude!"

Still smiling an "I love it when a plan comes together" smile, I said, "Bunch o' pussies. They ain't gonna do shit. Watch. We vets gotta teach these guys, right?"

He placed an arm around my shoulder. "Let's relax, dude," Besto said. "Just relax. It's nickel-beer night at Pig's. Let's just close it out and go have fun. We don't need this shit."

"They gotta learn *some* time, dude," I said.

He patted me on the ass with his mitt and ran out to his position.

Budski dug at the dirt in the back of the batter's box. His face burned with intense concentration. He was mouthing something over and over to himself.

Proud of the intensity of the reaction I'd incited, I covered my mouth with my glove, and said into it, "Let's go!" I mounted the mound. I balanced myself over the center of the rubber.

Skybrando pointed out to me. Time in.

Semzy squatted back down. He called for a curve and set the target right down the middle.

Fuck it, I thought. Fine. I gripped the seams, wound up and threw.

The pitch started a foot behind Budski. He jumped out of the way. The ball crossed the middle of the dish. Strike one. On the next pitch, he flinched a little less, but still could not jerk the bat off his shoulder to swing at the called strike. On the third, he timed it, but the ball swerved wide off the plate, and he could only fan the air with his bat.

A bullet of adrenaline raced through me. I pumped my fist through the air. "Yeah!" I yelled. "Siddown!" I glared at their now silent, mopey, and glum bench. Don't *ever* disrespect the game in my presence, I thought. Semzy was right. That *was* better than seeing Budski hit the dirt a few times.

I jogged off the field, sat on the bench. Semzy walked over and said, "You know you gettin' thrown at now."

"Yeah," I said. "No doubt. Let 'em bring it."

Sitting on the bench, still riding high on adrenaline, I kept making eye contact with Jennifer in the first-base stands. I couldn't really explain it, couldn't really make logical sense of it, but I just felt an electric charge between us. There was something magical there, something divine. I just knew there was. Troublemaker pride swelling my chest, I swished my clenched lips at her, made eyes at her, anything to keep the sparked connection alive. I wanted to run over. Wanted to talk with her for hours. I wanted to do a lot of things.

As she flirted with me, she shifted her body onto the top plank of the stands. The girl just loved to perform, it seemed. The wind whisked up her honey-brown hair. She winked at me. A mischievous smile broke out on her wayward-girl lips. An eerie light beamed from her eyes, beckoning me. She could have just been messing with me—teasing—I knew, but damn if I didn't want to find out for sure.

After a while, Budski ran in to the mound from his second-base position. He had a long, animated discussion with the pitcher, a hard-throwing lefty named Charlie Reilly. It wasn't hard to tell from his body language that he was telling the kid to knock me on my ass when I came up.

When my turn came around, I looked out at Reilly, an ugly kid with a face like a pizza, as I dug into my stance. His face burned red. His eyebrows were mashed together, like some conflicted soldier ready to do battle with an uncertain enemy. He inhaled a violent deep breath, and expelled it with a boxer's force.

My mind raced along in its muscle-memory self-dialogue: "Wait and be quick, it's coming up and in, hands back, take the slider to right, hands back, wait and be quick, hands back..."

Reilly stared in for the sign. Face scrunched, he nodded, then exhaled. He wound up and unleashed a pitch that zoomed toward my head.

A fear-flash, and then I flinched away from the vengeance-pitch. I heard the baseball strike the chain-link backstop behind us.

The catcher, freshman Max Fayner, ran out between Reilly and me.

I jumped up. Looking Reilly in the eyes, I laughed. "So fucking obvious!" I said.

"Easy fellas, easy," warned Coach Skybrando.

"Take it easy," said Fayner. He walked back toward his position.

I tried to keep myself calm, deeply inhaling and exhaling.

"Ain't no thang!" said Semzy from the bench. "Dirt off yo' shoulda, soulja!"

Reilly snatched the ball thrown by Coach Skybrando. He brushed some dirt off the rubber with his spikes.

Budski came running in again from his position. He

grabbed the ball out of Reilly's glove. He tossed it up and caught it, with a menacing look on his face.

I walked a few steps out toward the mound. "Oh, what, *you're* gonna knock me down, too? With *your* pussy arm?"

"Fuck you, asshole!" Budski said, a jealous hate on fire in his eyes. Then he chucked the ball toward me. I ducked, but it sailed way over my head. I turned and watched it zip through the air toward Jennifer. She ducked to avoid it, but as she did, she fell backward off the stands. She thumped onto the grass.

Stunned for a millisecond, time crawled to a slow-motion surreality. I took a step toward Jennifer, but saw a bunch of the guys running over toward her. I stopped. Blood-red rage erupted inside me. I felt an intense heat infusing every molecule of my body as it throbbed with pulsing aggression. I turned toward Budski.

Budski

My anger transformed into anxiety as I watched the ball flying toward Jenny. "Oh shit," I said, softly.

She ducked it, in an awkward body contortion. She toppled out of the stands and onto the ground. She seemed hurt, even though she landed on her side.

I started to run toward Jenny, but then I looked at Enzo. His eyes seemed to be burning up with rage. I stopped. I was going to have to deal with him.

Some of the guys and the coaches ran toward Jenny.

I braced myself. I watched Prinziatta's face burn red as he took off running right for me. As he approached, I turned slightly so that he would still tackle me, but because of my angle I would maintain the leverage. We both hit the ground. I struck precise blows with my fists, while Enzo just flailed about randomly. Before long, there was a scrum on the field, with the entire team either joining in or trying to pull people off each other. I got up with a few scratches and nothing more.

Prinziatta, however, wasn't so lucky. When everything calmed down, he stayed on the grass. He was the only one. Coach Hicks and Jill Mackinot, the trainer, ran over. After a few seconds, he opened his eyes. He sat up.

I ran over to Jenny, who was still on the ground. She seemed to be that way by choice, rather than because she couldn't get up. Tears streamed down her make-up-free face, but her eyes told me that she was more angry than actually physically injured. Everyone else had left her there, so I figured she was probably fine. "Jenny, you okay?" I said.

"Fuck you, Barr," she said. "Fuck you with a fucking crowbar."

"Come on," I said.

"What the fuck is your God-damned problem, you little bitch, huh?" she said.

"Oh, stop being dramatical," I said. "You know I was aiming at Prinziatta's dumb ass. I mean, you know that's what I was doing, right?"

Her lips fluttered. Her eyes watered. I really couldn't tell if the tears were genuine or not.

"I'm *hurt*, Barry," she pouted. "You...you hurt me!"

"Not on purpose," I said.

"Still!" she said. "You're the last person who's supposed to hurt me. On purpose or not. You're supposed to *protect* me, not be hurting me!"

I felt like Donald Trump when he went bankrupt. I felt like Ken Lay after the Enron collapse; Michael Milken in '80s handcuffs; Bernie Madoff being pushed around by cameramen on the streets. I felt the need to atone for my rage outbreak. I had to   mother   my   girl.   I   got   down   on   the ground and engulfed her in a loving embrace. "Aww, poor baby. Needs daddy to kiss her boo-boo and makes it aaaall better?"

"Yes!" she said, sniffling as she snuggled into me. "You dumbass."

"Aww, there there," I said. "There there, now. Daddy will make it aaaall better for his boo. Let's get you to the trainers' room. They can have a look atcha."

"Do they have aspirin?"

"Course," I said.

"Vicodin?" she said.

"Let's go, crazy," I said.

She pulled herself up, and we started walking toward the gym.

"Why are you even here today, anyway? Didn't I tell you to go to that open audition in the city?" I said.

"Barry, I'm hurt here," Jenny said. "You pegged me with a baseball! I need comforting, you dickhead. Not condemnation."

"Okay, okay," I said. We continued to walk toward the gym where all the coaches had their offices. "It's just that, if you do what you're supposed to do, good things tend to happen. If you don't, bad things tend to happen. Or so I've noticed. That's all."

"Bad things?" Jenny said. "Bad things? What, like having your boyfriend hit you with a baseball? Those the kinds of bad things you're talking about, Barr? You get that from watching an episode of *Cops* or some shit?"

"I was aiming for Prinziatta," I said. "I already told you that. It was an accident, that's all."

"Yeah, right, sure, Barr," said Jenny.

Once we hit the gym, she stormed off toward the trainers' room, clearly pissed at me.

Subtle, Barry, I thought. Verrrry subtle. I need so much

work. I threw myself against the wall near Coach Hicks's office door, and slumped down to the linoleum floor.

After a few minutes, I heard sneaker-squeak footsteps getting louder in the hall. Then Coach Hicks stood above me. "Budski," he said. "I don't think I can have you on my ballclub."

Prinziatta

"**I**'m all right, I'm all right," I said. The hum of the training-room ice machine made me shudder, somehow, bringing a coldness to my skin. "I blacked out for, like, a second, it's no big deal." I felt a thumping ache on my left side, but I didn't want to tell Jill, the trainer, about it. I thought I'd be fine. No need for Jill to think otherwise.

"Still," said Jill. "Follow my finger with your eyes now."

I did. "Nothing but a scratch," I said. "That guy ain't nothin'. Just lemme get one night's rest, and then we'll see. Sucker-punched me's all. Then we'll see what's what. He's nothing but a chickenshit motherfucker."

"Guys and their pride," she said, shaking her head. "Christ. Can you Band-Aid yourself up?"

"Yeah."

"I gotta check in on some of the other guys," she said. "Just do me a favor and chill here for a second. Calm down a bit and we'll see how you're doing in a few minutes."

"Fine," I said. I laid back on the trainers' table. Budski got the better of me, I thought. Okay, fine. But there's a last time for everything.

Jennifer Burnette's voice shattered my ego-pumping reverie: "Oh God, not *this* fuckin' guy!"

Anger cut through my brain like an explosion of shrapnel. I looked over toward the direction of the sound of her suburban-theatrical voice. "You're not an athlete," I said. "Get the hell outta the training room." Dressed in all white, she was a walking contradiction.

"Not that it's any of your concern," she said. "But I'm just gonna grab some Tylenol or something."

"Good for you," I said. "Then get the hell out."

"You know, this is really all your fault, anyway, so you shouldn't be telling anyone what to do. Really."

"You're giving me a big headache, big mouth," I said.

"And another thing..." she said.

"Oh God." I leaned back and laid down on the trainers' table. Then I closed my eyes, and put my hands over them. For additional emphasis.

"Barry said he was trying to hit *you*. Now, why would he want to go and do that for?" Jennifer said.

My head pounded with a duality of ache, the kind of affliction that flares up when you're simultaneously repulsed by and attracted to someone. It was killing me. "I dunno, maybe because you were flirting with me from the stands?" I said. "Guys kinda don't like it when their girlfriends do that kinda shit. Y'know?"

"Me!?" she said. "What about you, you jerk!? Take responsibility for your actions like a man, you little bitch."

"Please," I said. "That's your response? Calling me a bitch? You're really pathetic, you know that? Why don't you get out of here already, you non-athletic person."

"No, *you're* pathetic!" she said. I heard her footsteps stomp
away. "Keep your damn eyes off me! You make me so mad!"

"I thought you were getting some Tylenol!" I said. I heard
the footstomps return. Then I heard the sound of a pill bottle
shaken. The footstomps receded again. I barely caught her voice
shrieking from the hallway, "He is a such a jerk!"

Girls, I thought. Fuck 'em. My mind drifted, hazy and
fuzzy, into an HBO day-dream.

*I am staring at Dr. Melfi's pretty legs in some sterile therapy
office.*

*"And why do you think you're so attracted to this girl, Enzo?"
she says in that gritty voice she has.*

*"Doc, that's a very good question. So good, in fact, that I can
only answer it with another. Do you believe in magic?"*

"You mean, like, David Copperfield?"

*"No, I mean like the magic that happens for two people who
are, I dunno, say... standing beneath the Manhattan Bridge Over-
pass in Brooklyn, and you hear that F train rumbling over the
bridge, that subway-track-rattling you've heard your whole scrap-
ping Noir York City life, but at* that *moment, that sound is an
orchestral symphony because at* that *moment you're kissing a girl
who elevates even the most ordinary of urban soundscapes into
masterpieces of multi-sensory artwork. That kinda magic."*

*"Oh, uhh, welll..." Dr. Melfi says. She shifts those pretty legs
of hers, and re-crosses them the other way. "I'm not so sure about
that."*

*"I am," I say. "Because I've felt it. I've felt that kinda magic.
And once you feel it, you can never again doubt its existence."*

*Dr. Melfi says, "So, if there's a Magic Girl involved, then you
may need to employ some magic tricks. Some slight of hand, cut a
girl in half, these kinds of things. Get tricky."*

"Right," I say. "Of course. Get tricky."

"Ennnnzo!" I heard a voice saying, almost singing, lullaby-sweet. "Eeeennnnzzzooo!" I heard again.

I peeked open my eyes. I saw Shannon Hestian, unfocused, standing over me. "Hi," I said, grog-voiced.

She smiled in a Florence Nightingale kind of way. Very caring, very compassionate. Very boring. "How ya doin'?" she said softly.

"Fine," I said. "Ain't no thing."

"Rub some dirt on it, huh?" she said, teasing.

"Yeah, exactly," I said. "Dirt works."

"Don't worry, Enzo," she said. "I'll take really, really good care of you."

"Heaven help me," I said.

Budski

I could hear my dad's voice in my head almost immediately. "What do you mean, you got thrown off the team? You weren't even on the team in the first place! Why are you such a screw-up, Barry? Why can't you do anything right, Barry? How many times do I have to bail your sorry ass out, Barry? I think the mailman's your real father, Barry. No way you could be my genetic creation, Barry. We need to go get our D.N.A. tested, Barry." Blahzay blahzay motherfucking blahzay.

"Coach, I think if you just hear me out for second..." I said to Coach Hicks, sitting uncomfortably behind his disheveled desk.

Jenny Drama stormed into the office. "He is such a jerk!" she said, red-faced, with a bottle of Tylenol in her hand. "Oh my God!"

"Yeah, can you give us a minute, babe?" I said. "We'll be done in a hot sec."

"Okay, whatev," she said.

"And close the door behind you?"

"Sure." She stomped out, the door rattling shut.

"Coach," I said. "Look, I'm a positive person. Let's think positive, and work this out."

"I really don't think so, Son," Coach Hicks said. "We got what happened today, and I also saw something in the paper about an incident at the Sammy house..."

I dipped my head and then brought it back up. I looked Coach straight in the eyes. I needed him to trust me. "Coach, I can understand that, but it's nothing, really."

Coach said, "Nothing? I don't think it's nothing."

"I know, I know," I said. "I didn't mean it like that. It's terrible, what happened with that girl. I feel badly for her, I really do. Apparently, she had some substance-abuse issues and she came to the house high as a freakin' kite, and started dancing, and next thing you know, she goes down. It's tragic, it really is. But we, the fraternity, had nothing to do with it. And it would be unfair to hold it against people who can have a good time responsibly, just because of one stripper with a substance-abuse addiction."

"And the M.E.'s report confirms that?" Coach said.

"I resent the implication, Coach," I said. "But, it's not back yet. And we think it's pretty obvious that she had a drug overdose that caused what happened. Unless she ate, like, three Big Macs and super-sized fries for breakfast, lunch, and dinner her whole life."

Coach said, "And there was no chance that any of your people gave her anything?"

"There were an awful lot of people at the party. If anything like that happened, I'm sure someone would come forward and say something. I know I would, anyway. Any reasonable person would, I think," I said.

"I guess," said Coach. "But if anything comes of it, if anyone comes forward, or the police find anything against you guys, you'll have no leash with me. Not a short leash. No leash. You understand me, Barry?"

I felt the pressure lift. Relief set in. "Gotcha," I said. "Absolutely." On his face, I could see him letting go of his concern for the issue.

"But now, about your relationship with Prinziatta. Seems to be a lotta tension there. As a ballclub, we can't be having serious stuff like this going down between teammates. I believe in chemistry, Son. I think, above all, a ballclub must be comprised of guys who are willing to stand up for each other. Certainly can't be guys fighting with each other. The fighting we do against the other teams out on the field is tough enough. So, we can't be having any in-fighting within our own ranks. You see what I'm saying, Barry?"

"Coach, seriously, I agree with that. And that's why I'm telling you that this is a one-time thing that happened, and it's never gonna happen again. I'm definitely gonna go to Enzo and I'll apologize and let him know I just lost my temper for some reason out there, and that we should put our differences behind us, and be cool from here on out."

"I'm not sure that's good enough," Coach said.

My mind started racing. Its soundtrack was my stupid father's disappointed tone of voice. And then the light bulb sparked to life. "Hey," I said. "How about this. If Enzo's cool with me, then you're cool with me, right? I mean, doesn't that make sense?"

"Well, sure," said Coach. "Course."

"Okay, so, lemme do my thing, and if Prinziatta comes to you and says he's cool with me, then that should take care of everything. Right?"

Coach thought it over. He tugged on the bill of his cap. "Okay," he said. "Fine."

"Maybe I'll get him to join Sammy, even. I'll call him a little later and see if maybe he'll consider it," I said.

"Okay," said Coach.

Sometimes a win is a loss. Because now? Now I was going to have to go smooth things over with that hothead, Enzo Prinziatta. The little fucker.

The problem with pepper-pots like him was, you never knew what could set them off. They were unpredictable. And unpredictability's bad for business. So, I'd have to finesse it, somehow. Always some crap to plow through, it seemed.

Prinziatta

"Hey, wanna see some titty?"

I looked up, mouth open, from my textbook. I saw Semzy's hulking body dominating the entrance to my room. "Not right now, thanks," I said. "Keep your titties to yourself, dude."

"C'mon, man, let's go to Rolando's," he said.

"Rolando's? On a Tuesday night?"

"Yeah," Semzy said.

"Those girls are all skanks," I said. "And on a weekday? C'mon, man."

"Yeah," he said. "But they gots a new girl there. Alice. Met her in one of my Psych classes. Baby-girl's putting herself through school."

I raised my eyebrows in deep suspicion. "Alice?" I said.

"Bad name," he said. "Great body."

"That's nice," I said. "And lemme guess. You just wanna contribute to her ongoing education? Throw a few bucks at her, just

59

to make sure she can continue to improve herself? That what you're thinking?"

"Yeah," he said. "Like, you can't be strippin' fo'eva. Gotsta get a real job sometime, man."

"Uh huh," I said.

"And, uhh, this girl, man? She fine as hell."

"Alice, huh?" I said.

"Alice!" he said. "Can't go wrong with no girl go by the name of Alice. Belie' dat."

"There it is," I said. I remembered the imaginary Dr. Melfi's legs, and then something she told me. *Get tricky*, my substitute mom had said. I needed to get some dirt on Budski. Seemed to me that one good place to start would be Rolando's. Maybe one of the strippers was friends with the dead girl. Maybe she wanted to talk. Couldn't hurt. "All right. Gimme like a half hour to finish with this shit here, then we'll bounce," I said.

"Bet."

Rolando's was a tiny strip club on Route 299, a.k.a. Main Street, past the Super 8 and right next to the crappy new EconoLodge, about three miles off campus. They didn't have a liquor license, they didn't have a giant flashing billboard outside, they didn't have premium dancing talent. What they did have was dim lighting, loud music, and sparkly girls motivated to be mile-high mileage.

"What about Janeece? She approve of this little outing here? Or did you not even tell your girlfriend we're even going?" I said to Semzy after we took our seats up front by the stage. One of the less well-endowed girls was writhing to a Kid Rock song.

"Naah, she thinks I'm at the library," Semzy said. "This here be between you and me. You be sure to keep it that way, ya heard?"

"Yeah, yeah, I gotcha," I said. "Listen, while I'm here, I

think I'm gonna try and find out about that stripper that died at the Sammy house. When they beat the crap outta me?"

"Dawg, let that shit slide already, damn," Semzy said. "Whatchou gonna find out? What, no, serious, whatchou gonna learn?"

"I...I dunno," I said. "Hey, I gotta get along with this guy, and that means interacting with Sammy, and that means...the more I know, the better off I'll be, right?"

"Wrong."

"Wrong?"

"Wrong, cuz the more you keep snoopin' around into shit that ain't none o' your business, the more you gonna keep gettin' yo' ass kicked. You feel me?" Semzy said.

"Yeah," I said. "I feel you. You're right. Still, I feel like I need to know more information."

"That's yo' problem, right there. That feelin' shit. Stop feelin' so much, relax, and watch some titties bounce. That's the thing to do. Not go askin' all kindsa questions you don' want to hear the answers to, anyway."

"Yeah," I said. "Yeah." But I needed to know. I needed to get some context on this Budski guy. How did he get Sammy up and running so fast? How did he grab so much power so quickly? What really happened with that stripper?

One of the girls—blue-eyed, thin to the point of titlessness, heavy-perfumed, sparkly—sat down next to me. She smiled with all her charm. One of her front teeth was chipped. "You want a lap dance, baby?" she said.

"Sure," I said.

She grabbed my hand and led me to a secluded area in the back of the club. I tried to extract some info out of her while she was maneuvering herself near my mid-section. No luck. This happened three more times. These girls just weren't talking.

"See?" Semzy said.

"What?"

"You're just givin' yo'self a headache, 'steada enjoyin' the show," he said. "And fo' what?"

"I know, I know," I said. "You're right. Just watch the titties bounce. So, you're a genius, that what you wanna hear? Bouncing titties. Got it." I leaned back in my seat, and watched the sparkling carnality. I felt a sinking sense of saddening disappointment. If I couldn't get any dirt on Budski, how could I possibly get tricky? And without getting tricky, how could I get with Jennifer Burnette? It seemed impossible. I felt lost, homeless, like I'd been picked off first trying to steal, and my legs couldn't decide whether to fight or surrender. And this place didn't even serve beer. Fuck, I thought.

"Let's go to Pig's and get drunk, man," I said to Semzy.

"Nah, Alice ain't even been on yet," he said.

"Damn. Okay." Down and Sober was a helluva corner.

One of the dancers leaned in toward me and whispered into my ear, "I heard you been askin' about Chardine. If you want, we can talk. In one of the V.I.P. rooms."

"Okay," I said.

She led me back there.

"So, what are you? Huh?" she said, in an accusatory tone of voice.

"What?"

"FBI, CIA, NPPD, Sherriff... NPFD, what?" she said.

"No," I said. "I'm just a guy, that's all. Just a regular person."

"And why you askin' all these girls about Chardine?" She was better-looking than the rest of the dancers. Her eyes were clearer.

"I'm just curious about her, that's all," I said.

"Curious," she said.

"Yeah," I said. "See, I was there at the party the night she died. I saw her, actually, before all the chaos and whatever."

"Yeah?" She planted a firm hand on a firmer hip.

"Yeah, and, so, I'm just kinda curious, that's all," I said.

"You wearin' a wire, huh?" she said. She rubbed her hand down my chest and all over my pants. "No one just be curious for no reason."

"You're kinda turnin' me on there, babe," I said, laughing. "Look, I told you, I'm just a guy. I'm not wearing any wire. I was just at that party when this happened, and, uhh, this Budski guy, Barry Budski, he's the President of Sammy, and he's trying out for the baseball team this year, so I'm just wondering if anyone here knows anything about the guy, and also what happened that night. I kinda just need to see what's up with this dude."

"Budski, huh?"

"Yeah, you know him?" I said.

She scrunched up her face as if she were tasting something disgusting. "Sure, we know him," she said. Her tone of voice suggested revulsion at the thought of him. "Rolando has a deal with him for the house. Girls go over there all the time. And then he makes sure a couple of his bros come in, regular-like, and spread their money around."

"Kinda sounds like you don't like the guy much," I said.

"Honestly?"

"Please."

"He's a pompous jackass," she said. "Thinks he's God's gift or some shit. Sorry if he's your buddy."

"No, yeah, that's my take, too," I said. "I damn sure don't like the idea of being the guy's teammate, that's for sure."

"He's a jerk."

"Yeah, but a lotta guys are jerks," I said. "Lotta chicks *dig* jerks, actually. What makes him especially repulsive, y'know?"

Her green eyes narrowed, as if she were trying to assess my trustworthiness. "Hey, look, I know a lot of the girls are into some of the hard stuff, I'm not saying they're not," she said. "They are. But that guy? A lot of the girls say when they went to the house, he encouraged it... encouraged them to use more."

"But why? What would he care?"

"The guy's a jackass. How the hell should I know why? Maybe that's what gets him off, the little prick," she said.

"Oooh, okay," I said. I felt her getting worked up, and I didn't want to set her off. Strippers don't exactly have the best reputations.

"I never liked it," she said. "I always said it was bullshit. I always said something was gonna happen. And now it has. He usually gave 'em a T-shirt, as, like, some kinda prize, some form of payment."

"A T-shirt?"

"Yeah, everybody loves T-shirts, right? And Budski, he gets a little free advertising. Everybody wins," she said. "Total turdball."

"I guess," I said.

"Everybody except Chardine," she said.

I said, "You ever tell anybody about what was going on at the house?"

"Rolando didn't wanna hear it," she said. "He had a good deal. Plus, I like this job. I make a lotta money for what I do. I don't exactly wanna screw it up, y'know? But I always said something would happen. And now? Now it is what it is."

"Didn't the cops come through here, ask you guys some questions?" I said. "Why not tell them any of this?"

"Oh, they came through here all right," she said. "Asked Rolando a few questions, and then rolled on out again."

"Oh."

"Like I said, I like my job, I don't wanna cause no trouble," she said. "And I don't get into any drug stuff, so ain't no problem for me. I just feel kinda bad about it, with what happened and all."

"Yeah," I said.

"But y'know, I really wanted to get all this off my chest," she said. "So, thanks. I'm gonna give you a lap dance for free, big boy."

"Sweet," I said. And it was.

The next morning, I went to see the Director of Greek Affairs, Professor Gembull, during his office hour. I thought I'd try and feel him out about Sammy and about Budski, since he was the administration's liaison with the Greek community.

I sat down in the leather chair in front of his desk. "Professor Gembull, can I ask you a couple questions about Sigma Alpha Mu?" I said.

"Sure," he said. He was rummaging through a filing cabinet, apparently searching for something. "God damn it!" He slammed the drawer shut, and walked toward the desk. "What do you wanna know?"

"Problem?" I said.

"Just misplaced something," he said. "I hate it when I lose things. It's just so annoying to know you have something, like an envelope or something, and then the next minute, *poof!*, it's gone without a trace."

"I can imagine," I said.

"So, uhh," he said, "how can I help you?" He sat in his high-backed, ergonomically designed black office chair behind his desk.

"Well, I was thinking about rushing Sammy this year," I said. "But then I saw this thing in the paper about an incident with a stripper who died in the house or something. And I was just kinda wondering whether I should go ahead and rush."

"You're Prinziatta, right?" he said. "Enzo Prinziatta?"

"Yeah," I said. "Why?"

"No reason," he said. Behind his John Lennon rims, his eyes held a stern, authoritarian gaze upon me. It felt like he was a cop trying to beat a confession out of me. "But as to your question, yes, they did have an incident there recently. And we, the college, looked into it very closely, as you may know. And the thing with it is, it was just an unfortunate accident that happened. This girl apparently had some issues, some problems, and things of this nature, aaaand... before you know it, bad things happened. It's sad. But, as you may also know, especially since it's in Chapter twelve of your student handbook, page two thirty-one, paragraph four, clause D, we do have programs in place for students that may need it. Students who have these kinds of problems. This girl, however, she wasn't a student here, so we were very limited in terms of what we could offer her for some assistance with her, umm, rather significant problems."

"Yeah, I get that," I said. "So, Sammy? You figure they're not a bad organization to join?"

"Oh, no," he said. "I would advise you that they're a fraternity in perfect standing with this university."

"Perfect standing," I said. "Didn't even know there was such a thing."

"I would also advise you that snooping around at gentlemen's clubs is certainly not advisable," Professor Gembull said.

"Excuse me?"

"Just in general," he said. "You'll be better off minding your own business. As a point of advice to you. A dime's worth, as it were, for free."

"I'm just curious, y'know?" I said. "Just cuz I was thinking about Sammy, that's all it is. I'm just a curious guy."

He nodded his head in recognition. "Oh, and one more thing," the Professor said.

"Yeah?" I said.

"Bartholomew knows."

Budski

I knocked on the son-of-a-bitch's door. Control the anger, I reminded myself. Keep it cool, man.

He opened the door wearing only his white sliding shorts, his beer gut flopping over them disgustingly. "Hey," he said. "Come in."

The room was in disarray, clothes and empty beer bottles everywhere. I stood close to the door.

He walked over to a small fish tank and sprinkled some food into it. "I'm exhausted, dude," he said. "I'm about to pass out."

"This'll be quick," I said.

"Okay," said Enzo.

"I understand you've been making certain inquiries," I said. "At certain gentlemanly establishments?"

"Barry," he said. "I'm just curious. No disrespect."

"Maybe there are times when you shouldn't be so curious. Know what I'm sayin'?"

"I understand," Enzo said. "But a girl is dead."

"We understand this," I said. "We're all upset about it. Nobody wanted that. It's not like any of my guys wanted that to happen."

"Yeah."

"People have problems, and it's too bad that they have personal issues," I said. "But if she didn't pass out there, it would have been on the street, or in some parking lot, or in Murphy's, or some other damn place. Just so happens it happened at my place. And, as you well know, we immediately called nine-one-one, and did everything we could for the girl. There's nothing there. Nothing there, *hombre*."

"I know," Enzo said. "Okay, I get it. I just felt bad for her, I guess. And nobody told me anything, anyway."

"All right, so let's put that behind us then," I said.

"Sure," he said. "No problem."

I was relieved. "Soooo, listen, have you given any more thought about joining the frat, like we talked about on the phone?"

"I remember," he said.

"We don't need any more of this cloak and dagger stuff, y'know, Enzo? Just come on board, we'll skip all the pledge stuff for ya, and just make it quick and easy. It'll be a new day for me and you."

"I dunno," Enzo said.

"Do you even understand how the connections we have with sororities work? Do you understand how many hot girls you'll have access to? Exclusive access, I mean? These are girls who will *not* date guys who aren't in a frat. I don't care who you are, they just won't even look at you. I'm telling you, they won't. And these are girls just as hot as Jenny. If not hotter."

"Yeah, but..."

"And that's just with girls. Papers, tests, all that stuff, we got filing cabinets fulla stuff for *any* class you're taking, and we got guys who already took that same class before," I said.

"The thing is..." he said.

"And then there's the kick-ass parties, where we blow it the hell out..." I said.

"I know, I know..."

"And we got all kinds of connections through the national, guys you can call for advice," I said. "Y'know... for whatever it is you might need."

"Wait. National?" he said.

"Yeah, the national headquarters. And..."

"Oh," Enzo said. "I never really thought about it like that."

"Well, maybe you should."

"Maybe," he said. "Y'know, I feel like I should tell you... ahh, never mind."

"What?" I said.

He smiled, real wide. Like he had ideas. "I'll think about it," he said. "But let's say I do. Then what, y'know. I was thinking, and what *I'd* like to see is, I'd like to have, um, kind of open elections next year. So I can run for President, myself. See if I can give you a good run for your money. Know what I mean? How 'bout that?"

I felt like I had just been gut-punched. This guy had no freaking clue about anything, and he wanted to run for President? I played it cool, though. "Sure, yeah," I said. "That sounds good. Let the guys decide. Democracy in action, right? Yeah, that's cool."

We slapped hands. I got out of there before I said anything I'd regret later. What I really wanted to do was give this guy another beat-down, but that would have to wait for another day.

Elections, I thought. What a bunch of nonsense.

Prinziatta

I blinked. The world was fuzzy haze. "Ahh," I said. My room. It seemed like I was in my room, in my bed. My brain clicked and rotated, spun and spazzed. No traction. I couldn't get my brain to click into reality. I gave up trying and drifted back into a deep sleep.

Cold. I am cold. I hug my black ski jacket tighter around me. No use. Cold, shivery cold. I look around. I'm in some kind of white tube, with freezing cold air shooting down at me from the top, some sort of refrigeration technique. It ices me down, this weird-ass cooler, like an upside-down MRI machine. Numbness dawns on me, preserves me.

I feel a violent urge to get out of this crazy chill chamber. I feel an overwhelming, burning hot need to move, to get going, to break free from this ice prison. My chest burns with this desire, a fiery, char-smoked passion to go. I try to break free, but I can not. I can not.

I scream, or try to scream, but my voice, effectively frozen inside my throat, has no power. It stays iced, stays chilled out. No sound escapes.

Snap.

I woke up cold, shivery cold. I was naked. I scrounged around the floor with my hand until I found a pair of boxers and slipped them on. Scratching my pot belly, I made my way to the suite toilet and extracted last night's beer intake. Then I, groggy and foggy, went back to bed.

Back inside the dream, *I sit down at the dining room table of my childhood Brooklyn home. Tony Soprano sits at the opposite end of the table. He is nine months pregnant. He wears a pink T-shirt with an Italian flag logo on it. He chugs an entire bottle of Guiness beer. He looks at me and says, "You're fucked."*

"Gabagool?" I say.

"You're fucked," he says, emphasizing the second word. "Unless you kill the anger and flex your muscle, you're fucked. You. Fucked."

Snap.

"You up?" Barry Budski's face floated above me like a freaky nightmare.

I thought it was the dream, lingering.

"Enzo," Budski said. "Hey Enzo, you up? Can you hear me, buddy? You up, dude?"

I stretched open my eyes to make sure what they were seeing was real. "Yeah," I groaned.

"Enzo, hey, listen man," Budski said. "I just wanted to come back here and say that I'm sorry for what happened out there, y'know?"

"Out there?" I breathed.

"I meant to apologize before, but I forgot. I meant to, but, I just kinda forgot. So I wanted to come here and let you know that I *am* sorry for what happened during that intrasquad game. It's, like, we're teammates and everything and we need to be cool, so we can put this thing behind us and shit. Let's just be cool, and let's go win a bunch of games and be B.M.O.C.s, right, bro?"

He held out his fist. Slowly, I reached out and tapped it with my own. "Yeah, we're good, I guess," I said.

"Okay, cool," he said. "Feel better and whatever."

"Hey," I said. "But what about Jennifer? She okay?"

He looked at me, hard. "Bitches ain't shit, right?"

"That's what Snoop Dogg says," I said.

He laughed a bit. "Okay, well. Later, bro."

I heard his footsteps fading from earshot, then they stopped. I thought I heard him talking on his cell. I sat up, sitting over the side of the twin. My mind was working better, slightly. I moved over to the mini-fridge and extracted a can of Budweiser. The beer felt good going down. My brain relaxed and my thoughts flowed more coherently.

This Budski guy reminded me of some low-level boss from *The Sopranos*. He carried around that weird mix of authority and immaturity that defines those guys. Weird.

I felt that burning anger rising in me, but I gulped down some beer to quiet it the fuck down. Besides, anger wasn't going to get me anywhere. All the anger had done for me so far was get my ass whupped a couple times. So, angry, violent confrontation of the boyfriend was *out*.

I needed something else, something more subtle, something sneakier, stealthier. Something like a direct but undetectable attack. *Gabagool*.

"Barry!" I yelled at him.

Budski walked back into my room.

I put down my beer. "Remember that T-shirt?" I said.

"Not exactly."

12

Budski

"**I** grabbed it out of the trash that night, the night of the stripper. I kept it. Fuck knows why, really," Enzo Prinziatta said. "But I just found out Chardine was wearing it that night." He stared at my face like he was looking for tell-tale signs of what I knew, or didn't.

I didn't give him any. "Uhh," I said.

"So, I put it in a safety deposit box. Just, y'know, F.Y.I. Since we're at the dawning of a new day and all that good stuff."

"Okay, bro," I said. "Good to know. Check ya later." I walked out. My head buzzed with all sorts of sound bites in my father's voice, all echoing and bouncing off each other, creating an insufferable din. They were all, "Confiscate all the evidence" and "Don't leave anything to chance" and "Don't get lazy — it'll bite ya in the ass." They pounded and echoed in my head until it felt like it would explode.

I stumbled over to a garbage can in the corner with a small crack on the lip and heaved up everything in my gut in a volcanic spew. It wrenched my insides out. And then I heaved some more.

Once my clenched stomach calmed down, I told myself to do the same. Relax, relax, relax, I said to myself, hoping no one would pass by and witness my compromised state. Everything can be fixed. Nothing is ever finished. Everything can be fixed. Get a grip, man. Jeez. This is nothing. Just get back in there and negotiate your fucking ass off. Damn it.

I also remembered that Jenny had wanted to talk to me about something to do with this guy that night. We had forgotten about it. But it was probably the T-shirt.

I swallowed a bunch of times, flushing the remnants back down. I ran into the dormitory bathroom off the main stairwell, next to the dilapidated, humming vending machines. I turned on a rusty faucet, stuck my mouth under it, and flushed out the lingering putrid taste with cool water. Peering into the tendril-cracked mirror over the faded-rust-covered sink, I made sure my eyes, the whites of which were now tarnished by forked red lines, were done watering. Relax, I ordered my harried reflection. Re-the-fuck-lax, and handle this.

I sauntered, all forced confidence and good humor, back into Enzo's room. I leaned in, holding onto one of the doorjamb posts. "Almost forgot," I said.

Prinziatta put down a can of beer on the night table. The guy was *always* drinking it seemed. "Yeah?" he said.

"Y'know, I just have to tell you, *amigo*, I feel really guilty about something else, too."

"That's nice," he said. He grinned like the smug bastard he was.

"I mean, I'm not really responsible for what happened to you at the house, those guys just took a disliking to you for some reason, I guess. But still, I'm the President of the fraternity, so it all comes back to me in the end, anyway. So, there's that. And now we have this baseball thing. So I just wanted you to know that I feel very badly about all of it."

"Okay," he said. "Duly noted."

"Y'know, when we were starting the chapter last year, I was kind of unsure about it, too," I said. "I was asking myself, Why am I doing this? Isn't it just another place where a bunch of low-achievers can have a place to hang out and drink beer and watch football?"

Prinziatta snorted and laughed.

"And then...then I talked to some folks, and they told me they had felt the same way before they joined their frats. So I decided to go ahead with it. And now? Now I feel like it was the best thing I could have ever done. Because the thing is, I've found that the brotherhood acts like a support system for everybody's individual goals and aspirations, their unique qualities, all that stuff. All those things are actually enhanced because you know you got a group o' guys who are always gonna have your back, no matter what. No matter how 'out there' it may be. It's kinda like having a second home, where the guys just are all real supportive and cool."

"Uh huh," Prinziatta said. His face and tone told me he wasn't buying the pitch.

"Look, I know the perception out there may be something different. But a lotta times what you hear is false because it comes from guys who didn't get bids because they're not good guys or whatever, and they get bitter," I said. "And they start these things going around, just to get back at the frats. It's no big thing to me, but you should at least understand where this stuff comes from, and the truth of the whole situation."

"The truth," Prinziatta said. He crossed his arms against his chest.

"So," I said, "just think about it. I'll see you later."

"Later, bro."

I walked out, then back in again. I felt around in my jeans front pocket, found what I was looking for. "Almost forgot this," I said. I tossed his #42 pendant at him. "Here's this. You dropped it at *mi casa*."

"Oh," Enzo said. His face brightened, like he had opened a gift on Christmas and it was exactly what he wanted. He uncrossed his arms from his chest, resting a palm on either side of him. I had a shot. "Thanks, man."

"Coulda gotten a lotta *dinero* for that thing, too, dude," I said. "But I figured it wasn't right, what my boys did. Picking it up when you, uhh, dropped it. So, there ya go."

"Yeah, no," he said. "I appreciate that. This thing means a lot to me. It really does."

"Oh yeah?" I said. "Big Jackie Robinson fan?"

"Mo Rivera," he said. "Best reliever of all time. I thought for sure this was gone forever. I kinda need this. It's kinda like my good-luck charm out there. I feel naked without it when I'm throwing. Y'know, it's just...it's just, like, kinda comforting or whatever. So, yeah. Thanks again, man."

"Gotcha," I said. "See, I'm not such a bad guy, after all, huh?"

"I wouldn't say that much," he said. "Let's see what the new day brings before we make any judgments."

He did not offer to give me back my T-shirt.

"When do you want me to come down there, to the house? We gonna do some kind of ceremony at least?" Enzo said.

Prinziatta

With a rumble in my stomach worse than the time my mother tried to make Rachael Ray's stuffed tomatoes, I trudged up the ornate marble steps of the Sammy house. I smoothed out imaginary infield dirt with my imaginary cleats as I stood there on the landing. I rang the bell and smoothed out some more dirt. Some dude answered eventually.

"Budski around?" I said.

"Maybe," he said, a hard look in his eyes. It felt like he was trying to determine if I was a threat.

The look only made my anxiety about this union increase by a degree. What were these guys hiding? What were they protecting? "I'm Enzo Prinziatta. We're, uhh, teammates. I just need to talk to him is all."

"Okay, come in," he said, his look softening. "I'll see if I can find him."

We walked through a large foyer, into a living room area

tastefully decorated with expensive-looking leather couches, matching coffee tables, and chairs. Pimp my mansion, but classy. When I was at the Sammy party where the boys made pugilistically sure I understood not to get involved with fraternal business, I hadn't realized just how magnanimous the place was. A massive Victorian job, it felt more like an estate than a house, like a manor home you'd see out in the Hamptons. Looking around, it seemed like there were at least a thousand rooms going off long hallways above the winding stairs off the living room. A distant buzz-hum floated in the air as faint footsteps and voices taut with stress added to the old-money, business-like feel of the place.

It made me feel small, intimidated, like some kind of an ignoramus. Why wasn't I building my own corporate fraternal empire? "Cool digs," I said to the dude.

"Thanks. Have a seat," the dude said. "I dunno if President Budski's around, but I'll go check."

"Thanks," I said. I sat on the edge of one of the black leather couches.

Soon the dude returned. "Prez Budski's out, sorry. Anything you want me to tell him?"

I stood. "Oh, uhh, well," I said. "Naah. Just some stuff we had talked about. I'll just get with him later. Nothing urgent."

"Okay," the dude said, his face brightening. He walked over to a coffee table and picked up a brochure. He walked back and handed it to me. "Meantime, check this out," he said. "Gives you some of the info about our organization. What's your name again? Edgar, is it?"

"No, it's Enzo," I said. "Enzo Prinziatta."

"Oh right, sorry. President Budski knows how to reach you?"

"Yeah, he knows."

"Okay, check ya later, dude."

As I was about to leave the house, I studied the brochure. Professionally done, it threw me off. It seemed like this fraternity was operating like a business. I mean, normally, frat rush procedures were supposed to be somewhat secretive, or at least so I thought. You don't print up a brochure listing all the benefits of brotherhood. Do you? It's the kind of thing you pass around orally, because you gotta be in the know to be in the know. Isn't it? One of those types of things, like a Greek version of *Omerta*? Something seemed super-weird about the whole thing.

I didn't even see Barry Budski walking in.

"Hey, Prinziatta!" he said, a black backpack slung over his right shoulder. "Ready to do this thing?"

"Yeah," I said, coming out of my trance-like stupor. "Uhh, pretty much."

"Why don't we go talk about it in my room? You got anything right now, or you wanna hang for a few *minutos* and chop it up?" he said. He was dressed like Donald Trump on casual Friday, a pink sweater vest fronting a white polo above khakis and penny-loafers.

"No," I said. "I'm done for the day. Yeah, y'know, I'd like to know how it works and what I'd have to do, and all that stuff."

"Yeah, sure," he said, a broad smile beaming a reassuring quality at me. "*No problemo*, bro."

We headed upstairs, into his bedroom. It was a massive space with a high ceiling. Classy. He had one of those Heineken BeerTender taps on a serving cart type of thing, only it had the Sigma Alpha Mu logo all over it instead of Heineken's. He also had about twenty Sammy short glasses, pints, and shot glasses on the little server cart.

I still felt like something was off, even if I couldn't quite figure out what it was. I shoved my hands in my front pockets. "Great space," I said.

"Thanks," the Prez said. Budski set his backpack down on his king-size mahogany sleigh bed. He walked over to the Beer-Tender and said, "Care for a beer? Think I got an Amberbock in there right now. I try to mix it up with different stuff. Keep from getting bored, y'know?"

The whole scene creeped me out. Why was there so much money here? Everything in the house screamed money: the bed, the house, the customized BeerTender, the fact that he wasn't drinking cheapo beer like everyone else, his mannerisms, the ceilings. Everything just screamed out, *money*! I mean sure, frats have money, they have to operate and throw parties and do whatever else they do, but everything here just seemed to be on a whole other level. I couldn't make sense of it. "Yeah, sure," I said. "Sounds good. Long as you don't mix in some arsenic."

Budski laughed. "Been watching a lotta late-night T.V. lately?" he said.

"HBO," I said. "*The Wire* and stuff like that."

"Gotcha. Y'know," Budski said, "I'm glad you came here. I think it's really great that you're gonna be able to put our differences behind us. Let's get past what happened and just be on the same page going forward, you know?"

"Right," I said. He handed me a beer, dark and luscious. "Thanks," I said. I took a sip. It was shockingly tasty. It felt like having filet mignon after a months-long diet of hot dogs.

Barry said, "Like we talked about before, we'll just forgo all that rush crap with you. No initiation. Put you on the fast track. That way, we can get started quicker."

I felt off-kilter, like a boxer after being struck by a surprise cross. "Oh, okay," I said. "Well, if that works for you guys, then it works for me."

"Cool, great," said Budski. "Now, regarding Jennifer..."

My anxiety drowned itself in dread over what was surely

coming. Here's where he pulls out the gun and caps me, double-oh-seven-style, I thought. Cool as Marlo Stanfield. And all of his fucking cronies would help him cover it up, yeah, make it look like an accident, look like I came here with blood in my eyes, hate in my heart and, because of my unrequited love for his sweet girl with the fiery eyes and apple-curve cheeks, I tried to take out their belovéd leader, their belovéd *El Presidente*, their belovéd fraternal father, the one who made everything possible, and I would be framed as the one who tried to take all of that away, but somehow everything got all screwed up and I turned the gun on myself, cuz I had, like, emotional problems, yeah, severe emotional problems, I mean, hey, look how much the kid drank for God's sake, no one who's stable, no one *normal* drinks like that, I mean come on now, cases at a time, who the hell does that? Only the criminally insane, don'tcha think, ain't that right, Mister Doctor of Psychology?

My God.

My nerves relented and the fear, all shards of dirty glass and balls of sweat, crawled around my stomach. My brain jumped into high-alert mode. I downed the rest of the dark beer. "Yeah?" I said, exuding my trademark brilliance.

"Yeah, well, I think we better put that on the table right now, just kinda get it out in the open so that it doesn't come back and be a problem down the road, don't you think? 'Nother *cerveza?*"

"Uhh. Yeah," I said. "I mean, sure, yeah. Of course. Yeah." I handed him the emptied Sammy-logo glass.

He refilled it and handed it back to me. The look in his eye made me think of the kiss of death Michael Corleone gave to Fredo in the second *Godfather* movie. It broke my heart. "Thank you," I said.

"*No problemo*," Budski said. "Now, the way I see it is, you have an interest in my girlfriend. Am I understanding this properly?"

My stomach tightened a twist. Here it comes, I thought. Here's where they come in from the hidden secret doors and take me out with silencered nines and make my body disappear, make me go swimming with the fishes. I could hear the college President explaining it to my mother: "We can't be held accountable for the students 24 hours a day and everything they do, Mrs. Prinziatta. Especially considering the nearly debilitating dependence your son had on alcohol. Did you ever try to get him any professional help, Mrs. Prinziatta? There there, now. There there."

"Uhh, well," I said. I drank from the Sammy glass. "Umm, I guess you could kinda say that, maybe, I mean, I didn't know..."

"Look, you don't have to rationalize it," said Budski. "Let's just put this all out there. It's okay, man. I'm a laid-back guy, really. I know you don't really know me yet, but I'm really laid-back and cool. Now, that day when we had the intrasquad game, I admit, I had a little too much, umm, coffee that morning and I was just kinda all jacked up, and I saw the two of you doing whatever the fuck it was that you were doing, and I kinda lost it, I just flipped out. But that's not really who I am, I can promise you that."

It felt like a sales pitch, but I didn't think I could resist it without being swarm-ambushed on my way back to campus. As it was, I didn't even know if I would make it through this meeting. "Oh, okay," I said. "I, uhh. Okay, that's cool."

"So you have an interest."

"Yeah." I looked around. No frat ninjas flew into the room.

"Enzo, do you know how many girls there are on campus?" Barry said.

"More than one?" I said.

Budski laughed. "Good one. No, but really, there are about six thousand."

"Okay?"

"Okay, so Jennifer's one. One of six thousand. Just choose one of the other five thousand nine hundred and ninety-nine. Okay?" His tone and expression made it clear that he was telling me, not asking.

The thought of it hit me like the news of an unexpected death in the family. My mind blanked for a second. The weight of the situation pulled on me like an anchor chained to my ankles pulling me down to the ocean bed. I tried to prevent it from showing on my face. "Um, sure," I said. "Okay. Simple math, right?"

"Precisely," he said. "No abacus required, even."

Of course. It was just that simple. Something slithering in my belly vehemently denied this. I told it to shut the fuck down so I could get out of there alive. "Right," I said.

"So, we're good then?" Budski said. "No misunderstandings?"

"Yeah, man," I said. "We're good. Total ceasefire."

"Cool, I gotta go work out," he said. "You know your way out?"

"Yep," I said. "Thanks for the brews, man."

"All right," he said. "I'll let the guys know you're on board, and then you'll have access to the house and all that stuff. When you come back get with my man David D. He'll hook you up with everything you need."

"Cool," I said. "Later."

I wandered out of the frat house. I heard and felt the big front door bang shut behind me. It was over. No ninjas had attacked me. I was still alive.

14

Budski

After that prick Prinziatta left, I felt elated, victorious, untouched. Untouchable. Prinziatta was dead, done. Or a dead issue, at least. The threat was neutralized. The prospect of him reneging on the deal did not phase me. It wasn't that I thought he had too much integrity to be dishonorable, it was that I had one hell of a back-up plan in mind just in case he was.

I walked into the room of the house that I considered my business office. I had a computer station, phone, and filing cabinet in there. Pretty basic, but good enough for the size of our current operations.

I sat behind the desk and picked up the phone. I dialed Dmitri's number.

"D.B. Studios, Barbara speaking," said a voice at the other end.

"Hi, this is Barry Budski calling for Dmitri, please," I said.

"Please hold." Some cheesy music came on.

Freshman Billy Libergo poked his head in the doorway. "Barr?" he said.

"Yeah, I'm on hold," I said. "What is it?"

"I got a problem with some of these invoices—" he said.

"How many times I gotta tell you guys?" I said, cutting him off. "All that stuff goes through Charles, not through me. He handles that."

"I know," he said, "but he's not around right now, and—"

"Call him on his cell, then," I said. "If it's important enough to bring to me, it's important enough to raise him on his cell."

"It's just, he's got his Psych class—"

"Did I fucking stutter, motherfucker?" I said. I had to be firm with the guys or they'd lose respect for me. I had learned that lesson already.

"Okay, boss," Billy said. His head disappeared from the doorway.

The cheesy music played on through the receiver.

Freshman Ritty Banche stepped into the doorway, looking down at a file folder full of papers. "Barry, I got a question, this guy's calling up asking for our E.I.N. and how many employees we got and all these kinds of questions. Should I—" He looked up. "Oh, you're on the phone? Sorry..."

"No, I'm on hold, it's okay," I said. "But you can ask, uhh, David F. about your question, since Charles isn't here. Okay?"

"Oh, right, I forgot," he said. "Thanks." He walked away.

"Fucking freshman," I said. I wondered if all businesses were this bogged down in trivial crap. How did anyone ever make any money if all you did all day was answer stupid questions from new employees and listen to crappy music while on hold?

The music stopped. "Dmitri speaking."

"Hey, Dmitri, it's Barry Budski, how are ya?" I said.

"I'm good," he said. "Except your girl never showed up today. We were expecting her this morning."

"I know, that's what I was calling about," I said. "Jesus. I wanted to see how it went. Shit. I'm sorry, man."

"No skin off *my* nose," he said. "But I just don't know when I'm gonna have time to fit her in now. I'm pretty booked up. Till next month, anyway."

"I know, I know, you're a busy man," I said. "Well, this sucks, but lemme get in touch with Jenny and see what the heck happened. After I talk to her, I'll get back to you and try to schedule something for next month, I guess."

"Okay, buddy," he said. "You know I can't refund your deposit, though. I'm sorry about that."

"Yeah, I know," I said. "Don't worry, I'll make Jenny repay me somehow."

He laughed. "All right, man. Take it easy."

"See ya."

I slipped the phone receiver into the cradle slot. I picked up the miniature rake from my tiny Zen Garden Desk Set and started raking the sand in the box. "Akal, maha kal," I said to myself, trying to sedate my mind through mantra. "Akal, maha kal. Akal, maha kal." My mind relaxed and then flexed back to the frustrating reality that was dealing with Ms. Jennifer Burnette. "Fuck me!" I yelled, as loud as my voice would go.

Junior Kenneth Listowitz came running up the stairs, and stuck his head into the office doorway. "What?" he said. "What is it, man?"

"Nothing," I said. "Something with Jenny. And my dad's gonna kill me if he finds out."

"Always something with that girl, ain't it?" he said.

I shook my head. "Sometimes I wonder if she's really worth all the trouble."

"And then you look at her, right?"

We laughed.

I picked up the receiver and dialed the Fatherhood Foundation, again. I was trying to have them broker a meeting with Chardine's father. I wanted to let him know how sorry I was. I wanted to let him know that despite the circumstances, I thought Chardine was a really cool girl. But mostly, I just wanted to let him know that I felt morally, if not legally, responsible for his daughter's death, and that I would do whatever he wanted to try and make it up to him. I knew a loss like that couldn't be "made up," but still. Sometimes you can soften it a little, at least.

I got my contact's voicemail again and left my fifth urgent message about it.

Prinziatta

Outside the Sammy house, I felt my breath coming short and reedy, like I had been running uphill for miles through two-hundred percent humidity air. I bent over, grabbed my jeans at the knees. I felt like I was on the mound, watching the ball leave the park after I made a gigantic mistake, like starting an at-bat with a get-me-over fastball to a first-ball fastball heel-swinger. A dumb mistake born of hubris. I felt devastated, defeated, beaten. How could I agree to be Barry's brother? A man so clearly full of deceit and lies and irrational violence? It didn't make sense. Trusting this guy was a mistake. I knew it was. But what else could I do?

Sometimes the ninjas in your own head cut you up worse than any actual martial artists ever could.

I thought about the girl in question. Jennifer Burnette and I had actually smoothed things over since the training room. We decided to be friends. *Just* friends. The ceasefire with Barry actually made that situation easier for me to accept. At least, logically—for my brain to comprehend. It didn't do anything for my heart, though.

I walked back to campus in search of Semzy. I needed his sage wisdom. When I got back to the suite, I found out that he was in class, however. As a substitute, I simply and astutely collapsed on the suite couch and ever so smartly fell asleep.

"Hey, wake up! Wakey wakey! Let's go smack some blue balls around!" I heard a Long Island-accented female voice prod, vaguely. I opened my eyes and turned around. Jennifer's head was poking through the doorway of the suite. Goofy goggles lay around her neck. Her chestnut hair was pulled back from her face into a pony tail. The only make-up I could detect was a shiny lip gloss. Not that she needed it. She was the kind of girl who could come home after three days of not sleeping in the woods and still look like she had just walked off a magazine photo-shoot set.

I felt hot all of a sudden, flushed. No, I thought. No, I can't deal with seeing that face just yet. This isn't right. "Uh, nah," I said, sitting up. "I, uhh, forgot. And plus, too, I'm waiting for m'man Semzy to get back."

She walked into the space, dressed retro-athletically in '70s-era short yellow terrycloth workout shorts with white trim around the bottoms and white stripes down the seams, a tight-fitting T-shirt with faded lettering that read "Bada Bing! Gentleman's Club" and high tube socks with yellow and pink stripes.

The impact of the image hit me in the face like a Joe Pesci-wielded Louisville Slugger. It hurt just to look at her only because I knew that beneath that obvious physical beauty swirled the kind of spirit that could set a man rocket-flight free. I wanted to jump off the couch and unleash her wild, savage spirit. But I couldn't. I'd made a deal. I stayed chained to the couch as she hovered above me, just out of reach.

"Whaddaya mean naah?" she said. "I'm looking for a partner, and you said you played."

"Yeah, I know. I do," I said. "But I, uhh, I have some studying to do."

"Studying?" she said. "You said you forgot, and you're waiting for Semzy. Now you've got to study? Forget that, let's go play!"

"For class," I said. I quickly moved off the couch and hunted around, unsuccessfully, for my book bag. "Uhh, I have to go now. Gotta hit the library. Excuse me, if you don't mind." I hurried toward the door.

Jennifer blocked it. "Excuse you, but I do mind!" she said. "I wanna go play. And you don't even have your books." Her face expressed a combination of little-girl poutiness and dominatrix anger.

I tried to ignore it. I needed to be out of her vicinity or I might do something that would get me ninja-sliced in nineteen places. "We'll play some other time, Jennifer," I said. "It's no big deal."

"But I wanna play now!" she said.

"Well, you can't always get what you want." I tried to move past her, make my way out the door and out from where she could hurt me just by being there, but she blocked the way.

"Man, you're frustrating," she said.

"Yes," I said. "And the seventies called, they need their clothes back. Don't make me shove you."

She moved over a bit. "Not funny, Enzo. This is in style right now. What the hell do you know?"

What the hell did I know? "I know enough," I said. I slithered past her, into the large hall.

"What is this?" she said, calling after me. "Why you acting all squirrelly? You're weirding me out, dude!"

"Maybe you're weirding yourself out by dressing like it's freakin' Halloween," I called back.

"I don't think—"

I stopped and turned around. I looked at her. Big mistake. "Or nineteen seventy-five," I said. "Maybe you don't feel weirded out, but simply... anachronistic."

"Look, *dick*-tionary boy, we're supposed to play," Jennifer said. "Unless you're scurred. But if you're scurred to lose to a girl, just say you're scurred!"

"I ain't scared, Jennifer," I said. "I just have to study. You might wanna familiarize yourself with the concept. It's kinda like, the whole reason we're here at school. Y'know? It's not just to party, you might be surprised to learn."

"Blahzay blahzay blahzay," she said. "Now you're sounding like my stupid parents, squirrel boy."

I felt like I would explode. I couldn't take it. The pressure was too much, like a steam rush against a weak governor. I thought, Fuck it. The time is now.

Budski

"You have reached Jennifer's voicemail. Please leave a message. Unless you're creepy. In which case, fuck off. *Beep!*"

I felt like punching a wall, but I managed to hold myself back. For God's sake, I thought. What is this bitch doing all these times where I can't reach her? I hated when she turned her phone off. And she knew I hated when she did that. Because I had told her so.

I exploded off my chair. It was time to take some action. I decided to race to campus and stake out her dorm suite until she showed up, maybe even recon her like a Navy SEAL. If I didn't start getting some demonstrable R.O.I. on our investment in her enhancements, my dad was going to kill me. Enough was enough.

I ran as fast as I could out of the house.

Prinziatta

I sprinted up to retro-Jennifer, caressed the back of her head with my right hand, and kissed her with as much violent power as I could while maintaining a fragile edge of tenderness. I pulled back, expecting her to slap me.

Instead, she looked at me with those live-wire eyes of hers and kissed me back, even more passionately. Her aroma, some Long Island touch of intoxicating perfume, just fueled my passion. The kiss lasted, in serene bliss, for what seemed like a century. It felt like a wholeness, a completeness. It felt like *home*. Like this great big sense of belonging in the place you were cosmically meant to be, a sense of yin-yang circular fullness. It felt like serenity and electric energy at the same time, two polar forces pulling in opposite directions but, somehow, toward the same goal. Strange, incredible, wrong, right. A swirl into a gigantic ball of conflicted, aligned emotion.

I heard the hallway door slam open. That broke the spell, snapped the illusion. We stepped back from each other, awkward and tender in the afterglow of passion. A girl scuttled past.

I was seized by a swirling mix of emotions—horror, joy, lust, shock. I felt confused and angry. Cock-sure and happy. I was *all* fucked up. "I... I," I said. Jennifer's face looked oddly blanched under the fluorescence. "I'm sorry." I ducked away, toward the exit.

"Wait. Enzo!" she said. "Wait a sec, Jesus!"

"Going to the library," I said. "To study!"

I slammed open the heavy door, skip-step ran down the stairs, and bolted out of the building. I stopped and bent over, grabbing my jeans at the knees, again. My breaths came short and heavy. I felt like I had gone fifteen rounds with the heavyweight champion of the world. But. But it was only a kiss. A kiss that killed the ceasefire, but still. Still just a kiss.

I heard the door slam open and then that Long Island voice streaming at me: "Hey! Hey! Don't just run off!" I didn't want to turn around and face it. I didn't want to turn around and face what I'd done. I didn't want to turn around. I didn't want to turn around and face her face. I didn't want to confirm a growing suspicion that I just couldn't take it. "Squirrel boy!"

I felt dizzy, ditzy. I didn't know exactly what was going on. I hadn't thought it through. I had no plan. My life felt like it was spinning out of control into infinite, inky, star-dotted space. I stared out into a vapor of nothingness, trying to wrap my head around this. It didn't work.

Jennifer jumped on my back and tackled me to the ground, giggling all the way.

I turned over, to face her. "Hi," I said.

"Hi," she said, breezy. "So. What's new?" Her smile, impish and grand and maddening, beamed in the night.

"I honestly have no earthly idea why I just did that."

"Then let's pretend," said Jennifer. Her goggles and racquet were gone.

"Pretend?"

"Pretend we're on Mars," she said. She leaned down and kissed me. Deep and hard and long. Then she pulled her head up, eyes and smile sparkling. "Pretty good for a Martian."

"Yeah," I said, full of the wisdom of the ages.

"Yeah," she said. She leaned down for another kiss.

That confused, rattled state hit me again, but this time, I was able to overcome my more carnal instincts, somehow. "No," I said. When I heard it, it sounded like I had said it through a pocket-comb wrapped in tissue paper. Phony.

"No?"

"No, I mean, yes," I said, smart as Einstein. "I mean, I can't. I got a deal."

"I know," she said. "I can feel your deal." She leaned down again.

"No, I mean, yeah, it is, but, no, no, I got a deal, a different deal."

Sarcasm-dripping, pillow-soft, she said, "Yeah, okay, Howie Mandel."

"No, I cut a deal," I said. "I cut a deal with... with Barry."

"WHAT!?" she said. She jumped off me, with gymnastic deftness. "What the fuck, dude?" Her face was red with anger, her eyes full of rage.

I hauled myself off the ground, still somewhat elongated. "I know," I said.

"Then why the fuck did you kiss me then?"

"I dunno," I said.

"You don't know?" she said.

"I, uhh..."

"God," she said. "And what kinda deal is this, anyway? Like

I'm his *property* or some shit like that? And you agreed to not fuck with his *prop*erty? That what we're talkin' about here?"

"Well, it's not," I said. "That's actually...uhhh...you don't understand," I said.

"Then *make* me understand, Enzo," she said. "Please. What, like I'm some fuckin' physical *ass*et he thinks he can just appropriate however he wants to? That little fuck-face."

"No, no, certainly not."

"I am so *furious*!" she said. "I am gonna straighten his ass out, right now!" She stomped off, feminine power and fury trailing behind her.

"No!" I yelled after her. "Jennifer, don't say anything to Barry! Don't...don't...." But it was too late. She was back in the building.

I felt awful, worse than failing a cup check. I knew what was coming. And it wasn't going to be pretty.

Budski

"Did you enjoy it, at least?" I said.

Jenny was stomping past me, oblivious to my presence, as I stood in the Bevier Hall second-floor stairwell by the big window overlooking the building's side exit. A window out of which I had just witnessed her cheating on me with someone with whom I had negotiated a deal about the very subject. "Broken promises need to have consequences," I said.

"Wha..." she said.

I was playing it cool, concealing the conflagration deep beneath the surface. "Looked fun from here," I said. "But did *you* enjoy it, though? That's what I really wanna know. What makes *Jenny* happy. That's what's important."

"Barry? What the hell are you doing here?" she said.

"Looking for you, my dear," I said. "You're a hard woman to find, I guess. Unless you look in the right places. Like on top of Enzo Prinziatta."

103

She looked down, hiding her eyes from me. "Yeah, well, y'know," she said.

"Please tell me you had a better reason for missing your photo session with Dmitri Bardopoulos than jumping on some guinea greaseball," I said. "Please tell me that. *Por favor.*"

"Oh, yeah," she said. "About that. Uhh, I forgot to tell Danny I needed to re-sched. Wasn't feeling like it was a photo-graphical day. I'm, uhh, sorry." She crossed her arms against her chest, burying her hands under her thin biceps.

"It's Dmitri, not Danny," I said. "And you forgot?"

"Dmitri, right. Yes. I'm sorry, Barr, I just forgot. Yeah." Her eyes remained fixed floor-ward.

"You do know that we have a deal, right?" I said. "Or did you forget that, too?"

"I know, I know," she said.

I flung a pointed index finger toward the general direction of her upper body. "Those, uhh, things on your chest that you love to show off? They're because of me," I said. "What *I* got done for you. And you have your end of the bargain to uphold."

"I know, I know, jeez," she said. "It won't happen again, I promise!"

"Promises, promises, promises," I said. "Pretty worthless coming from you, don't you think?"

She finally looked up at me. "Oh, don't be so dramatical, B.," she said. "I'll just get them done next week or whatev, it's no biggie."

"See?" I said. "This whole attitude of yours, this whole thing, this is the problem."

"What?" she said.

"I mean, when we agreed to finance those, *things*, of yours, you promised us that you'd be pursuing a career. That you would be ambitious, and go after stuff. Auditions, photo shoots, local stuff, whatever you could get," I said.

"I know!" she said. "And I am... my Facebook stuff, I did some YouTube videos, I mean, some of the pics I take of myself, they look pretty cool, I think, and professional-looking. I'm doing stuff, you can't say that I'm not."

"What kind of strategy is that?" I said. "Random YouTube videos, Facebook pics? I mean, what the hell? You're kidding me with this shit, right?"

"Kidding?" she said. "Hell no, I am not kidding! And I said—I said—I'll definitely go for the next time! I said that, B. I'm not being difficult, I'm really not. Look at L.C. or, uhh, that Sterzer girl, someone like that. You think they're out there hustlin'? Hell's no! You just put yourself out there and you get discovered by someone else. But it just takes time. It'll happen! You'll see."

I couldn't stand how difficult she was being, playing it off like this. It made me think she thought I was some kind of tool. It felt like an entire city was burning down inside of me. "I'm invoking the implants contract clause," I said. "You'll receive the legal language of the agreement in the mail. Be sure to look for it."

"The Booby Clause?" she said. "You're invoking the Booby Clause? Gimme a break!"

"Watch your mailbox," I said, as a warning.

She uncrossed her arms, and balled her fists. Ready to rumble. "Okay Barry, okay. Do you...do you remember the night that, uhh, that stripper died?" she said.

"Yes," I said. "Course I do. Why's everybody gotta bring that shit up?"

"I told you I knew something, but we never got around to talking about it?"

"Okay?" I said.

"Yeah, well. I know that Prinziatta knows something about what happened that night," Jenny said. "And if I get those papers in the mail, I'm gonna start having reeeeaaally long conversations with him about exactly what he knows, and what he saw, and whatever whatever whatever. And I think, too, I just *might* be able to convince him to go to the girl's family, or the police, or whatever."

I shook my head. I couldn't believe she was going to out-negotiate me. It was a hard loss to swallow. "I understand," I said. "Well played."

"Huh," she said. She ran upstairs.

That city kept on burning down. I couldn't put it out with a thousand fire trucks. I walked outside with my face feeling like it was the charred remains.

Prinziatta

I stared up at the unsympathetic stars. "Why?" I said to no one. "Why? Why is this so hard?" Then I saw Barry standing over me. Here it comes, I thought. Maybe I can get Semzy to sneak me a Guiness when I'm laid up in the hospital.

"Come on, dipshit," he said. "Let's go back to the house and figure this out."

I was stunned, numb-brained. I couldn't come up with anything to say. Barry and his trademarked mysteriousness. He sure knew how to keep a guy off-guard, no doubt about that. The walk to the house was long and silent and sweat and jangly nerves.

As we entered the house, Barry said, "*Mi casa es su casa*, eh?"

I walked in full of jittery anxiety, fully expecting to get jumped. This had to be some kind of set-up. Plausible deniability or something. But I knew he'd make me pay the price,

somehow, for breaking my word, for breaking the ceasefire.
"Right," I said.

"Have a seat, *compadre*," he said.

"Okay," I said. I sat—edge-balanced and spring-loaded
ready to react to sudden violence—on one of the leather
couches.

"So, wazzup, *mi amigo*?" Budski said. His off-key, friendly
confidence continued. It felt like a tiger about to rip a rabbit
apart for brunch.

"Dude," I said. "I don't know what you saw, but I wanna
just come totally clean, or whatever. I broke our little ceasefire
over Jennifer."

"Really?" he said.

It seemed like he was trying to sound surprised. The look
in his eyes was my first clue. Still, I had to play it straight, had
to do my penance.

"Yeah," I said. "I feel terrible about it, and I want to just
let you know that I didn't mean for it to happen, and that I'm
sorry about it, and it won't happen again, and, you know... I
just made a mistake. And. I'm sorry."

His face registered no emotion whatsoever. "I see," he said.
"Very interesting."

I felt my anxiety ratchet up into pure terror. My leg
wouldn't stop bouncing.

"Lemme get this straight. You broke our agreement, yes?"
Barry said.

"Yes," I said.

"And, how, exactly? I mean, did you *fuck* her? By accident?" he said.

"No," I said.

"Did you, I dunno, finger-fuck her?"

"No."

"Did she, uhh, maybe blow you?"

"No."

"Did you eat her out?" Budski said.

"No."

"Did you, ummm, I dunno, see her naked? In all her glorious nudeness?" he said.

"No."

"So, what happened, exactly?" said Barry.

"I kissed her," I said.

"You kissed her," Barry said.

"I kissed your girl, and that was my bad, and I'm really, really sorry," I said.

"You kissed my girl," he said.

"Yeah, dude. And I am sooooo sorry."

"I can see that," he said. "Tell you what, *mi hermano*. You broke our agreement, but I can see that you're sorry, and I know it'll never happen again, right?"

"Right, yes, absolutely."

"But, still and all, you broke our agreement."

"Yah," I said. Nerves started coming on strong again.

"So I think you should still pay some kinda penalty." He paused for what seemed to me like dramatic effect. "Enzo, did you know that Gatorade was invented on a college campus?"

"Uhh, no," I said.

"It's true," Budski said. "University of Florida. The Gators. That's why it's called Gatorade."

"Ah," I said. Confusion racked my brain.

"But that was, like, a million years ago. And while there have been little tweaks and improvements in sports drinks and the like over the years, there hasn't really been a major leap forward. Gatorade is still number one in the sports drink market, after all," Budski said.

"Be like Mike," I said. "Heh."

"Exactly. And it's time for that shit to change," he said. "We've been working with a company to try and develop the next evolution of energy sports drink, a kind of high-performance beverage that you take before a workout to improve your performance dramatically."

"Okay?" I said. "But what's in it, though?"

"B vitamins, electrolytes, minerals, anti-oxidants. Great stuff like that. And now we're ready to market it," he said. "Only problem is, we need a spokesman."

"Uhh, okay?" I said. "I'm sure LeBron James could use another endorsement deal."

"Exactly," he said. "How do we get someone who can make an impact, and yet, who'd be willing to agree to our, admittedly less than lucrative, terms?"

"Hell if I know," I said. "You're the business major, Barry."

"So, here's the business major's proposition. How about you volunteer to help us with this product?" Budski said. "All you have to do is drink the drink, then work out on the treadmill for about an hour."

"Why not have one of the other brothers do it?" I said.

"Between you and me?" he said. "This isn't a very athletic frat, not this local chapter, anyway. I don't have a lotta athletes on the roster right now. And the ones that are, they hate doing cardio. They like to lift, get big, look at themselves in the mirror and preen. But you, you're a pitcher. You need to be, like, a marathon runner anyway—get those legs in shape. So I figure, it's kind of a win-win deal here. You atone for your transgression, I get my spokesman, and you get to get yourself into better shape for the upcoming season, maybe get back some o' that shine you had on you in high school. Back when you had a future. Win-win-win, actually. See?"

I wasn't sure I could trust him, but it did seem like a fair deal. I wondered, for a split-second, how he knew about how good I was in high school, but then I remembered we lived in the Age of Google. "So how many times would I have to do this?" I said. "I mean, how would it work, exactly?"

"First, you need to move into the house," he said. "We got a whole gym set up here in the basement, and it's way better than that Mickey Mouse stuff they got on campus. Then, it's just an hour a day, five times a week. Basically, wake up, stretch, drink the drink, run on the treadmill for sixty minutes, and you're done. Easy cheesy."

If he was leveling with me, I couldn't find the downside. "Lemme think about it," I said.

"Not to mention, dude," Budski said. "But another thing?"

"Yeah?" I said.

"You're lookin' kinda, uhh, chunky these days," Barry said, his eyebrows raised accusingly. "*Un poquito gordito.* Hate to break it to you, bro, but it happens to be true."

"Ain't nothin' but livin'," I said.

"From what I understand, Enzo, you were one helluvan athlete back in the day," Budski said. "Back in high school. Heard you could really blow people away with that fastball of yours."

"I was all right," I said.

"Looks like your conditioning has, shall we say, gotten away from you a bit? *Un poquito, si?* All's I'm saying is, let's get it back. We're teammates. Your gain is my gain, in a sense."

I needed time to formulate an intelligent response, perhaps a counter-proposal even. "Umm, lemme think about it," I said. "What's with all the Spanish, by the way?"

"Getting my language out of the way this semester," he said. "*Este* semester. See?"

"Yah," I said. "It's kind of annoying, though. F.Y.I."

"Okay," Budski said. "But, look, think about it. Think about my proposal. And F.Y.I. to you, *mi amigo*? Lay off the *cerveza* a bit. Your gut's got enough of that stuff in there, looks like."

"*Cerveza*," I said.

"And if not, I'm sure I can come up with some other type of punishment for you, *amigo*. Since you did mess around with my girlfriend and all," Budski said. "*Mi corazon*?"

"Right," I said.

"Look, why don't you sleep on it tonight, and lemme know *mañana*. 'Kay?"

"'Kay," I said.

Think. Think about it. Yes, that was what I had to do. Think on it some. Simple as a dimple.

I went home, back to the dorm, and Googled everything I could think of about new developments in sports drinks. Coconut water, glucose polymers, PolyLactate, citrus-infusion, proteins, carbohydrate levels, B vitamins for sustained energy. Blah blah blah. All the normal stuff. Nothing unusual.

If Barry was lying, it could only be one thing. Steroids. It had to be illicit steroids, right? This guy was putting together a sports drink with some sort of steroid in it. That had to be it. What, was he going to develop an underground Gatorade? Who the fuck would buy that? But you promise athletes an undetectable steroid in a sports drink form, and that's a hella-good black-market product.

I leaned back in my desk chair, picked up a tennis ball, and started throw-and-catching it off the wall. It helped me think: Was it fair? What was the fair thing to do? How could I face this with integrity? Was it fair that I hurt my arm right when the scouts were looking at me? I trained every single day, was in remarkable physical condition, and then *boom!* my elbow goes.

It was after that surgery that I started wearing the #42 pendant. Mariano Rivera had the same surgery I had when he was in the minors, and went on, obviously, to become the greatest relief pitcher in the history of baseball. I thought, if he could do that, maybe I can come back, too, and at least be drafted.

I mulled this a bit. Then I punched up his Wikipedia entry on my laptop, to confirm something I thought I remembered, but wasn't completely sure about. And there it was. The Yankees were thinking about trading him after he had mixed results in the high minors and majors, but then "...a surprise improvement prompted a change of heart. In one minor league start, Rivera suddenly began throwing 95-96 miles per hour."

So in the middle of the steroid era, after he came off Tommy John surgery, Rivera suddenly started throwing harder out of nowhere, when the team was thinking about getting rid of him? Hmmm.

I rubbed that pendant between my thumb and forefinger and wondered. Who would care? What would it matter? I'd get in shape, and play better on a baseball field monitored by no one of significance, during games attended by no scouts, watched over by no one for no one. So I'd have more fun, maybe we'd win a few more games. And I'd avoid getting my ass beat down again by the Sammy thugs.

But what if he was giving me an exceptionally dangerous drug? What then? I'd have to take some precautions.

A little while later, Semzy walked into the room, his satchel strapped over his rather large midsection. "Yo," he said.

"Yo, Semzy, lemme holla atcha for a sec," I said. "I'm thinking about juicing."

"Good," he said. "Lemme get a grape while you at it."

"Nah, man, the good juice," I said. "Steroids."

"Don't be no fool."

"I'm serious," I said.

He raised his eyebrows, realizing I wasn't kidding around. "'Bout damn time," he said.

"For what?" I said.

"You rehabbin', right?" he said.

"Yeah, kinda," I said.

"Need to get yo' cheese back?" he said.

"Yeah," I said. "It'd be nice."

"Get drafted and get yo' cheddah right," he said. "Right?"

"Well. I mean. Yeah," I said.

"Do whatcha gotta do to gets paid, man," Semzy said. "Gotsta keep Ben Frank on the brain, yo."

"Right!" I said. Huh, I thought. The big man made a lot of sense—even if it was an unexpected angle for him to take.

"Doc Conti writin' you a scrip'?" he said.

"Not exactly," I said.

"Who then?"

"Umm," I said. "I'm gonna be drinking a new kind of sports drink that I *think*, but don't know for sure, has steroids in it."

"You jokin', right?" he said.

"Nope."

"Then you just straight-up stupid?" he said.

"Uhh."

"Don't do that shit to yo'self, dawg. Really," he said. "You can't be *that* stupid."

I said, "But, the thing is, and I was researching this, you'll be fascin—"

"'Ey, I gotta go, but just don' do dat shit. Don't care whatchou been reading or whatever. You should know right from wrong. Go to the doc. If you needs it, he gives you a scrip' for it. Get it legal. That's all I gots to say about it. Later."

He threw his black satchel over his shoulder and walked out. Just like that.

"Semz! Hey yo, Semzy!" I said. "Yo, Lakewood!" I couldn't get his attention. "Damn it, Semzy."

Our suitemate, Steve "Blondie" Oakridge, walked in. "What's with the yelling? I'm working on my short game over here."

"God damn it, Blondie," I said. "My fucking catcher. And he just disappears? Fuckin' fucker. I mean, he's my catcher!"

"What?" Steve said. He ran a hand through his fluffy blond hair. "What are you talking about? So what? What does his baseball position have to do with anything?"

"Man, see, that's the problem with golfers," I said. "What the hell do you know about team sports?"

"I know plenty, I mean—"

"Nah, I'm sayin'," I said, "you need personal experience to really *know* something. And the bond between pitcher and catcher, dude, that's like a sacred thing. Like maybe if you had a caddy or somethin', it might be close."

"Sounds kinda gay," Blondie said.

"Man, whadda you know? How hard can it be to hit a ball that's just sittin' there waiting for you to hit it?" I said.

He laughed. "Harder than you think."

"Okay, so just like that," I said. "You don't know what it's like when your catcher just walks off and leaves you all alone out there."

"Your catcher, Enzo?" Steve said. He wrinkled his eyebrows in mock-concern. "Or your father?"

"Man, get the fuck outta here with that Doctor Phil bullshit," I said. "Before I shove a tee up your ass."

"Gayyyy," he said. He strolled out like some sort of a dandy.

I walked over to Fred the Attack Tetra's tank and sprinkled in some food. "Everyone's a fuckin' psychologist these days, right Fred? He ain't my father, right? Yeah, he ain't my fuckin' father. And you know what? It's time to take back what I lost. It's time to get on with it. It's time already."

Budski

I was seething, but trying to channel it into a hard, Sammy-Ade-aided workout on the fly machine. Turning anger into pecs. "That fucking stripper," I said to no one in the gym. The thought that one stripper-girl was going to ruin everything I had worked so hard to build up from scratch disturbed me. What made it worse was that my father had already been here to help me work around the situation, and now I probably had to go back to him for even more advice. Plus, the Fatherhood Foundation still couldn't coordinate a meet for me with Chardine's father. I did more flies, trying to burn off all the anger. It wasn't working.

"Bitches," I seethed. "Total waste of time and money. All that money we invested in Jenny? And this is how she repays us? By running her filthy mouth? Ain't right, it just ain't right." I kept pumping out flies.

Sophomore Jimmy Jenkins came into the weight room.

"Hey boss, just wanted to let you know that the shipment you were waiting for is here," he said. "I just signed for it."

"Get the fuck outta here," I said. "And tell everyone else not to fuck with me right now. I gotta work some shit out."

"Uhh, okay, Barr," he said. "Yeah, no problem." He slinked away, hands shoved into his front jeans pockets.

I kept working out and thinking, but I couldn't come up with an alternative solution. I exhaled, loud. "Fuck!" I said. I'd have go back to the old man. There was no other way. I fished my cell out of my pocket and dialed my father's work number. When his secretary put me through, he said, "Barry?"

"Dad, I think I got a bit of a problem here."

He sighed or exhaled, I couldn't tell which. "Yeah?" he said.

"Unfortunately," I said.

"Well, okay. What is it?"

"I was getting on Jenny like you told me," I said. "Trying to get her to be more proactive. Get her new pictures done, go on auditions. Stuff like that."

"Barry, I'm getting a little tired of this, honestly."

"I know, Dad, but see, she got all mad at me and stuff, for getting on her so bad, and I was like, well, either do what you're supposed to do, or I'll pull the trigger on the Booby Clause."

"Barry, Jesus Christ, you're not talking about what I think you're talking about?" he said.

"Yeah, the stipulation we put in her contract when we gave her the money for the implants. That if she didn't live up to her end of the bargain, we can legally recover our losses."

"Oh yeah," he said. "*That* Booby Clause."

"Yeah, and anyway, soon as I brought that up, she went ballistic."

"Son," he said. "It might be time we cut our losses with that girl."

"But she's so..."

"Hot?"

"*Hell's* yeah, but she can be a great revenue-generating asset for us too," I said.

"Potentially," he said.

"Potentially," I agreed. "I mean, we spent eleven grand on those things!"

"I know it, buddy," he said. "I know it. But you gotta push it. You have to sweat and hustle twenty-four-seven to make things happen, and even if you do, even when you do *all* the right things, it's no guarantee of success. Keep that in mind. That's just, uhh, that's just the reality of business. It's dog-eat-dog, Son."

"I know Dad, and I been trying, I really have. But I mean, I need to know, what else can I really do?" I said. "What else can I realistically do?"

There was a long pause on the line. "Son, lemme tell you a little story about your mother," he said.

"Umm, okay?" I said.

"Y'know, your mom was pretty attractive herself, back in the day," he said.

"Dad, I'm not sure I need to hear this," I said.

"Just listen to me, Bartholomew," he said.

I hated when he called me that, even though it was my given name. I'd adopted "Barry" at age ten—on my tenth birthday—and he was the only one who still consistently used that long, ugly version of my name.

"Once your mom started getting a little older," he said, "especially after she had you, her body began to...let's say, sag, a little."

"Gross, dude," I said.

"So naturally, she wanted some, uhh, enhancement," he

said. "And I figured, hey, why not? We have the money, and it'll
be fun for me, too. So why not, right?"

"Uhh," I said.

"So, she gets them, and she's happy, and I'm happy," he said.

"Can we get to the point any time soon, please?" I said.
"This is creeping me out, Dad."

"Point is, when we started to go to functions and dinners
and events, stuff like that, black tie affairs or what-have-you, she
wanted to show them off. And so here I was, with this middle-
aged woman on my arm, showing off a massive amount of obvi-
ously-augmented cleavage..."

"Oh shit," I said.

"Exactly. It was quite embarrassing. But no matter what I
said, no matter what argument I made, she did not want to hear
it. She had them, she was going to show them off and have people stare at them, stare at her, no matter what. She was insistent.
Did not care. Needed the attention and was not ashamed about
it, either."

"So wha'dja do?" I said.

"This is the point, what I did," he said. "She'd been bugging
me for years to get an Escalade. She wanted to ride up high over
everybody on the road, and in a luxury vehicle as well. She's high
maintenance, your mother."

"Yeah."

"So I made her a deal," he said. "Calm down with the cleavage and you get your Escalade. And it worked. We both got
what we wanted."

"Oh," I said.

"So, the lesson is this. Take your useless emotions out of
the deal, and deal with her like you would in any other business negotiation. Negotiate from the position of her having no
sexual appeal to you whatsoever," he said. "Otherwise, you're in

a one-down position the whole time, and you can *never* win a negotiation that way."

"But Dad," I said.

"Barry, that's really all there is to it," he said. "It's a simple give-and-take knife fight. Like everything else. You know it's right when everyone involved's equally unhappy."

I exhaled. There was no use arguing with him. "Fine. Got it. No emotions. Knife fight."

"Right," he said.

"Thanks, Dad. I'll make it work."

"Okay, Son," he said. "Remember, our money's on the line with her, so it's imperative that you do. Not to make you nervous or anything." He laughed.

I pressed the END button on my cell and stood up from the fly machine.

Now all I needed to do was figure out what the hell Jenny Drama wanted but couldn't have, and propose to give it to her if she did what we wanted. The good thing was, I had a pretty clear idea about exactly what—or who—that might be.

21

Prinziatta

"Hey man," I said. "I just wanted to apologize for not being around much lately."

"Ah, don' sweat it, dawg," Semzy said.

Our favorite bar, P&G's, was the best place for me to try and make amends with my catcher, I figured. We had taken a corner booth in the back and a tray full of fifty-cent beers. "No, really, I know it ain't right or whatever. You know I just have my head all mixed up with this thing with Jennifer and Barry and all that."

"Yeah," he said, his know-it-all eyes full of pity. "Ain't no thing, dawg. Don't sweat it. I don't care 'bout that shit right now. Let's just concentrate on getting shitfaced, yo."

"All right," I said. "But I wanted to tell you something else, too."

"Yeah?" Semzy said, sipping from his beer cup.

"I'm thinking about rushing Sammy," I said.

"Yeah?"

"Yeah, and, so you know. What do you think about that?"
I said.

"Why you wanna do that shit?" he said.

"I dunno, I talked to Budski about it," I said. "He kind
of convinced me it's a good idea. He can be pretty persuasive,
actually."

"So?" Semzy said. "He came at me too with that nonsense. I
told him forget that shit."

"Well, that's you. Woulda been me to, before all this stuff
happened," I said. "So now, now, this is where this whole juicing
thing is coming from that I told you about before. He's got this
new sports drink thing that he's developing, and he wants me to
be a spokesman for it, if it works. Do the treadmill thing, maybe
get back into some kind of decent shape while I'm at it."

"You know how fucking crazy that sounds, Enzo?" Semzy
said. "That ain't you. Me and you, we ain't treadmill dudes. We
like to party too much."

"Well," I said. "It's a bit of a risk, but from what he's telling
me the risk is minimal."

"What's in this thing, anyway?" he said. "You ask your new
bes' friend that?"

"He's not my best friend," I said. "But he's just saying,
y'know, it's some new kinda sports drink. Helps you train better.
Vitamins, minerals, all that good stuff."

"Uhh, don't you watch the news, or what?" he said.

"Huh?" I said.

"Do the word 'Balco' ring a bell, dumbass? Bonds, Giambi,
that runner-girl, Jones or whatever, that weird guy with the mus-
tache? He-llo?"

"Yeah, yeah, I know," I said. "That's what I thought, too. But
so what? I'll drink the stuff, work out, and get in shape..."

"Or get dead," he said.

"Any of these guys, are they dead?" I said.

"Uhh, that Caminiti cat's dead."

"Caminiti? First off, he was an M.V.P., okay? And second, he died after his career was over. He was a coke-head, and God knows what else he was doing," I said. "That the newspaper *didn't* report."

"Seems like a big risk to take, bro," Semzy said. "And for what? To pitch a little better in a D-3 school? Why risk it?"

"Yeah," I said. "I know. I thought about that, too."

"Look, why don't you hold off on making this decision for a while? Just chill a little. Let's have a few drinks, let's think it over. Let's chill and talk about it some more," Semzy advised. That's what it felt like—legal advice.

I noticed a look in his eyes that struck me as unusual. It seemed like a strange combination of nervousness and desperation. I felt the rise of an old familiar feeling—a cold, creeping sensation of being sold out. Here I was listening to my alleged best bro telling me to drink my head off instead of getting in shape? How did that make any sense? There was something wrong, something amiss. I had no idea what it was, but I didn't like its stench. No matter how much cheap beer I drank, it just would not go away.

I kept drinking. Drinking and thinking. And then I realized precisely what the problem was. Sometimes the thing people hate most is a real chance at success.

"Is you okay?" Semzy asked me.

"Sure," I said. "Why not?"

"You look like you got ideas." He brushed something from the bottom of his retro Justin Tuck jersey.

"Ideas?" I said.

"Yeah, but you seem, I dunno, different."

"Different how?" I said.

"Just. Different," Semzy said. "Dawg, all's you got to be is the best damn drinker I ever seen in my life, which you already is. That's just what you is. Can't be all changin' and shit. Fish gotsta swim, you feel me?"

I felt the surge of an embarrassing truth realized shiver through me. I ran my hand through my hair once, then again. "That's not very helpful," I said. "Especially from a psychology kook like yourself. You're supposed to be the master of having worthless, nice-sounding theories, or theorums, or whatever the hell you call 'em. The kinds of things some douchebag'll pay a hundred bucks an hour for. Like, some magic dust you sprinkle on someone, and suddenly, all the issues they had when they walked through the magic door disappear! C'mon, man, I thought you was better than that."

"Hey!" he said. "I was complimentin' yo' ass, man. You can drink anyone on campus under the table, I don't care if the dude's seven feet tall or some shit. You got talent like that."

"Okay, so what about you, big man? Back to what *you're* good at," I said. "Let's get back to why you think it's okay to charge people hundreds of thousands of dollars just to have someone to bitch and complain to."

"Dude, a lotta people need and benefit from psychological counseling," he said. "It's serious business, yo, and it be helpin' a ton o' people every day."

"If you say so," I said.

"Best believe it," he said. "Thing is, people where I'm from, a lotta them can't afford it, even though they the ones most needin' it and stuff. It's fucked up, cuz they need to understand why they do what they do, or why it's mad important to stay home and be a good dad to they children instead of bein' out drinkin' with the fellas and playin' gangsta fo' no reason. See what I'm sayin'?"

"Sooo, you're gonna be like, the poor man's Dr. Phil from the 'hood?" I said. "Am I understanding this right?"

"Yeah, som'in like that," he said. "And you? You be the modern-day Arthur or whatever that dude name was. Funny-ass drunk dude."

The nobility of his idea to be a Dr. Phil in the 'hood had always made me choke up a little. But now I saw it from a different angle—the angle that affected me. If I could become what I was pre-injury, scouts would be crawling all over this tiny campus, and then Semzy would have a real moral dilemma to deal with. Pursue baseball or finish his schooling and then start his practice as soon as possible. "A'ight," I said. "That's cool, though. But just remember this—avoidance is a bitch, too. If you have talents, plural, you should pursue them all, homie. This or that? Yes, both."

"Agreed," he said. "Now what was we talkin' 'bout?"

I shrugged. "Avoidance?" I said.

"Oh yeah!" Semzy said. "Now, I remember."

"Oh, goodie," I said.

"Wanted to holla at you 'bout how you wanna go all Roger Clemens on us."

"You mean by dominating on the mound? Blowin' the ol' speedball by everyone?" I said.

"Not exactly what I had in mind," said Semzy.

"You mean by being a huge inspiration to everyone with my extreme training, and with my intense workouts, and by having this great body all the girls want to get their hands all over? That what you mean?" I said.

"Not it," Semzy said.

"Well, then," I said, "you must be mistaken, big fella. You must be mistaken."

"I really don't think so," he said.

"Well, I do," I said. "So, okay, see ya!"

"Wait, wait a minute, Enzo," Semzy said. "We got a lotta drinkin' to do yet."

I stood up. I was tired of it. Even if I knew *why* he was being like this, I still didn't like it, and I needed to do something drastic about it. I needed to create a massive barrier to self-sabotage. Enough was enough. "Geez, you're such a nag, man."

"Just be careful, dawg," he said. "'Sall I'm sayin.'"

"Gotcha!" I said.

I walked over to the bar, determined to do the right thing. Small piles of dollar bills were scattered across the bartop. I looked at Hank, the bartender. He walked toward me.

"Hank," I said, "if I took all the money here on this bar, each one of these little piles here, you'd ban me from ever coming in here again, wouldn't you?"

"Course," he said.

"Cool," I said, "let's do that, then." I ran up and down the bar, taking each and every money pile and stuffing it into my jeans.

"Hey!" Hank said.

Then I ran the hell outta there, grinning like the Riddler. Behind me, I heard Semzy holler at me, "What the fuck, dude!?"

I hit up every bar in town in the exact same way, barely avoiding a violent confrontation each time. I cut myself off, permanently. Last call at the bar at the end of the universe.

I liked it even more for its symbolic value, as a great, real reminder of which direction I needed to travel. When I got back to the dorm I had a text message from Semzy on my phone: "U lost it, dawg. Hit me up whn u get yo mind back. Til then, fuck off"

Budski

"I just want to get this thing going already. In a celebrity-worshipping culture, the most lucrative thing you can be is a respected celeb—and the management behind a respected celebrity, in a more behind-the-scenes way. So, while the things I've done so far with the frat are nice, they're really just small potatoes. Celebrity brand management and extension—that's where the real dollars are," I said.

Jenny said, "So you've said." She adjusted her white Bouclé sweater so that more of her tanned shoulder was exposed.

My heart jumped a little. "Yeah, well," I said. "I'm getting damn tired of waiting around for other people to make moves." I fake-coughed.

Jenny and I watched the hazing from way in the back of the basement, but we could still see and hear pretty good. Five pledges were bent over a table with their naked asses exposed to the haze-master, Senior Mark Gluttealle.

"How many hours of practice does it take before you can master a craft and who is the author of that theory?" the haze-master said.

"Sir, twenty-thousand and Malcolm Gladwaller, sir!" said the pledge.

The haze-master whacked him on the ass with the pledge-paddle. "Wrong!" he said. He moved over to the next pledge. "Who is the author of *Permission Marketing*?" he said.

"Sir, Chris Brogan, sir!" Pledge Number Two said.

The haze-master whacked him on the ass with the pledge-paddle. "Wrong!" he said. He moved over to the next pledge. "Who uses the term, 'zombieconomy' to describe the state of the American economy circa 2006 to present?" he said.

"Sir, Umair Haque, sir!" Pledge Number Three said. "Of the Havas Media Lab at Harvard Business School."

The haze-master whacked him on the ass with the pledge-paddle. "Co-rrect!" he said. He moved over to the next pledge. "Who wrote, *Freakonomics*, and what is its overall theme?" he said.

"Sir, Steven Levitt and behavioral economics, sir!" said Pledge Number Four.

"Hazing's going pretty good, don'tcha think?" I said to Jenny.

She shook her head. "How come Enzo's not with these guys?"

"We're, uhh, being a little more innovative with his pledge status," I said. "After all, in today's business climate, innovation is the most vital and important element to any successful venture."

"Borrrring!" Jenny said. "Where the hell's the fun in this shit? Usually, hazing involves getting *fucked up* and doing crazy-ass, fun shit! This? This is just plain stupid."

"Yeah, okay," I said. "I just wanted to check how it was going in here, anyway. Let's go hang out in my room."

"Fine," she said.

Once we got up there, I was determined to exert my managerial influence over her. To let her know I had everything under control, managerially speaking. "Uhh, so, how'd it, like, go today, or whatever?" I said.

"Huh?" she said.

"How'd it go today?" I said, louder, angrier. "Please tell me you went to that open audition in the city this morning."

"Oh, uhh, yeah," she said, diving her big eyes toward the ground. "Yeah, it was fine. Lotta girls there. Lotta waiting. You know how it goes."

I could barely hear the words. "What?" I said.

"You heard me," she said. Her eyes were still locked on the carpet.

Suspicious, I handed her a beer from the BeerTender. "Mm-hmm," I said.

"Thanks," she said. She forced a smile, but it lacked the eye engagement of a real smile.

I tried, hard, not to lose my cool. It took a good amount of discipline. My rage boiled beneath the surface. I thought about my long-term plan, though, and that cooled it down some. "So, how did you do?" I said.

"Huh?" she said.

"How do you think you did? At the audition."

She touched her neck with her index finger, then tried to make it seem as if she had an itch there that she was scratching. "Okay, I guess," she said. "You never really know. You just do your thing and hope they like it, I guess. Right?"

"Can I ask you a question?" I said.

"Mm?"

"What the fuck do you want, exactly?" I said. "I'm racking my goddam brain, and I can't seem to figure it out for the life of me."

"Oh, stop being so dramatical, Barr," she said. "I'm a girl. It's like Cyndi Lauper used to say. I just wanna have fun. Or something."

"Just stop it," I said.

"What?" Jenny said.

"I thought you wanted a career," I said. "Thought you wanted to act. Like it was your *calling* or some shit. Isn't that what you told me? That that's what you *really* wanted most in life?"

"I do!" she said. "And I will. It's just gonna take some time. You think, you think these people who make it, you think they just, *poof*, snap their fingers and it happens? It takes time, Barr, that's all it is. Quit being so impatient. For God's sake."

The career angle seemed like it wasn't going to take, not yet. For some reason, I just couldn't connect with her on that level. I had to switch tracks, messy though it would probably be. "Yeah, okay," I said.

"Besides, I thought we were going shopping. No?" she said.

"Yeah, we are," I said. "I mean, we were. I mean, uhh. Lemme ask you something."

"Okay?"

"What color shirt was the casting director wearing?" I said.

Her eyes shifted up and to the right. "What?" she said.

"You heard me," I said.

"Uhh, green," she said. "And what difference does it make, anyway? You think I remember shit like that? *Hell's* no! Damn. You're being too controlling, you know that? You're stressing me out big-time, Barry."

That made for a reasonably realistic cue. "Know what I think?" I said.

"What?" she said.

"I think we need a break," I said.

"A break?" she said.

"Yeah," I said. "You wanna see Enzo anyway, right? So, we need to stop seeing each other for a while. We can continue on professionally, but personally, I think we need a break."

"Professionally?" she said. "Barry, you ain't my manager, and you do not control me. How many times I gotta tell you that? It's not hard to understand. This little fuckin' Double B Management idea you got in your head? It's nothin'! It's just an idea. It's like you're this little boy saying he wants to be an astronaut. That doesn't mean he's actually an astronaut!"

"Everything has to start somewhere," I said. "Microsoft didn't..."

"Yeah, but what are you actually *doing*? Telling me to go on auditions? Getting my pics taken? Anybody can do that shit. That's not management, Barry. Management would be getting me meetings with famous directors, getting me real exposure with real players in the game," she said. "And don't ask me how, that's supposed to be *your* job! Damn it, Barry, step up! You're putting all this shit on me, when all you're doing is sitting here with your plans and your nagging and and whatever! I mean, what the fuck, Barry? You wanna manage me? Then *manage* me, dumbass. Do something I can respect. Not this little garbage bullshit you been doing. That ain't gonna cut it!"

"I, uhh..." I said.

"You want a break? Well, guess what? I want a break too, Barry. You *got* it, dumbass!" she said. She stomped out of my room, and the house. She slammed the front door behind her. I heard it all the way up in my room.

Perfect, I thought. My little trap worked. Now the only problem was it meant she'd be going after Enzo Prinziatta. Risk, no matter how well managed, was still a bitch.

Prinziatta

The Saturday-morning Sammy kitchen looked like a beer-can junkyard. I had played the role of keg-master the night before, and I had managed to prevent any of the fermented stuff from trickling down my gullet. I felt strangely proud of that.

"Trivia question," I said. I sat down, split-legged, on a Sammy barstool.

"All right, sir," Barry said. He cracked an egg on the rim of a Sammy bowl. He let its gooey contents drip into the depth.

"What's the best way to defeat an enemy?" I said.

"Hmmm, let's see," he said. "Hire a covert operative to kill his entire family, and then, um, watch him hang himself because he can't deal with the pain?"

I recoiled, my face clenched. "No!" I said. "Make him a friend. Jesus Christ."

"Oh, uh, yeah," Barry said. "You could go that way too, I guess."

"So, in that sprit of frenemiship, I heard you got a vacancy at this here Bates Motel," I said.

"Ah, the prodigal mutt returns," Barry said. "Domestic *problemos* in the dorm? R.A.'s catch you with a beer bottle or something?" He whisked the egg goo in the bowl with a Sammy fork.

"Nah, this way I can keep an eye on what you're putting in the SammyAde," I said. "Make sure you don't give me the batch with the poison in it."

Barry laughed. "Cha," he said, "like we manufacture it here. No, but y'know what? This is gonna be great, *amigo*. You can really focus on your training this way."

"All right, thanks," I said. "I'll bring over some of my stuff this afternoon."

"Sure," Barry said, smiling like a madman. "My pleasure."

So, my period of intense physical training began on a mild January morning in the year of the Flying Spaghetti Monster, Two Thousand and Seven. The gym equipment at the Sammy House was actually much better than what they had on campus, believe it or not—and it wasn't even close.

It felt good. All my anger, all my frustration, all my rage against the world could be channeled into the energy I needed to get through the grueling workouts. And when it was over, the result of that anger-pouring was making my life better, not worse. It was replacing the negative of alcohol anesthesia with the positive of physical exertion and endorphins. And if it meant avoiding looking like Tony Soprano for the rest of my life, all the better.

The sports drink itself tasted like Gatorade minus the high fructose corn syrup. I didn't really notice any effects other than that as time went on, my workouts got longer. But that's hardly unusual. The more you work out, the more you *can* work out. And the weight. Started. Coming. Off.

One night about a month after I had moved in, Jennifer Burnette strutted through the door of the gym, wearing a "sexy cop" Halloween costume. It included a utility belt complete with a holster, fake gun, and handcuffs. Her hair was teased up to the heavens. I seriously doubted any real female cops, even on Halloween in Bohemia, wore their make-up like she did, with thick black eyeliner and long lashes, a little too much sheer blush, and gaudy blue eye shadow. But still, for all its over-the-top, Long Island sluttiness, it turned me on. It really did. "*Some-body's* up late," she said. "And lookin' fine." The barely-buttoned cop uniform shirt tied up above her little belly button showed off the top of a butterfly tattoo coming out of her *Reno 911*-type short-shorts.

I put the bench press bar back on the rest. "Ha," I said. "Nice and subtle. Reliving Halloween in January?"

"Stop! Or I'll shoot!" she said, pointing her gun-fingers at me. "You like?" Her proud smile made it clear she knew that I did.

"It's a'ight," I said. "The boots are what sell it, though. Forty-Second Street all the way. Super-classy, Long Island Lassy." The black patent-leather jobs went all the way above her knees.

"A'ight?" she said. "Yeah, right." She swished her way over to me, snuggled herself into me on the press bench. "How you doin'?" she whispered into my ear.

I scrunched over a bit, away from her. "What's all this?"

"Havin' fun," she said. "Why not join me?"

"Join you? What, like, good cop, bad cop? That the idea here?" I said.

"Now you're starting to get it," she said.

"As much as you need to be punished, I think I'll pass," I said.

"Why? You...scurred? Scurrred of a...a...gurrrrrl?" she said. She batted her enhanced eyelashes so that the cuteness of the gesture was obvious even to the last row of the imaginary theater stage on which she perpetually performed. "Why you keep resistin' for, Enzo?" Her pupils were penny-sized. Her breath reeked of beer and tic-tacs.

This whole situation made me feel like the stone-cold sober guy walking into a bar at 2 A.M. Disquieting and awkward. "I ain't scared," I said. "I just, uhh, need to get back to my workout."

"Ain't nothin' goin' on but the lovin', baby," Jennifer said.

I didn't want her like this, definitely drunk and probably high. Maybe I was old-fashioned, but it didn't feel right and it wouldn't be the same as if she were sober. It just felt plain wrong. "Uhh," I said, unable to verbally overcome her sensual charms.

She stood up and moved right in front of me, about six inches away. She swayed her hips slowly back and forth, in rhythm to the beat of some song playing in her head. Then she inched her way closer to me and whispered, "Pour some honey on me, baby!"

Despite my gentlemanly reservations, my animal instincts shot up through me on their own command. I wanted to rapture her, right there, with complete abandon. I wanted to let my inhibitions run vulture-dive wild. But, somehow, I strapped a leash on the scavenger and locked it back up in its cage. "Jennifer," I said, in a calm, fatherly voice. "You know I shouldn't be with you. Get off me."

"Get off? That's what I'm *tryin'* to do, get off, silly!" She continued to writhe and grind into my lap.

"Hey!" I said. "Stop it, Officer Slutty."

"Now, you're getting' it, big boy," said Jennifer.

"No," I said. "I said no. Get the hell off." I pushed her away from me. "No means no."

She fell on the floor. Her face beamed confusion and determination. "Oh, now you're gettin' rough, huh?" Jennifer said. "You're finally getting' good now. Took ya long enough, but whatevs." She lunged at me, lioness-like, albeit clumsily.

I slid out of the way and watched her crash onto the floor again. "Just stop it, Jennifer," I said. "You're making yourself look ridiculous. Hot, yeah, but also too, ridiculous."

"Hot. See I knew it," she said.

"Don't make me spank you, now," I said. The conflict of the situation—red devil versus white angel in a no-holds-barred death-cage match for my soul—made my chest hurt. Everything was a fight, even within yourself, I thought. *Every*thing's a fight.

"There you go with the promises again," she said.

"I'm turning in for the night," I said. "Good night, Officer Slutty. Go home."

"Turning in? Okay, Urkell. Yeah, g'night!" she said. She stayed there, splayed out on the floor, somewhat awkwardly.

I noticed a mischievous look in her dark, bright eyes. I walked out of the gym wondering what was really going on with her. It was hard to tell. She ran hot and cold for me, it seemed. Maybe Budski the PuppetMaster was controlling her like some warped Svengali man, maneuvering her for ends only he fully understood. Maybe Jennifer was bi-polar. Maybe she had a serious drug problem, which caused occasional schizophrenic episodes. Maybe. Maybe a hundred things. With this girl, who knew? Maybe that was a part of her alluring, mysterious magic.

Why was it that *she* moved me like no other girl moved me? Why was it that she left an indelible mark on me? Why did it feel like if I didn't make this woman my wife, my life would be more fetters than wings? Where did that feeling come from?

Why did she conjure it? Who the fuck was she to do all this to me, with such grace and ease and thick perfume and make-up? These things I pondered as I walked, sweaty and exasperated, toward the bathroom. Maybe I'm going right out of my freaking mind, I thought. I started the shower.

Whenever I felt like this, whenever emotions of anxiety or fear or sadness or joy or excitement seized me, my normal reaction would be to reach for a beer, and to keep on reaching for a beer until there were no more beers left or I couldn't remember what had driven me to drink in the first place, whichever came first. There was a behavioral aspect to it, which felt like a strange kind of emptiness. It was like reaching for something you think is there that's not and your clasping hand grasps only air, or when you sit down expecting a chair to be there and it isn't, so you crash to the floor like some kind of klutz. Living like this— sober—was like living in that moment of complete unexpectedness all of the time. It was more than a little bit scary.

I heard a knock on the bathroom door as I was taking off my "Anger Management Tour" T-shirt. I didn't want to answer it. "Eeenzoooo!!!" I heard in Jennifer's sing-song voice. I didn't want to answer it. "Go 'way!" I yelled. "Nobody home. *No en casa, señorita!*" I didn't want to answer it.

"Enzo!" I heard. "Come out and plaaay!" Pounding knocks and echoes reverberated from the door.

I needed a drink. Bad. Instead, I went to the damn door and yanked it open. "Yes, Officer Slutty?" I said, innocent as you please.

"Lemme in, silly," she said. She forced her way by me, under my arm. "Oooh, nice pecs, dude."

A strange sort of ache pounded in my heart. I was tired— tired of trying to figure this girl out. There was a perfectly good girl—Shannon Hestian—who wanted to be with me, a girl most

guys on campus would kill to be with, so why couldn't I just let
it go at that? Why couldn't I be happy with happy? Why was my
soul not content to settle for excellent? Why did I feel the need
to reach for perfect? And who was I to make these stupid value
judgments anyway? It made my heart ache and my head hurt.

Jennifer strutted into the bathroom.

I followed, dreading what was sure to come. I took off my
shorts and underwear and entered the steaming shower. The
room already smelled like her perfume waft-mingled with the
smell and damp of the shower steam.

"Oh," I heard her say through the shower curtain. "That
how you gonna play this? Wet? Fine with me." I heard the hurm
and thrush of her disrobing.

She came into the shower, tripping a bit on the top of
the tub, a giant smile beaming at me. "That's right," she said.
"Thaaat's right." She started to run her hands down my chest,
water wetting down her hair, her body.

"No," I said. I pushed her hands down. "Why are you doing
this, Jennifer?"

"Doing what?" she said, playing innocent. The context
made the question comical. It would have been more so, if so
much anguish hadn't been involved in it for me.

"Why are you doing this now? You're with Budski, I've
promised not to see you. Why would you wanna do this now? I
don't get it," I said.

She grinned sexily. She leaned her body into mine. She
whispered in my ear, "Don't you see? Forbidden fruit." She
kissed my neck.

"Stop, stop it Jennifer, stop it," I said.

"Oh, and we're on a break, anyway," she said. She pulled her
head up. "And if you tell me to stop one more time, I swear to

God I'm gonna fucking explode in your lap, so stop it with the stop it!"

I couldn't take it anymore. The golden eagle broke the kangaroo-leather leash, exploded free from the falconer's gauntlet, and soared into the sky of his desire's delight. I gave Jenny Drama the performance she'd been begging for.

After it was over, sweaty and exhausted, I felt complete. I had never felt that way before, but it was exactly as I had imagined it would be the moment I had seen this girl at the Sammy Halloween party. She had this unique quality: she allowed, or damn-near forced, a man to be free as flight.

In the morning, she awakened me with a steaming coffee cup in my face. "Morning sunshine," she said. "Wake up and sniff the java!"

"Blurmnn mmmgnnn neggeggl llnnnn ndddebbb," I said.

"Precisely," she said, leaving the cup on the nightstand by the bed and tramping off into the bathroom.

I gathered up my dream-yarn and pulled my consciousness together. I sat up on the bed and sipped from the mug. It was good coffee. I smiled widely, thinking about how maybe sobriety led to good decisions, good relationships. Maybe it was true: drinking solves nothing, and in fact only makes things worse.

Jennifer came out of the bathroom just in time to catch the mood of my grin and whatever my face was translating from my brain. She said, stern as steel, "Hey! You do know that this does not mean we're together now, right? We can just be, like, friends with benefits and stuff, okay?"

Crushed, I felt like a deflating balloon with all the air rushing out of my backside, desperately in need of some Bailey's Irish Cream for the stupid fucking coffee. "Not okay," I said. "That just ain't gonna work for me."

"Oh, don't tell me you're one of those intimacy junkies!" she said, protesting in a crimson bathrobe. "Enjoy the ride! You just hit the motherfuckin' lottery, baby! And you're sittin' there pouting? It's commitment-free sex!"

My brain felt like a black void. It was hard to think, hard to speak. I mumbled something about being used, about a piece of meat. Being gut-punched before 8 A.M. is a special, cruel, and unusual proposition.

"Holy shit, man!" she said. "You're an athlete! You ain't supposed to be all sensitive! Jesus Effin' Christ, man!" Jenny Drama melodramatically slammed the bathroom door. I heard the screech of the shower knobs and then the water pouring down.

My first thought was to find the nearest keg and empty its contents into my stomach. My brain felt like it was constricting, somehow. It felt like blackness was pressing down on it. I fled the bedroom in my boxer shorts and headed for the kitchen in search of anesthetics.

"Hey, slow down there, chief," Barry said, leaning against the kitchen counter. He took a sip of what looked like a protein drink from the Sammy blender. "What's up?"

"You know that ex of yours?" I said.

"More than likely." He sipped.

"She's fucking crazy!" I had my head in the fridge. "Where's the beer, man?"

"Dude, it's eight in the morning," Barry said.

"I don't care!" I said. "Where's the fucking beer?!"

"Relax, man," Barry said. "Have some SammyAde instead. Then you can, uhh, go workout. Trust me. You'll feel better. Burn it off, dude. Beer won't help you, man. Trust me. I been there with Jenny Drama. Alcohol don't solve nada with that chica."

There was no beer in the fridge, anyway. "Okay, fine!" I said. I grabbed a 32-ounce bottle of the stuff and began to chug.

"Whoa," Barry said. "Take it easy, there, chief. Not so fast with that stuff. Or so mucho! Damn."

I stopped chugging long enough to say, "Fuck you," then went back to chugging until there wasn't anything left to chug. "Fuck you," I said again—for good measure—and headed back to my room. Jennifer was still in the shower. I threw on a pair of shorts, socks, and my high-tops. I went to the gym in the basement. I started the treadmill rotating, which got my mind moving, too.

Eventually, sweat-soaked and grimy, heart chugging like the rounds of a machine gun, the solution became clear as crystal.

Budski

"How can it be done?" I asked myself, hoping for sub-conscious guidance.

I raked gravel around the black boulder in my bedroom-set Karesansui Zen gravel garden, slow and steady. I raked all the gravel around that boulder left-to-right. Then I went over to the white boulder on the other side of the garden and raked the gravel top-to-bottom. Slow, steady, careful. Back and forth with that rake, working it like the work was artistry of the highest importance. Back and forth, forth and back. Then I went back to the black boulder and reversed the pattern. Back and forth, forth and back. Then to the white and reversed it. Slow and steady. Combing down to my serenity.

"God grant me the serenity to accept the things I cannot change; the courage to change the things I can, and the wisdom to know the difference," I whisper-prayed to myself. "Be not angry that you cannot make others as you wish them to be, since you cannot make yourself as you wish to be. Seek freedom and become captive of your desires. Seek discipline and find your liberty." I repeated my serenity prayer over and over until it seemed burned onto my brain.

How could I engineer an "attention event" for Jennifer that would make her understand my legitimacy and jump-start her career at the same time?

I kept on raking and thinking. And then it hit me.

I picked up the phone and dialed. "Cindy, m'love! How are you this fine morning?" I said.

"Barry Budski," Cindy said. "Don't you ever go to class?"

"Ah," I said. "Class is overrated."

"So what can I do for you, sweetie?"

"I heard the Student Union building entranceway is in need of some new artwork," I said.

"Perhaps that could be true," she said.

"And I also heard, on a related note, that your funding situation is in a state of disrepair."

"Perhaps," she said.

"Well, it just so happens that we may be able to be of some assistance to you."

"And for this assistance, what price would the Student Union need to be ready to pay?"

"Funny you should ask..."

FADE TO BLACK.
FADE IN FROM BLACK.

"Ohhhkay, so we're all on the call," I said. "Well guys, I'm glad you were all available because I wanted to discuss the Tucker Max appearance. Once that becomes a reality, which I anticipate it will, I'm planning some fun stunts that *may* piss off some of the femiNazi groups, which will probably be coming out in full force to protest. So, here's what I need from my fellow members of the Hellenic Co-Operative..."

FADE TO BLACK.
FADE IN FROM BLACK.

"Hey, Professor Gembull," I said. "Just wanted to let you know that the Student Union board and the Hellenic Co-Operative are both now one-hundred percent behind the Tucker Max thing."

"Great," Professor Gembull said. "I'll let it be known in administrative circles, such as they are."

"Okay, great. Thanks."

"One more thing, Barry," he said.

"Yeah?"

"You should watch your back with that Enzo Prinziatta fella."

"Oh yeah?"

"I got the feeling he's kind of a... How shall I put this? A rottweiler."

"A rottweiler?"

"Yeah, a sort of runner-up attack dog. Mean, ornery, with a chip on his shoulder. The kind that won't let go once he gets his teeth into something."

"Um. Okay. Well," I said. "Thanks for that..."

FADE TO BLACK.
FADE IN FROM BLACK.

I raked gravel around the black boulder in my bedroom-set Karesansui Zen gravel garden, slow and steady. I raked all the gravel around that boulder left-to-right. Then I went over to the white boulder on the other side of the garden and raked the gravel top-to-bottom. Slow, steady, careful. Back and forth with that rake, working it like the work was artistry of the highest importance. Back and forth, forth and back. Then I went back to the black boulder and reversed the pattern. Back and forth, forth and back. Then to the white and reversed it. Slow and steady. Combing down to my serenity.

First Jenny, then Enzy, I thought.

Prinziatta

"**L**et's go!" I said to myself, trying to psych myself up. "A change-up with the same arm speed, choked back ten or more miles per hour."

I knew good-girl Shannon always did her laundry on Saturday nights, so I figured the laundry room—full of dirty things getting clean—would be a good place to execute my pitch. As I treaded down the central Bevier staircase to the basement, I felt pangs of guilt in my recently dwindled gut. I shut them down with the idea that the Shan relationship wouldn't last long, and to help her get over things, I'd buy her a really nice guilt gift. I turned the corner into the doorway of the laundry room, and heard the washers and dryers banging and water-swishing, doing their thing. The smell of soap and apparel and water and hot machinery infiltrated my nose. Shannon Hestian—alone— was bent over a folding table, sorting her dainties.

"Okay!" I said, faux-arrogance in my voice. I leaned, faux-arrogantly, on the door jamb.

She looked at me. "Okay what?" she said.

Even in the simple, uncoordinated outfit of beige UGGs, skinny jeans, and a baby T she looked stunning. "It's your lucky day, young lady," I said.

"Why, is Usher doing a concert on campus?" she said.

I made a mental note: Usher tickets. "Nope," I said. "Even better."

"How could anything possibly be better than that?" she said.

"You got some pretty low standards there, you know that?" I said.

"Anyway..." she said.

"Anyway, I've decided to grant you your wish and go out with you."

"Ha," she said. She went back to her folding.

"No, seriously," I said. "Your ship has finally arrived, babycakes."

"Cha," she said.

She was right. Every God-damned thing was a fight. I felt a sense of disappointment slowly eroding my faux-arrogance. I crossed my arms against my chest, already zipped up in an Adidas track top. "Hey, I was expecting at least a coherent sentence. C'mon," I said.

"You're not serious," she said.

"No, really, I am," I said. "Why not? Everyone says we should be together, so let's get together and see."

"You really think I'm that dumb?" she said. Her eyebrows scrunched together on her make-up-free face. I didn't understand the meaning of this facial expression, but I didn't like it.

"No. Uhh. Of course not," I said.

"You can be so frustrating, you know that?" Shannon said.

"What?" I said. "I'm doing a good thing here. Or trying to. Giving you what you want."

"That's not what you're doing and we both know it," she said. "The only difference is, you think I don't know it, but I do, so you can stuff your sorries in a sack, mister." She finished up with the folding.

A heavy, sinking feeling made me dip my head for a second. I jammed my hands in front jeans pockets. I felt weakened. "Shan, that doesn't even make sense," I said.

"Like this does?" she said. "Whatever you wanna call it. I call it pathetic, personally, but that's just me." She turned toward me, gave me a look I couldn't quite translate, again, and then hopped on top of one of the rumbling washing machines. Rough and tumble.

"I really don't see why you're so upset," I said. "You're not making any sense. You having your period or something?"

"Enzo?"

"Yes?"

"Please leave me alone," she said. "I don't have time for your crap. I have laundry priorities to handle."

Desperate, I said, "You gonna give me *any* kinda clue, or just be all mysterious and junk?"

"You think I don't know you're just saying this, and wanting to do this, just to make Jennifer jealous? You think I'm that slow, like I'm some kid on the short bus?" Shannon said. She folded her right leg over her left as the washing machine rocked on beneath her.

I looked down at the linoleum, ashamed and disappointed. I smoothed out some imaginary infield dirt with my imaginary cleat. "Short bus?" I said.

"I mean, it's really insulting, this whole thing here," Shannon said. "You just stroll in here and think I should just, like,

bow down in front of you and kiss your feet just because you're
Enzo Freaking Prinziatta or something? I mean, please. Just get
outta here before you make me even madder. Like you're Jon
Bon Jovi or something? Please. You're not even close to that
cool."

"Christ," I said. I turned, and walked out. Everything's a
fight, I thought.

"Get real, dude!" Shannon shouted after me.

Budski

Saturday night in New Paltz. I knew exactly where Jenny Drama would be. Before I went to see her, though, I watched the Alec Baldwin clip from *Glengarry Glenn Ross* on YouTube, the "coffee's for closers" scene. I needed to amp myself up. I jumped in the Scion with a huge smile on my face. I couldn't wait to see the look in Jenny's shocked and amazed pretty little face. Always be closing, I thought. Always. Be. Closing.

As I approached her suite, I heard music thumping and the rise and fall of raucous, coed voices in full-throttle party mode. Saturday night in New Paltz. I knocked on the door. Jenny opened it, her smile mile-wide, hair inartfully mussed.

"Hey!" she said. Her breath reeked of cheap beer and faint aluminum. Her eyes switched instantly from high-octane party girl to half-ashamed ex-girlfriend. Her body language was loose and unguarded—more than usual. "'Sup?"

"Hey, look," I said. "I can see you're, umm, busy here but I just wanted to let you know that I made some calls, pulled some strings, and it now looks like the Tucker Max thing is going to happen." I beamed a proud smile.

Her face scrunched up in a display of drunken confusion.

Frustrated, I exhaled and said, "He's this...this guy. The, uhh, the important thing to keep in mind, though, is he's controversial, there's gonna be, like, a lotta protests, and that's gonna bring, umm, a big media presence on campus. Perfect opportunity for you to get some exposure *if* we can play it right. See, what we need to do is..."

"Exposure?" she said. "Fuck Tookie Whoeva. I can get my own exposures. Pff." She slammed the door.

I flushed my anger down with brass-balled resolve. I thought for a split-second about why I loved New Paltz College, *espec*ially on a Saturday night. It was brimming with drunk and hung-over kids—easy targets. For a closer, that is. I rapped on the door again, louder this time.

Phillip Donpiseo—known to the New Paltz community as "Flipper the Swimmer"—opened it, with his head and conversation still turned toward a girl inside the room. Flipper was the school's best athlete, by far.

"Flipper!" I said. I shifted my pitch plan.

He turned toward me. He held a clear plastic cup of clear liquid.

"Flipper the Swimmer! How you doin', man?" I said. "I'm Barry Budski. Baseball team." I held out my hand.

"Ah," he said. He shook it.

I pushed my way past him, into the raging party. "What's that?" I said, turning back to him. "Vodka or somethin'?" Cheesy, '80s pop music filled the air.

"Just water," the chlorinated one said. "I'm in season now."

"Oh, hey, that's right," I said. "Flipper plays it clean!

Everybody knows that. Hey, didn't I just read about one of your, uhh, matches in *The Oracle?* You almost *won,* man!"

"Yeah," he said, agitation flooding his face. "Guy from Binghamton beat me by three-tenths of a second."

"Wow, that's close, man," I said. "You almost had 'im. Next time, know what I'm sayin'?"

"Yeah," he said. "It's my only loss this year. And if I didn't screw up my first push-off, he woulda been toast, dude."

"Hey, I believe you, man," I said. "I believe you. I'm'a get a drink. Be right back, bro."

"'Kay," he said.

I got myself a cup of water, and made my way back to the man. "Y'know, if you want to avenge that loss you might wanna step up your training some. Believe me, I know what it's like staying sober when everyone else is partying hard." I held up my plastic water cup as proof, flimsy as it was.

"Step up?" he said. "Step up how? I train three hours a day, six days a week as it is now."

"Yeah, give you an edge over that competition," I said. I sipped some water. "Like those, uhh, Binghamton guys."

"What are you talking about, exactly?" he said. His eyes hardened into a look of extreme interest with an edge of cautiousness. He was on the damn hook, I just had to reel the big breaststroker in.

"It's, uhh, this new kinda energy sports drink. Makes you train harder, longer," I said. "Gives you the energy you need to take your training program to the next level, instead of hitting that plateau. Know what I mean? Maybe three-tenths of a second's worth of an edge."

"I ain't into that Balco shit, man," he said. "I'm straight edge. Everyone knows that."

"So? Who *is* into that shit anymore?" I said. "That's old

news. Yesterday. Nobody's doing that shit anymore. This here's new. And ain't nothing illegal about it. It's like, uhh. Think of it as a different kind of Red Bull, like, but for athletes. Got all kindsa vitamins and stuff in there. Anti-oxidants, too."

"Like B-12?" he said. His look suggested all the recent headlines about athletes claiming to have taken B-12 shots after they test positive for performance-enhancing drugs.

"Hey, I'm just sayin'," I said. "Even Gatorade started out on a college campus. University of Florida. The Gators. And all the ingredients are listed on the label as per FDA regulations, of course. You think I'm gonna risk going to jail just to make a few bucks?"

"Still," he said. "I don't like to take chances with that stuff. I always competed clean and never had any issues."

"Just think about it, dude," I said. "That's all I'm sayin'. This stuff *is* clean. Gatorade's clean, isn't it?"

"I don't think so," he said. "Why would I trust you? We just met two seconds ago."

"No, I get it," I said. "That's really logical. But don't worry, you'll be hearing more about it soon. We're growing pretty good right now. We're gonna be doing a pretty aggressive advertising campaign pretty soon. Just keep it in the back of your mind, dude. Okay?"

He shrugged and sipped his water.

A pang of frustration hit me, but I let it dissolve. I reminded myself to think long-term. "I'll check ya later, big man."

"Okay," he said. He sipped water again.

"Oh that reminds me," I said. "One more thing."

"Yeah?"

I smiled. "We're already selling to Binghamton," I said. "Cortland and Oswego, too, in case you might have any matches coming up against those guys."

"Uhh," he said. He squinted and hardened his eyes. It looked like he was seriously considering the implication.

"Y'know, I'm also the President of Sigma Alpha Mu. You know the Sammy house?" I said. I gulped down some water.

"Yeah, sure," he said.

"So you know where to find me if you change your mind," I said. "I'll even give you a free sample, dude." I slapped his shoulder. "That way, you can try it out. If it ain't for you, no sweat, *amigo*."

"I won't change my mind," he said. His face, however, said he might.

"A'ight," I said. "Well, I tried, right?" I smiled. "I gotta bounce. Nice chatting with you."

As I walked toward the door, I heard Jenny screech-singing along to Foreigner's "I Wanna Know What Love Is." I looked around to source the noise, and I saw her—spotlit her—in the middle room off the common area. She was belting out the lyrics and somehow gut-laughing at the same time. Some people I didn't know were gathered around her like a fan club, egging her on and laughing like jackals at the various peaks and valleys of her vocally histrionic performance. The song ended, and she curtsy-twirled herself off-balance, then came stumbling out of the room. She spilled onto the floor of the common room, drunkenly hysterical. Her fan club added a backing chorus of hysteria.

I looked at her, looked at Flipper, raised my eyebrows, and said, "Allll righty then." I walked out. Oh for two, I thought. Fucking sales. Just when you think you're a brass-balled closer, one bad "sit" and you feel like a loser. No coffee for me.

Prinziatta

I felt confused and guilty and more than a little mixed up. I felt lost and neutered. I felt *sick*. I should have known that the Shan Plan was far too simple to work. Shan was far too smart to fall for that. Stupidstupidstupid. Stupidstupidstupid. Damn. How could I have thought that would have worked? God damn, I need a drink, I thought. It felt like my mind was experiencing withdrawal symptoms, like it was, any minute now, about to make my whole body shake and sweat and ache and fret for alcohol. Booze. *Boooooooooooozzzzze*. I couldn't seem to coax my mind out of its crushing darkness. It was as if I, neurologically, needed the alcohol as a magical escape hatch—as if numbing the emotions, suppressing thought about the problem, would make it disappear. It seemed locked away, inaccessible, on its own turf yet somehow ruthlessly trapped by monster shadows and gigantic projections. On some cognitive level, I knew my dilemma wasn't as severe as all that, but biology's biology. All I know is how I felt, how *it* felt. I had to break through the wall

159

of black pain, somehow. I decided to do what I'd been doing
since I quit drinking—work out. I looked down at my track top,
jeans, and high tops, decided they'd do, and took off on a jog
around campus.

It felt like a bit of a relief to be on the go, to be *active*. To be
pounding on my muscles rather than pounding down beers. As
I trotted around The Gunk, I noticed a few clusters of girls surrounding solitary guys strumming a guitar and singing on those
large park tables they have around the pond. It reminded me of
that famous scene in *Animal House*, where Belushi smashes the
hippie dude's guitar. At first, I thought the modern-day versions
of Belushi's hippie dude were ridiculous caricatures. But then
I looked closer at the girls' faces as I ran. They were absolutely
enraptured by the guitar dudes. And the dudes weren't anything
special. Except that they strummed a guitar and carried a tune
on the back of romantic lyrics.

Well, I didn't have a guitar, but I did know where to go to
get some romantic lyricism. And also too, some advice on how
to deploy it.

But first, I had to get something else. I had to deal with the
alcohol thing somehow, and I couldn't work out twenty-four
hours a day. I needed something else to help me work past the
black times when the siren song of sweet inebriation might be
too tempting to resist.

When I got back to the house, I showered and changed,
then walked over to the Water Street Market on Main. I figured
an artsy-fartsy place like that should have what I needed—an
Alcoholics Anonymous pendant. I also wanted to get a military
beaded chain to put both it and my #42 pendant on. I wanted
them to "chink" slightly when I moved—as an audible reminder
of my new, clear-eyed, path.

I looked around the small shop, all wood and creak and the smell of some kind of hippie fragrance like patchouli, looked in all the glass-and-metal cases they had. I knew, with all due remorse, that buying the pendant was an admission: I needed help. Something was wrong with me, and I couldn't fix it by myself, so I had to admit that I needed help. Even if that help took the form of a stupid pendant chinking around my neck. It was still a form of admission. It made me feel contrite, humbled. It made me wish I could call my dad.

But I couldn't.

I found the items, and brought them up to the register. A half-baked-looking dude rang me up. His eyes contained something that looked suspiciously like compassion, but they were so bloodshot it was hard to tell exactly.

I strolled out of the shop, smiling in the sunshiny New Paltz afternoon. I noticed someone bum-rushing out of the door of The Gilded Otter brew-pub across the street. The person was in *such* a hurry, caused such a ruckus, that it halted me. I focused on the ruckus and something about it seemed familiar. Then it smacked me hard: It was Jenny Drama and she was headed right for me with a drunk, mischievous look on her theatrical face. My heart dropped off the roof of a nine-story building and splattered on the cement of my depleted soul. I closed my eyes tight and said, "Shit." There was no escape, no exiting stage left or right. I'd just have to face the daemon. A drunk Jenny Drama.

"Heyyyy! Wait up, Mr. Softee!" she screamed from across Main. She was waiting for the light to change, or more accurately, for cars to stop being in her way, dressed hair to toes in Noir York City black. Smack-dab in the center of Main in green New Paltz, her new "goth look" or whatever it was stood out like a soot-black second base on a baseball diamond. It looked

from where I was that she had even black-Sharpie'd her formerly
white Keds.

The light changed and she charged at me. "Hey! Hey! Princess! Whatcha got in the *bag*, Princess?" She landed near me, all
out of breath, yet still bouncing on her toes like a boxer. "Got a
present for me, Princess?"

"Not even," I said. "Got a present for *me*."

"Whatchagot?" she said. "Whatchagotwhatchagotwhat-
chagot? Huh?" She patted me randomly on different parts of
my body, half-petting and half-tickling me. How did anybody
ever deal with this insane chick? I played defense as best I could,
but eventually she got the bag out of my hand. "Hey, what's this
from, uhh, from The Tchatchke Shoppe? Huh? Let's see here..."
She pulled it out of the bag.

"Hey!" I said. "That's personal!"

She pulled out the pendant, a silver triangle within a cir-
cle. "Hey hey! Lookie lookie! Somebody's bein'a lightweight
rookie! Let's all do the Sober Dance! The Sober Daaance!
Essessess, Ohohoh, Beebeebee, Eeeeeeeee, Arrarrarr...."

Her body contorted into a series of maneuvers that could
best be described as a combination of the Elaine Benes barmy-
jig and some kind of a wounded-animal mating prance. "Let's
do the Sober Dance!" she said. "Essessess, ohohoh, beebeebee..."

I felt deadened, as if some essential part of me was being
snuffed out by her histrionic ridicule, as if I had no right to even
be in the same space with her, on the same planet with her. I
knew—thought, reasoned—it was a false notion, but that's just
how I felt.

"I cannot deal with you right now," I said. I grabbed the
pendant and sprinted—with her gut-laughter thunder-echoing
in my ears—to Scudder Hall where my good buddy, Jared Besto,
New Paltz Hawks shortstop, curly-haired man, and noted poet

resided. I say "noted" not because his verse was published in the most respected literary journals in the country, nor because he was the darling of poetry critics nationwide. Nope, his poetry was noted for one reason and one reason only—it charmed the panties off good-looking girls from Montauk to Bohemia, from New Paltz to Buffalo, almost every time.

This being the case, I had to go see the man. I needed to return to Shannon with something so unexpected, so ridiculously unlike me, that it would instantly reverse her sudden resistance to me. Like those magnetic goofuses with the guitars in the grass, but better.

I knocked on the curly-haired man's door. He answered.

"Bro," I said, indicating a manly need with my tone.

"Bro," said he, conveying his deep understanding of my problem. He wiped his mouth with the right sleeve of his LeBron James jersey.

"Need your help, dude," I said.

"I gotchou, holmes," he said.

"It's kind of a long story," I said. "And I don't have a lotta time."

"Girl trouble?" he said.

"What else?" I said.

"Who with?" he said. "Jenny Drama?"

Hearing her name brought back the sting of her recent assault. I closed my eyes and pursed my lips. "No, not her," I said.

"Who then?" he said.

"You don't know her."

"Try me," Jared said.

"Trust me, you don't," I said.

"You don't know everyone I know," he said. "You need my help, you're gonna have to give me a little more here."

I sighed with all the exasperation of a luckless gambler. I

felt, faint but rising, that old familiar feeling of a desperate need for an alcoholic beverage. "Okay, fine," I said. "It's Shannon Hestian."

"Hot Shannon?" he said. "Oh, hells no! You gotsta be kidding, bro. I'm'a get that girl myself. Uhh, some day." He closed the door. "Sorry, bro!" he said.

My head throbbed with pain. It felt like my brain was trying to explode out of my head, as an escape, as a fitting end to a noble effort at reform rebuffed. I looked down at my bag from The Tchatchke Shoppe. I thought about the A.A. pendant. "Fuck it," I said.

I knocked on the door, hard. "Yo, Besto, open up, man! I'm gonna make this totally worth it for ya!" I banged on the door again.

He opened it. "How's that, exactly?" he said.

"Look, this is completely confidential," I said. "You can't tell anyone. Agreed?"

"Fine," he said.

"I just need a poem so I can get Shannon to go out with me for a few weeks, and make Jenny Drama jealous. It's not gonna get serious, I'm not even gonna sleep with her—won't even touch her, really, and I'll get her something really nice, also, when it's over," I said.

"Still waiting to hear how any of this is good for me," he said. He blinked with intense indignance.

"This is it," I said. "After the two weeks, and after I get back in her good graces, I'll put in the good word for you."

"What kinda good word?" he said.

"Any kind you want," I said. "You think about it, come up with how you want me to present it, and I will. There's your opening."

"Hmm," he said. "Not bad. Okay, I'm in. Now, gimme some context for this poem."

"Context?" I said.

"Yeah, something to make it seem like you went out and wrote it yourself. Like, what she was wearing, or something she does, or where she was..."

The bright light of sudden inspiration excited me. "Oh, the laundry!" I said. "She was doing laundry! Laundry, dude!"

"All right," he said. "Calm down, dude. Lemme see what I got." He went back into his room.

From what I could see where I was standing, the room seemed disheveled, with beer cans, clothes, and textbooks cluttering up the floor space. I could hear him fumbling around in there, flipping papers and things around in search of something.

He returned to the doorway. He stuck out a piece of looseleaf paper toward me. "Here ya go, bro," he said. "Tell Shannon you wrote this for her, and maybe add in the fact that you were drinking your broken heart away and *bam!* this just came to you and you just *had* to get it all down on paper, and the words just flowed outta you like water. Like the ache in your heart was so bad, and the thought of her was so powerful, that you just had to express the intense feelings of, like, love in some kinda artistic way, and this is how it came out. Something like that. Eighty percent va-jay-jay rate, give or take."

My spirit soared. This is gonna rock, I thought. "Or beer," I said.

"Huh?" Jared said.

"The words. They flowed outta me like beer from a tap," I said.

"Ehh," he said. He frowned and gave me a look that said, Nice try, kid. "But water's better, maybe even better yet a waterfall. Something natural. Chicks dig that nature junk. They love nature, animals, all that crusty, granola crap like that."

"Right," I said. "Yeah. Makes sense."

"Anything else, bro?"

"Nah, that's it," I said.

"All right," he said. "Later. G'luck. Not that you need it, now. And, remember, don't be touchin' on my girl. She's, like, on loan to you and shit! We got an agreement, and a verbal contract is valid and binding in the State of New York!"

"Gotcha," I said. "No worries, bro. No need to go all Johnnie Cochran on me." I walked away, smiling.

Here is the poem crafted by the curly-haired ladies' man, with an eighty percent va-jay-jay rate, give or take:

Sunlight Interrupted

She was sunlight interrupted
    on the soft-wood floors of my mind.
She was a breeze on a humid day
    that blows itself into a winter
        gale force across your face.

She was the salt water
    surrounding the boat
        lost at sea for centuries.

She rose and fell with every breath
She sparked life and snuffed death
She captured the inmates and in stealth
Fed them bread and stories for their health

She was a white prom dress
    in the black breezy night

She was every footfall before the bedroom door opens

And she was the smoke rising from my cigarette

She was the dirt and detergent
    the goods and the money
    the race and the standings
    the inspiration and the song.

It was love from the rinse cycle
And now she's gone.

I crossed out his title and wrote, "Love on Top of a Washing Machine," so I could honestly say I had written at least some of it. I scribbled my initials onto the bottom of it, and *voila!* Poet-o-Matic.

I double-timed it back to Bevier with hope in my heart, my legs feather-light. I strolled into Shannon's open suite, which smelled flowery, clean, and girly. I stood in her room's doorway with a confidence tempered by my previous experience with her. "Shannon, I have something for you," I said.

Her back was facing me as she sat at her desk, highlighting in a textbook. "A diamond necklace, Enzo, you shouldn't have!" she mocked without turning around.

"Funny," I said. "No, that's not it."

"What then?" she said. She turned around in the wooden chair and looked at me.

"Something else," I said.

"What?" she said.

I walked in and handed her the loose-leaf paper. "Uhh, here," I said.

Her eyes made their way down the blue-lined page. I saw them shine, like a new baseball right out of the box. I looked down, unsure of what that meant, exactly.

Shannon stood up, and jumped onto me. I caught her,

luckily, in an athletic reflex. Sweet, I thought. I'll remember her terrific smell crashing right into me for a long, long time.

"This is the greatest thing anyone's ever done for me," Shannon said weepily in my ear.

I found that hard to believe. There must have been dozens if not thousands of guys writing mediocre love poems for her. It struck me as odd, but I didn't really care, either. Eighty percent, I thought.

Now, I just had to make sure the two-week Shannon relationship was visible enough to make Jenny Drama jealous. *And* not touch the very touchable Shannon Hestian simultaneously. Too easy.

I knew one thing for sure. To strike at Jenny's heart, it would need to be a bold—nay, dramatic—maneuver. Since I had worked at McArdle Theater freshman year, I had some insider's knowledge. Of course, for a non-performer, performing on stage could be mind-numbingly frightening. But if everything went well, that fear would be vaporized by the sheer audacity of the moment.

Budski

"**S**o's that it?" I said.

"For now," Kevin Sullivan of Sullivan Plumbing of Ulster County said. He clanged his wrench into his toolbox and shut its lid.

"Jesus," I said. "You mean even after a six-hundred-dollar repair, this stupid boiler *still* might break down?"

"That's the way it is with these old houses," Kevin said. "Especially if no one ever modernizes the boiler."

I shook my head. "Jesus," I said.

Kevin said, "Who built this house anyway, the Huguenots?"

I laughed. "Yeah, probably," I said. "There wasn't much to choose from on the market when we bought it, I can tell you that much."

"Anyway, lemme know if you wanna go the other way and I'll give you a good deal on the labor for it," Kevin said.

"How about you give me the labor for free?" I said.

He laughed. "Yeah," he said. "Good one."

"No, seriously," I said. "I can make it up to you in herbage."

"Look," Kevin said, "I don't know nothin' about that shit. But my nephew, Stevie, he might. I'll send him around and if he thinks it's worth it, we can do business."

"Sounds good," I said.

"Later, Barry," he said. He lifted his toolbox and left.

I paced around the boiler room and thought about that Ben Affleck movie with the same name. I had already tried the brass-balled approach with Jenny Drama, and it didn't work. I need something else.

I thought about Jenny Drama's indifference and drunken antics. I paced, hands behind my back, fingers fidgeting.

I felt and heard my dad's voice coming through the restraints of time and space: "Never show weakness, only strength. Be aggressive, always. Double down. Do it big and do it right or don't do it at all. Let one person take advantage of you, and your reputation is killed. Without your rep, you're done."

I felt the nerve-rattling pressure—C.E.O. Pressure—to come up with a solution, quick. I needed to solve this one on my own. I hated being haunted by Dad, but I couldn't seem to hunt and kill his ghost no matter what I did.

Then it hit me. Those "Boiler Room" guys were all about client acquisition for the phony firm. Well, in order to make *my* firm seem non-phony to Jenny, all I had to do was acquire a few more clients with which to work. My mistake was that I had been too narrow in my focus. If I could attract some new talent, then Jenny would see that Double B Management was a legitimate business. And even if she didn't, the business wouldn't be cripplingly reliant on one capricious-as-hell chick.

Time to put the scouting cap on.

Prinziatta

Sometimes class work is useful. I felt like infiltrating a new world, space-crashing a universe in service to a romantic faux-fight. I had to come up with—invent—something vaguely romantic without a hint of the physical in it whatsoever. That's what I had to do, but I wasn't so sure I could accomplish it. One of the classes I took that semester was Shakespeare I.

"He jests at scars that never felt a wound." – Romeo Montague

The Friday after the "Perfume Pop" (the ladies' version of the "Lambeau Leap"), I went over to campus to see Shan early.

"Wanna do something sneaky?" I said in her room after a dining-hall breakfast.

"Sneaky?" Shannon said. "What kinda sneaky?"

"Well, it's Friday, right?"

"All day."

"Well, since most people are sleeping off hangovers, there's not a lot going on right now. So, I thought maybe we'd sneak into McArdle, and horse around some," I said.

"Horse around?" she said.

"Yeah," I said. "Pretend like we're actors. Mess around like that."

"Um, I dunno," Shannon said. "That's not really my thing. That's more of a Jenny Drama thing."

A clench of angst crunched my gut. I crossed my arms against my chest. "Hm," I said. "Well, tell ya what. You can sit in the audience and watch me do a soliloquy."

"A what?" she said.

"I'm taking a Shakespeare class," I said. "It's like a speech by one person, one of the actors in the thing, made to, like, the audience."

"Oh, uhh," she said. "Well. What play?"

"*Romeo and Juliet*."

"Heyyy," she said. "Now *that* sounds romantic." She smiled.

Relief set in, and I exhaled. "Indeed," I said. "*In*deed."

We headed over to McArdle Theater. As we were nearing the theater, I saw Flipper the Swimmer, Phillip Donpiseo. "Be right back," I said to Shan.

I approached him and said, "Hey, Flipper."

"Hey, it's the Prinzess!" he said. "How you doin', man?"

"Good bro," I said. "Real good." We shook hands.

"Hey, you look good, bro," he said. "You lose some weight or something?"

"Yeah, couple pounds, as a matter of fact," I said. "Quit drinkin'. Workin' out more. Using this new sports drink for endurance on the treadmill, stuff like that."

His face scrunched up, as if he were trying to suss something out. "Wait, you're not talking about Budski's thing?"

"Yeah, actually," I said. "Y'know, I'm in Sammy now, and

he has this thing he's putting out. It's good. I mean, it seems to work, I guess. I'm just working out pretty hard and not drinking, though."

"So, you don't know if that's what's helping you or not?" he said.

"Yeah, have no idea," I said. "But it's not hurting. Why? Did he talk to you about it?"

"Yeah," Flipper said. "I thought he was out of his mind."

"Yeah, me too. At first," I said.

We laughed.

I said, "But, there's been no, like, side effects or stuff like that. And you can see the results. I'm pretty stoked about it, dude."

"Yeah?"

"Yeah, so, if you're looking to take your workouts to the next level, you might wanna try it," I said.

"Still," he said.

"Hey, didn't you lose your first race in, like, three years or something recently?" I said. "Saw something in *The Oracle* about that."

"Yeah," he said. "So?"

"I think you see what I'm saying," I said. "All I know about it is I've seen big-time gains, *and* my fastball is coming back. But that's me. It's up to you, what you wanna do. Way I'd look at it is, if you don't need it, don't do it. But if it could make the difference between the Olympics or spending your life in a cubicle waiting for someone to brush a few more breadcrumbs onto your plate, well. I guess cubicle people can be happy, too. You see what I'm saying."

"'Kay, well," he said. "I'll think about... hey, how hard you throwin' now? Like, what were you throwing before and how hard now?"

"Before, I was in the mid-eighties, tops," I said. "Now I'm throwin', like, low to mid-nineties."

"What the?" he said. His brow crunched down like he couldn't believe what he was hearing.

"Lates!" I said.

"Yeah, uhh, later," he said.

I jogged back to Shannon. "Fucking Chlorine Boy," I said. Shannon laughed.

We continued our stroll through campus, which felt lifeless. Stock-still quiet, like 4 A.M. on a Sunday morning coming down, the leaves danced in their winded circles, the air smelled clean and grassy and fresh. The relative lack of student density on the grounds was refreshing for its rarity alone, but it also made high jinks easier to execute.

I found the hidden side-door key in one of the plant boxes near the door. I unlocked it, and we walked in. I wanted to give the whole operation a covert feel, even though I knew we weren't really risking much. We probably could have gotten in through the normal doors, but I thought that by making it seem somewhat dangerous it would enhance, romantically, the event for Shannon. We had seven minutes before class was due to start—a fact I had withheld from Shannon to further increase the mysterious feel of the whole experience.

"Okay, so you go have a front-row seat, okay?"

Shannon giggled. Her face was pink with joy, her eyes smiling as well. It seemed like her entire body was smiling.

I jumped up onstage, and pulled a piece of paper from my pocket and read over the lines. I stuffed it back into my jeans pocket. "But soft!" I said. "What light through yonder window breaks?"

Shannon had a gigantic smile on her face, and the kind of look in her eyes that, frankly, scared me. It was beaming with all the things I needed her *not* to be beaming with: Adoration, Pride, Love. E*spe*cially not Love, that fucking bastard. Always showing up where it was least convenient. It was not at all clear that this gambit would work.

I continued: "Uhh. Arise, fair sun, and kill the envious moon, Who is already sick and pale with grief That thou her maid art far more fair than she." I reached out my arms toward Shannon, pretending she was on a balcony.

I heard the doors at the back of the theater bang open and saw a few students enter. They stopped short when they saw me on stage, then sat down in the back. One of them was Jennifer. Jackpot, I thought.

Shannon glanced at them, then back at me.

I said, "Uhh, be, umm, be not her maid, since she is envious. Her vestial livery is but sick and green, And none but fools do wear it. Cast it off." Increasing my volume, directing my voice toward the back of the theater, I said, "It is my lady; O, it is my love! O that she knew she were!"

As if on cue, Jennifer leapt up and ran toward the stage. Stopping right in the front of the stage, she looked me in the eyes, and said, "O Romeo, Romeo! wherefore art thou Romeo? Deny thy father and refuse thy name!"

The other drama students in the back, more of whom had entered and plopped down to watch the spectacle, snickered and laughed.

Jennifer Juliet said, "Or, if thou wilt not, be but sworn my love, And I'll no longer be a Burnette!" She laughed a joy-infused laugh. Then she turned toward the back and bowed, over and over and over.

The other students hooted and hollered, applauding. They whistled and catcalled and stomped and yelled.

I jumped off the stage to confront Jennifer. My plan did not include a confrontation contingency scenario, but I felt like I had to do *some*thing. I opened my mouth.

"Hey! Hey!" Shannon said. She stood up.

Both Jenny Drama and I shifted our focus onto her. I closed my mouth.

"You just *shut up!*" Shannon said to Jenny. "Go back to your, your exhibitionist pals!" She then put her arm around me, and we walked up the long aisle toward the exit. As we did, I heard Jennifer laughing even harder—howling—and then the rest of her thespian buddies howl with her. The sound took on a wave-like effect in my ears, cresting and resting only after Shannon and I had left the theater.

I felt as low as a trundle-bed.

Budski

Anticipating the difficult sell was like the feeling you get when you see a brand-new, shiny baseball atop the mound before the game. Bring on the fun. I headed up to campus to try to find my next client. On a campus full of gravity-defying women, there just had to be one or two who had that X-factor and who would actually work hard to make it—celebrity-worship culture did have some advantages, if you knew how to use them. Once I started filling up a roster, Jenny would naturally follow.

I meandered about for a while once I got up there. Then I saw—watched, witnessed—Enzo and some girl I had never seen coming out of the McArdle Theater building. She was hugging him like a corner man hugs his boxer when they lose a close, devastating decision—consoling him, it looked like. This could be tricky, I thought.

But, she did seem to have the components of a good modeling candidate: long blonde hair, thin but not without curvature,

fairly tall. I'd have to investigate further. I ran toward them with
a concerned look on my face.

"Hey buddy, you all right?" I said to Enzo.

Enzo looked up.

His face looked haggard, exhausted, beaten.

"Yeah, it's, uhh, it's no big deal," Enzo said.

"It's no big deal," the girl said.

Enzo said, "Barry, this is Shannon. Shannon, Barry. Barry
founded the New Paltz chapter of Sigma Alpha Mu a few years
ago."

"Nice to meet you," I said.

"Likewise," she said.

We shook hands. Looking at her close-up, her facial fea-
tures were indeed promising: creamy-smooth skin, icy-blue eyes,
prominent cheekbones, good golden-triangle ratios, plump-
ish lips, small nose, no weirdness in the teeth that I could see.
And a natural blonde to boot, it seemed. A nice rarity. Promising indeed. I'd have to do a screen test to make sure, but still. I
smiled.

"Hey," Enzo said, "I just ran into Flipper."

"Yeah?" I said.

"Yeah, I was trying to soft-sell him on the idea of Sammy-
Ade, but I dunno if he really, y'know, if it did any good."

"Well, thanks for trying," I said. "I appreciate that, *amigo*."
To Shannon I said, "I don't know if Enzo told you, but I'm a
serial entrepreneur."

Shannon said, "Look, no offense, but we need to get going.
We're kind of in a hurry."

I glanced over to Enzo, then back to Shannon again. This
was going to be difficult. They seemed as if they were sutured
together.

"Barry has, like," Enzo said, "a bunch of small businesses he's running. He runs Sammy more like a business than a frat, actually. Right, Barry?"

I said, "Hey, if you guys need to split."

Shannon looked at Enzo like he had an open chest wound.

"No, it's all right," Enzo said. "I'm fine."

I said, "Okay. But yeah, more or less. I've got a few projects going. One of them is this new, healthy sports drink designed to enhance athletic performance. That's what Enzo was talking to Flipper about. We're trying to get him to partner with us on some promotions."

"I see," Shannon said. "Like Gatorade?"

"Yeah, except Gatorade *advertises* itself like that," I said, "but if you actually ever take a look at the label, there's a lotta unhealthy crap in there."

"Huh," she said. "Okay, well, it's been nice to meet you, but we really need to be going. We, uhh..."

"No," Enzo said. "It's fine. I'm fine. Really, Shannon."

I said, "I mean, if you guys need to go, or whatever..."

"No, I'm fine," Enzo said. "Shannon's just doing her normal smother-mothering."

"Hey!" Shannon said. She yanked her arm off of Enzo's shoulders. She turned toward me. "So, what *other* projects do have? Anything to cure grumpy-ass boyfriends?"

"Ha! I like this one, Enz! She's a keeper!" I said. "But, it's funny you should ask that, because there is one project I think *you* in particular might be especially interested in."

"Oh yeah?" she said. "What's that?"

"And it happens to be my favorite of all the stuff we're doing. It's this talent agency where we really focus on the careers of each individual we have. I want to keep it really small and tight and be the spot where talent comes when they want laser-focused representation," I said. "Have you ever done any modeling, Shannon?"

She blush-smiled. "No," she said. "But I am smart enough to know that every third dude on this campus is a modeling scout."

I felt a pang-flash of anger. I knew that was one common perception I had to overcome. So many guys tried to bullshit their way—the "model scout" way—into girls' pants, it had become the modern equivalent of "What's your sign?" I said, "Fair enough. Except that I'm a business owner—"

"I thought you said you were a surreal entrepreneur," she said, smiling.

Enzo laughed.

"And while it's true that the talent agency hasn't taken off *yet*," I said, "several of my businesses have."

"Sure, well, I'll, umm," she said, "definitely keep that, uhh, y'know, in mind." Her tone and body language were telling me a different story, though.

"Well, I tell you what," I said. "Have you ever done a man's make-up?"

"Barry, I don't think..." Enzo said.

Shannon laughed. "What?" she said.

"Y'know, like for television. For lighting purposes."

"I see," she said. "For, um, lighting purposes. But no, I haven't."

"Would you like to?" I said.

"Um, I don't think so," she said.

I grinned and looked at Enzo. "Boy, I've never heard a woman say no to free make-up before, have you?"

Enzo shrugged.

"Wait," Shannon said. "You didn't say anything about free cosmetics."

"Well, it's understood—my bad for not being explicit. But,

yeah, there'll be all kindsa stuff there. Not just for men. And you can take whatever you want."

"Oh," she said. "Well, that changes the equation a little. Now it's a definite maybe."

"Heyyy," I said. "Now, that's something. Okay, I'll get at you later, Shannon. Nice to meet you. Enz, can I talk to you privately?"

"Later," said Shannon.

"Yeah, sure," Enzo said.

I walked him a few feet away and put my arm around him. "Listen, it looks like the Tucker Max thing is a go."

"Tucker Max?" Enzo said.

"He's this guy," I said.

"Oh," Enzo said. "That narrows it down."

"He's this... controversial guy," I said. "Writes about drinking a lot and sleeping around with a lot of chicks without cuddling with them after."

"How nice," said Enzo.

"Point is, he's controversial, and one of his books is a bestseller," I said. "And some women's groups think he contributes to a rape culture, or whatever they call it, and so they don't like him, and don't think that New Paltz should pay him to speak here—oh, he gives talks on college campuses a lot—and, anyway, umm, the thing is, because of all this controversy he brings to the table, there's gonna be protests, and local media and all this stuff."

"And I care... why?" Enzo said.

"Well the way I see it is this. The higher the profile of the school, the better *your* chances to transfer somewhere big, make the jump to D-1, maybe. Maybe even get drafted," I said. "I've seen you throwing in the bubble, man. That fastball is poppin' Semzy's mitt, bro. And we all know that one signing bonus alone could set you up for life, if you invest it right. Which I'd also be glad to assist you with. For a modest fee, of course."

"Man, just stop it, dude," he said. "You're gettin' way out ahead of things."

"Maybe. But look. Just do me a favor and talk Shannon into coming to the studio tomorrow. I'm shooting some promotional stuff. That girl has real potential. I can see it."

"I don't think so, dude," Enzo said. "If she want to, that's cool, but otherwise—"

I said, stern, "Do you want to succeed or not? You wanna stay here in Smallville or you wanna go big-time? We both know that right arm of yours is your meal ticket. *If* your head doesn't screw it up. I wasn't lying about the SammyAde, right, and now you're back where you were in high school, if not even better. Thanks to *me*. And I'm not lying about *this* either."

"Well..."

"I'm just saying have her come down," I said.

"Yeah, I'll see," he said. "I'll see. I will. I swear."

"Okay," I said. "Good deal."

"But maybe I'll come, too," Enzo said. "Seems like fun."

"Yeah," I said, trying to hide the disappointment I felt. With Enzo around, it'd be much harder to work my magic mojo. In fact, I wasn't even sure if it was worth it to have him be there. But a deal was a deal was a deal no matter the devilish details. "See you at the house later?"

"Yeah," Enzo said over his shoulder.

Budski

Back. I needed to head back to the house to plan this out properly. Boiler and other old-house issues aside, there was something about that damned house that gave me a tremendous amount of protection and solace. It was like a huge barrier against any of the outside forces that could press down on me at any moment. The wolves—Visigoths, Huns, tax-zealot hippies, women waving restraining orders, for example—were always, always, always at the door. But the fact that there *was* a door, a protective, lockable barrier, between those evil forces and the gold housed on the other side was a huge comfort to me. Without that door, there'd just be an orifice for any kind of monster to waltz right through and gobble up anything he or she wanted.

So, I went back to my fortress to throw back a beer, relax for a second, and consider my alternatives. I went up to my room, and poured a cold one from the BeerTender. But I couldn't stop thinking about Prinziatta. Here I was, trying to run my goddamned businesses, and motherfucking Prinziatta sticks his goddamned nose all in it? What the fuck was it with this kid? I felt like punching him in the God-damned neck. The little greaseball. I get him in shape, I give him a place to live, and he thanks me by wanting to chaperone my thing with Shannon? Who the fuck was this kid? I went over to my dresser and unsheathed my Grayman. I flicked it into a log I kept in there for that purpose. I yanked it out, and gripped the handle, running my left index finger along the tang. Should just take this bad boy out and give it a workout, I thought. I brought a finger to the blade, lightly touching it. I ran it back and forth across the spine, and flicked it again into the log. Fucking good-for-nothing motherfucker.

I sheathed the knife and tucked it into my travel bag.

I had to map out a vision for Double B that would be cool, compelling, and different. I needed to, mostly, differentiate it in the marketplace. For a start-up in this space, I knew I couldn't compete with the established brands because they had too much size and market recognition for me to win that way. On the other end of the scale, you had eight gazillion guys who were mostly bullshit—using the promise of their "connections" to get into a hot chick's pants. And a lot of girls knew that and looked at guys like me automatically as a poser, and rightly so. So, that was a major challenge I had to overcome with regard to Shannon Hestian.

I found Tanjeeb Punjabi, our techy geek extraordinaire, in the basement playing *Halo* on Xbox. "Pause that a sec, Tan?" I said.

"Yeah, sure," he said. "'Sup, bro."

"We ready for the studio tomorrow?" I said.

"Yeah, we're set," he said. "No problems. *You* ready?"

"No doubt," I said.

"Cool."

"But I got *uno* small *problemo*," I said.

"Yeah?"

"Well, I was gonna invite this girl Shannon down to the studio," I said. "Kind of let her see all that stuff, and try to convince her to do the modeling thing."

"Oh, cool," Tanjeeb said. "You thinking about adding clients to that?"

"Yeah," I said. "Ex*actly*. *Problem* is, this is the same girl that Enzo's seeing right now."

"So?" Tan said.

"Soooo, he's not exactly crazy about her being managed by me, as you might imagine."

"Eh, yeah, but I mean, it's just professional, right?" Tanjeeb said. "He'll get over it."

"Have you *met* Enzo?" I said.

He laughed. "Yeah, but I mean. So? So what? Like he's her keeper?"

"Yeah, I'm with you," I said. "And that's exactly what I'm thinking, too. But, the thing is, I think we've *really* got to impress her. Make her feel like Double B is on the verge of really blowing up."

"Is it?" he said.

An anger-flash pulsed through me. "Of course it is! What the fuck, dude?" I said.

"Okay, all right, relax, jeez. It's not exactly on fire right now, dude," Tan said. "That's all I meant."

"Yeah, well," I said. "That's all gonna change *once* we get the right models to represent. Right?"

"If you say so," he said. "You da boss, boss man."

"So, the question is this," I said. "How to do it up, and do it up right."

"Well," Tan said, "we could do limos, maybe fill 'em with some champagne. Maybe some, uhh, I dunno. Strawberries and shit? That sorta thing. I dunno, I'm more of a tech guy, Barry. Maybe Stinson, or..."

"Yeah, that ain't bad," I said. "But I got some other ideas, too. Hey, you think Professor Gembull would lemme borrow his Breitling?"

Tan whistled as he picked up the Xbox controller. "Sheeeeeet, pardner," he said. "Much as we've supplemented that motherfucker's income? I should hope so. He should let you borrow his *wife* if you wanted to, that slimy prick."

Budski

I shined my black Romano Marteganis to mirror-like status. I looked at them with pride and saw my smiling teeth gleam back at me in the reflection. I was going all black for the day, trying to dapper it up as best I could—black shirt, black blazer, black slacks. Plus, for added effect, Professor Gembull's sixty-three-hundred-dollar Breitling Chronomat. One look in the mirror told me what I already knew: I looked like a biz-shark ready to chow down on some prey.

I gathered together all the guys and all the gear and we hit the road. First stop, campus to pick up Shannon and Enzo. I called them on the way and told them to meet us outside the dorm. When we arrived, I got out and leaned back against the side of the vehicle. "Hey guys," I said, smiling my most suave smile.

"What up?" Enzo said, quickly. He opened the door.

Shannon was too wrapped up into Enzo to acknowledge

me. They clambered into the car as if they were in a cocoon, one co-mingled body. The day was off to a challenging start.

On the road, where I had hoped to impress Shannon with all of the high-end equipment and the roles of all of the brothers, and the sheer size and scope of Double B Management, she just kind of snuggled into Enzo and kept quiet, seemingly uninterested by any of it. It was like they had some kind of lovers' force field around them. I couldn't gain access, couldn't pierce the caul. When I did make thrusts, little conversation starters, like, "Shannon, this is Tanjeeb, he's in charge of all of our technology," she would just say, "Oh, cool," in a faint voice, and snuggle her head more into Enzo's chest, like a small, loyal dog. It was disgusting.

An angry image popped into my mind straight from a dream I often had, a flashback setting stemming straight from my Babylon childhood: The schoolyard where we played fast-pitch stickball, asses-up, and two-hand-touch Nerf football, exploding in red and orange flames, burning down behind me. I walk away from the fire, walk away from my past burning the fuck down, everything behind me in ruins. The frustration-cum-anger felt that hot inside me.

We arrived at the studio, this place in town called Groove-Shack. Local musicians used it to record their MySpace-destined folk/anti-folk/neo-folk tracks, but they also had a room to shoot video in a professional setting. You paid mostly for lighting, and it was worth it. Good lighting makes the difference between amateur and professional video.

Shannon and Enzo were still seemingly joined at the hip when we exited the limo and carried all the gear into the studio. I didn't even have a chance to ask Shannon to do my make-up; I had to do it myself. I felt a flash of anger, but then it was time to go with the scripts, and I had to flush that away to keep it from showing on-screen.

I sat down in the studio behind a desk, news-anchor-style. I waited for Tanjeeb to signal me that everything was ready to go.

He pointed at me. Show time.

"Hi," I said, smiling into the camera, "my name is Barry Budski, and I'm the President of Sigma Alpha Mu fraternity. As some of you may know, we're a young frat here at SUNY New Paltz. Young *here*, yes, but not nationally. Our national organization is a large, diverse, and well-connected syndicate that has a presence on college campuses from coast to coast.

"With that kind of support and the exponential growth we'll be experiencing here in this chapter, we think you'll find our fraternity to be one of the best investments you can make... in yourself. An investment that will yield dividends and pay-outs for the rest of your life.

"So, come down to Harrington Street and say hi to one of our friendly Outreach Advisors to see the great opportunities that await you if you become a member of the Sigma Alpha Mu family.

"Thanks for listening. I'm Barry Budski wishing you a profitable day!

Oh, and by the way, there's a link on the bottom of this video to a password-protected video that has even more in-depth information about us. If you have your password, you know what to do. If you need a password, come by the house and let's discuss it."

I smiled, feeling like it went flawlessly. "How was that?" I asked Tanjeeb.

"Looked good to me in the camera, Prez," he said.

"How was sound?"

Tanjeeb looked over to junior Lendill Johnstone in the

little sound and tech room off the studio. He gave a thumb-up. "Clean," he said.

"So, I can take off this lav?" I said.

"Keep it on for the next one," Tanjeeb said. "Might as well plow through all of 'em at once, no? Just gimme a sec to load the new script into the thing."

"Gotcha," I said. I was dying to get the stupid make-up off me. It felt really unnatural.

"Okay, we're good to go!" Tanjeeb said. "The TelePrompT-er's set."

I stood up and smiled at Shannon, who was observing everything from the tech room. She was watching, but was also cuddling and flirting with Enzo. "Jesus," I said. "Tan, lemme know when we're good on camera."

"Just get back into position behind the desk, Barr," he said.

I slid into position. "How's that?" I said.

"Ooookay," he said. "Looks good." He fiddled with the settings. "Okay, we're recording. Any time you're ready. Go for it."

I looked into the camera, flashed my mega-watt smile and said, "Hi, I'm Barry Budski, and I run a small talent management company right here in New Paltz. It's called Double B Management.

"Now, like I said, we're small. I'm not going to lie about that. But what that means for you, if you become a client, is a laser-like focus on you and your career goals. Let's face it, in this noisy society, it can be hard to get noticed no matter how lovely or talented you may be. But we at Double B Management will focus all of our resources and attention on getting you the best gigs, meetings with the best, most well-connected people, and we'll present you in the most professional light possible.

"Look, whether you're interested in becoming a model, a singer, a broadcast newswoman, an actress, or just a celebrity

who's famous for being famous, give us a call. The number's at
the bottom of the screen. We look forward to hearing from
you."

"Nice!" Tanjeeb said.

"Sound's good!" Lendill said.

I waited until Tan loaded up a new script, and got set. Then
I gave my compensated spokesman look into the camera, and
said, "Are you an athlete who needs to take his game to the next
level? Have you reached the dreaded plateau point in your workouts, and now, no matter how hard you work out, you don't see
any more gains?

"Hi, I'm Barry Budski, and I'm an athlete, too. I know what
it's like to be frustrated by putting so much time and effort into
something without seeing the results you'd like. So many of us
have been there, done that. Spending hour after hour at the gym
pumping away on the machines, only to see little or no gains
with your physique. You curse your heredity, your gene-pool,
and anyone who is bigger or more cut than you are.

"Well, no more. I decided to do something about that.
Decades ago, people on the campus of the University of Florida
came up with a new sports drink to give their student-athletes
an edge over the competition. You may have even heard of it. It's
called Gatorade. And today, Gatorade still dominates the sports
drink market worldwide.

"I thought maybe we could come up with something better, something designed for the twenty-first century student-
athlete. And we have. It's called SammyAde and it's packed with
vitamins, minerals, and that little extra *boost* you need to get
over that last hurdle in your training.

"Swing by the Sig House on Harrington Street and ask one
of the guys about it. And look for testimonials by New Paltz and

other-school student-athletes coming soon. You'll be pumped that you did!"

"Nice!" said Tanjeeb. "You're a one-take wonder, Barry! Looks good, man."

"Sound's good!" said Lendill.

I took off the mic, and placed it on the desk. "Gotta get this make-up off me," I said. "I feel like a total putz with this stuff on me."

"I hear ya," said Tanjeeb. He extracted the tape from the camera and handed it to me.

"That was cool, dude," Enzo said to me, after I had washed the make-up off my face. "Nice, nice job."

"Yeah, cool," Shannon said.

"We're gonna head to Corny's Cones, get some ice cream," Enzo said. "Check you later. We'll grab a cab back to campus. Thanks for...whatever."

"Later," Shannon said.

I started to feel that rising conflagration again. I mashed my lips together, unable to come up with anything game-saving at that moment. "Yeah. Uhh, later," I said.

They walked out.

I went back to Tanjeeb and the guys. They were packing up our equipment.

"Didn't go as planned, huh, boss man?" Tanjeeb said.

That schoolyard burned in heat wave after heat wave, the flames rising from the cement and painted bases. The wall became engulfed in flames and the strike zone was eaten away by the heat. "Things went great," I said. "Things went fine."

"Really, Barry?" Tanjeeb said. "Really?

"Fine!" I said. I grabbed my Grayman from my travel bag, and shoved it in my jacket pocket. "You wanna see how great things went, I'll go out there right now and sign Shannon to a damn contract! On the spot!"

I ran to escape, I ran to win. I busted out of the studio, exploding through the door. "Hey!" I said. "Enzo! Shan! Hol' up!" I looked around, but didn't see them on the street. Must be at Corny's already, I thought.

I ran to the ice cream shop, busted through the door. They were licking vanilla at a wooden table, goo-goo-eyeing each other like goofballs in love.

I heard Enzo say, "So, what's it like to be you lately? Hmm?"

"Stop eating ice cream!" I said.

"Huh?" said Enzo, looking at me.

I sat down at their table. "Enzo, SammyAde worked for you, right? I mean, your performance improved significantly, right?"

"Yeah, kinda," he said. "Barry, what are you doing here, we're kinda in the middle of..."

"I mean, I told you it would work, and it worked," I said. "I am a man of my word."

"Well, I'm working out more," he said. "Plus, I quit drinking. It's hard to say exactly what—"

"Enzo! It's because of *me*, you motherfucking liar!" I pounded the table with my fist. "What are you talking about?"

"Barry, relax," Enzo said.

"There's something going on with your eyes, dude," Shannon said.

"Don't fuckin' tell me to relax, Enzo!" I said. "You owe me, dude! And what I need right now is for Shannon to sign with Double B Management!"

"What?" said Shannon.

"You can really do it, Shannon. It's in you. Trust me. I can feel it," I said. "SammyAde worked for him, and Double B can work for you. Simple as that."

"Barry, if she doesn't want to, she doesn't want to," Enzo said. "I'd lay off it. Go find someone else. You don't want someone if it's not what they want. Find someone else out of the six thousand."

"Six thousand?" Shannon said.

They looked at each other, and then stood up.

Enzo shrugged. "We'll check you later," he said. "You need to cool off, man."

"Yeah, no offense, Barry," said Shannon. "But it's, I'm just not comfortable with it. But don't worry, I'm sure you'll find someone good. There's lotsa pretty girls around."

They walked out, still licking their stupid coned vanilla ice cream.

I yanked out the knife and thrust it into the wooden table. I placed my head down next to it.

"Sir, would you like to sample our new espresso coffee flavor?" a female voice said.

I turned my head, and looked at her. "No," I said. "Coffee's for closers."

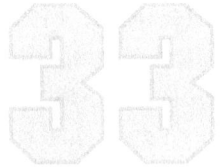

Prinziatta

I had started to feel it when we left McArdle and Shannon wrapped me up in the blanket of her compassion. It was smothering, but the kind of smothering that isn't *altogether* unpleasant. Nonetheless, I felt that it was too much. But before I could do anything about it, Barry showed up and diverted things. And then at the studio, things seemed so nice and natural and one thing flowing into the next that I couldn't bring myself to staunch the flow. Plus, Barry was recording, so I didn't want to start a big, noisy scene in the middle of his stupid promos. Fucking Barry.

And also too, I felt a sense of regret about the fact that I had accomplished exactly zero in order to get Jenny back. The Theater thing was a failure, and I hadn't done anything else to try to capture her gadfly attention. So now, if Shannon was falling into some kind of deeply committed emotional state with me, it would pose a dangerous problem.

The question was: What in God's name could I do about

195

it? It wasn't like I didn't enjoy it. Hell, I was *really* enjoying
it. Why, why, why did I even *want* stupid Jenny Drama? She
was so difficult, so out-of-reach, so alien to everything I had
ever known. But maybe that was just the thing.

I wasn't sure about it, but I thought back to my days
pitching for Xaverian High School. When you're a star athlete in high school, it becomes an upward spiral of goodness.
When it's clear you're going pro, a lot of things come your
way, costless: equipment, meals, rides, gear, girls. And while
the girl thing was cool, especially at first, I tired of it after a
while. It became too, I don't know, easy in a way. I guess I've
always been someone who enjoys the challenge of a fight,
enjoys overcoming adversity. And Jenny Drama was nothing
if not adverse.

And pretty Shannon was not.

Plus, there was the Barry thing, which just added an
additional adversarial dimension to the whole thing.

I was thinking this thicket of thorny thoughts as Shannon and I made our lover-bubbled way down the street in
town, licking Corny's ice cream, and smiling goofily at each
other. I said, "Wanna go shoot some pool?"

"Sure," she said. "The Corner Pocket?"

"Yep."

The New Paltz trees stood barren and the small-town
atmosphere dripped off the night everywhere I looked: the
words "Ariel Bookstore" hidden within the clock on the face
of the new Starbucks on the corner; the tiny, scrappy, ancient
storefronts; the narrow streets with neo-hippies smoking
neo-weed laced with the stench of unrealized dreams; the
shadows of the foothills of the mighty Shawangunks forever
nestled in a misty blur; the journey of the autumn leaves on
the flowing Adirondack air.

We racked up a game.

"Do you ever play?" I said. "Or are you, like, a novice?"

"I grew up with two younger brothers," Shan said. "I know how to handle myself."

"I like playing," I said, "but I'm not that great, really."

"You're probably better than you think you are," Shannon said. She winked at me.

As a test, as a *trial*, I insisted that she break. I watched her very closely: the way she gripped the cue, the velocity of her thrust, the angle of approach, the force of her power. It was quite clear she knew what she was doing. Her break, I witnessed, was hard, and it was true.

"Nice one," I said.

"Thanks," she said.

She lined up her next shot, a relatively easy one, and missed. "Damn," she said softly.

I looked at her with growing suspicion. I knocked in a few shots, then missed one from a difficult angle.

"Don't sweat it, that was a toughie," she said.

"Yeah," I said.

The shot mine left her with was a straightforward one, easy-peasy. She lined it up, and missed it.

"Be right back, babe," I told her. I ran into the bathroom and hovered, panting, over the rusting sink. My mind whirled and the walls and ceiling began to crowd me. They moved in creepy unison toward me like a Poe-esque torture chamber. I released several dry heaves in between panting spells, my body trying to reject the compression and constricting reality.

That's a tomb, that's a mausoleum, that's a sepulcher, that's a death sentence, that's the end of me. That's. That's the end, I thought. That's the end. And I wasn't ready for the end.

A slim glimmer of hope flashed through my mind. I rushed out of the bathroom.

"Uhh, hey," I said to Shannon. I tried to regain a smidge of composure in my body language. My shaky voice tone betrayed me, though. "You, uhh, do you remember the Halloween party last year?" I said.

"Uhhh," she said. "The one at the Sammy house?"

"You went as Queen Elizabeth?" I said.

"Oh yeah!" she said. "You went as a cuddly, corpulent Jesus Christ. And you got beat up by those Sammy guys. Shouldn't you, like, hate them? God."

"Yeah, but that was no big deal," I said. "You warned me not to interfere, and I got what I deserved, right?"

She shrugged.

"But, but do you remember that that night," I said, "you also told me that everything's a fight?"

"If you say so, En," she said.

"You did," I said. "And I was just thinking, I mean, it just kind of hit me while I was in the bathroom. The season's coming, and, y'know, this year I've been training pretty hard and I'm, I think I am anyway, I'm kind of back to where I was, or near it, and for me, y'know, baseball has always been like my sort of boxing ring..."

"Enzo," she said, "what the heck are you worried about? Your eyes. They look weird, sweetie."

"What I'm saying is that you're right," I said. "Everything *is* a fight, and I think for me, for me to be able to properly prepare for my fight, for my fights, just like Manny Pacquiao and all those boxer guys, y'know, I need to just, umm, slow this, slow this relationship down a little bit."

She smiled that reassuring Queen Elizabeth smile. "Is *that* all you're worried about, sweetie? Oooh, c'mere, c'mere," she said. She hugged me, tight. "We'll take it at whatever speed you want to, baby."

Now all I had to do was let Barry in on what else I wanted to do. And hope he didn't stab me in the eyeball with one of his three-foot hunting knives.

Budski

I headed back to the house with the thought rattling around my rattled mind and a sadness spiked through my heart that maybe I should cut my losses with Double B Management already—just consider it an unredeemable sunken cost and don't sink any more capital into the sinking proprietorship. Of course, there was the matter of the eleven thousand dollars from Dad for Jenny's enhanced front, so I'd have to reimburse him for that, which meant even more money down the drain. It never seemed to end with that girl. An unceasing money-suck. Sometimes, she hardly seemed worth it, but the potential, my God, the potential that girl had. If her chaotic energy could *ever* be harnessed into anything even remotely resembling focus, she'd be a world-stage dynamo. She was a high-risk, high-reward investment. But damn if it wasn't frustrating dealing with the market fluctuations.

As I walked through town, I played a thought-game with myself, a little brain strength training I did sometimes, called

"Know Your Ideal Customer." Gourmet Pizza: open until an hour after all the bars close to capture the drunk-hunger market of co-eds desperate for cheap, tasty eats after a night of binge drinking. Starbucks/Ariel Bookstore: capture the hungover kids who need a pick-me-up to help with studying and/or class attendance and participation. Partner the traditional "townie" bookstore with the new brand on the block to reduce consumer resistance to a national chain invading the local market. Jai Ma Yoga Center in a granola-rampant town like New Paltz: capture the new-age, feel-good demographic at a time when yoga has been well-established in the culture as a mind-body-spirit rejuvenator. Combine physical, mental, and spiritual exercise to create a loyal, perhaps even devotional, customer base. Express Yourself Tattoo: capture the "Dead Head" granola-creatives market, including musicians, or dudes who just keep a guitar in the corner of their place to impress chicks. They want a unique expression of their inner creativity in body ink... ... .

When I got back to the kitchen, I saw Enzo loading up the blender, fixing himself a protein shake, I figured.

"We'll be in that market, too," I said. "Soon." My voice sounded distant and fatigued.

"Yeah, g'luck with that," he said.

"Thanks," I said. "Do we have any of those Malbec bottles left?"

"Don't know," he said. "Check the fridge."

I exhaled, hard. "They wouldn't be in the fridge, you Neanderthal," I said. "They'd be...oh, forget it. What's the use?"

"Yeah," he said, dismissive. "Listen, Barry. I checked out this Tucker Max dude, and I want in."

"In on what?" I said.

"Onnnn whatever it is you got going on," Enzo said. "You

told me there's gonna be press coverage and stuff and that you were planning on doing *something*. Maybe ol' Mr. Baseball can help you out with whatever evil plans you're working on."

Evil plans. My mind and body deflated a notch, realizing I hadn't had time to come up with anything even close to an evil plan. Not even anything vaguely diabolical. All I had come up with so far were the broad strokes of an idea without any specifics, statistics, charts, graphs, studies, proofs, arguments, or *anything*. It was depressing. "Well, that's very nice, Enzo, but I'm not even sure what I'm going to be doing yet," I said. "I need to contemplate a refocus of my organizational priorities, and decide how best to allocate my resources in light of the facts about what's yielding results, and what isn't."

"Okay, well, as soon as you're done with your priorities and your resources and allocations and whatever, let's talk," Enzo said. "I'm here for you, bro." He took his protein shake and chugged out of the kitchen.

I went down to the dusty wine cellar to find that bottle of Malbec. Walking past cases of Lafite, Mouton Rothschild, Margaux, Petrus, and Latour, long-term investments all, I realized that a review of my cash flow seemed appropriate. It'd been a few days.

I found the bottle of Malbec and headed up to my office. I poured myself a glass and sat down at the desk. I opened Quick-Books on the computer. A quick perusal showed that the Ebay store was profitable, the gift shop items were profitable, the web design and S.E.O. piece, which was a joint venture with Tanjeeb, was barely profitable, and the pharmaceutical supply was, as always, massively profitable. In the red were the SammyAde manufacturing business and Double B Management. (I didn't care about the SammyAde situation, because I had a five-year plan in place for that, and it was still too early to make any judgments.) The main investments in Double B were Jenny's augmentation, Jenny's professional headshots, Jenny's cosmetics budget. Jenny, Jenny, Jenny. Without the cooperation of Ms. Jenny. I slugged down a hefty draught of the wine.

I clicked on the "Flex-Purpose" tab, and reviewed the contributions we'd made to our charity so far. Only five-thousand dollars to The Fatherhood Foundation U.S.A. I shook my head. We needed to grow and accelerate faster, much faster, so we could start fulfilling our overall mission to a much greater degree.

I clicked onto the "Long-Range" tab. The longer-term investments like the cases in the wine cellar, the sports cards, and the stock portfolio were separate. They didn't need regular management. I just made purchases every once in a while, and hung onto them for their potential pay-off years down the road. But I still liked to look at them occasionally. They were "funner" investments.

The money we saved by *not* going to an Ivy League school was really a great way to have some start-up funding. Gotta say, the old man was right on that one. Without that capital, very few of these initiatives could have been started.

Enzo walked in, a white towel wrapped around his neck. "Barry," he said, "I really think we should discuss this Tucker Max thing, and I think I can really help you."

"How?" I said. "You don't even know what's going on yet. *I* don't even know what's going on yet."

"Also, I want you to know that I'm going without sex till the season's over. Like the boxers," he said.

"Uhh," I said.

"And," Enzo said, "whatever's happening with Tucker Max, I'm sure that having *me* involved can make it better."

I was caught off-guard by Enzo's aggressiveness on this. I

couldn't see how he was trying to engineer leverage. It felt like he was, but I couldn't see *how*. "I think, honestly, whatever it is, it needs to be designed in order to significantly increase the number of pledges we get," I said. "That much I know right now."

"Okay?" Enzo said.

"I don't know if you've noticed, but I've been disappointed by our ability to recruit new members this semester," I said. "New, high-quality, high-profile members, anyway."

"No, I hadn't noticed," he said. "Don't know how I could have missed *that*."

"Yes, well, recruitment is essential for all of our operations to thrive, Mister Prinziatta," I said. "So, whatever I come up with for this, it *has* to involve a huge pledge push."

"Are you including Jenny in your plans?" he said.

This hit me hard. His angle was Jenny? Was it ever not Jenny? Were we ever going to get past this girl? "Not sure," I said. "Why?"

"Because, she's kind of difficult to deal with," he said. "But also. A, uhh, natural attention-getter."

"You're tellin' me?" I said.

"But," he said, "you, like, you're not wanting to get back with her, right?"

"Me?" I said. "No. Course not. And you, uhhm, you're with Shannon Hestian now, right? Abstinence not withstanding?"

Enzo said, "Yeah, well, kind of. I dunno. We're not *serious* or anything."

I said, "You guys *looked* pretty serious today. Are you sure Ms. Hestian would agree with your assessment?"

He grunted. He said, "But, like, what are you trying to do? Just, like, give the frat a bigger profile? Get some free publicity?"

"Yeah, pretty much," I said.

Enzo said, "Well, how 'bout something like this..."

Prinziatta

"Yeah, but what I'm saying is, we can use him for his connections, let him pay for the thing, and then we'll have the pictures and we can decide what to do with them," I said.

"Or *not* do with them," Shannon said.

In her dorm room, on opposite sides of the of the uncluttered space, I was trying to be ever not-so-intimate with Shannon. "Exactly, right," I said.

She exhaled weightily. "Fine, I'll think about it. I will. I promise."

"Good," I said.

"But Enzo, I'm hungry," she said.

"Oh, uhh," I said, "I think Has-Puke is having meatloaf today. Hang on, lemme check."

"No, not Has-Puke," she said. "Let's do somethiiiing, umm, a little bit more, y'know, ro*man*tic?"

"Romantic?"

"Yeah," she said. "Candles, coat check. No plastic trays. Y'know, romantic."

"Oh, *that* kinda romantic," I said. "Yeah, uhh, sure. That's no problem. But where? I mean, are you hungry for Mexican? Chinese? Italian? Tai? Japanese? Asian Fusian? French? Malaysian? Pizza? Burgers? I mean, there's a lot to consider."

"Yeah, but..." she said.

I said, "And what if you're hungry for something I'm not, or I'm hungry for something you're not, or *vice versa*, y'know? Then one of us is gonna be upset, and do you really want to upset one of us? Cuz I definitely don't."

"Enzo, honestly, I don't care, just pick—"

"See, because, I think that the safest thing to do, actually, would be to go to Has-Puke, because that way, like, we can each get what we want to eat, and no one gets hurt that way," I said. "See what I mean?"

"Enzo?" she said.

"Yes, Shannon?" I said.

"It's not about the food."

"When I'm hungry," I said, "it's *always* about the food."

She crossed her legs with angry force. "Enzo," she said, catching herself from saying something. "Fine. Let's just do Has-Puke then."

"That's a quality dining choice that you're making right there," I said. "Don't hate on the Hazz."

"Yeah, whatev," she said.

"And don't worry," I said. "You'll be in a lot better mood once you get some food in that tight stomach of yours."

The Hazz: The sound of metal clanking against metal, glazed ceramics, and hard plastic; the smell of meatloaf, potatoes, and onions wafted in the air; hungry co-eds carrying food trays to over-large tables, moving with youthful exuberance and cliquish allegiance.

I opted for meatloaf and potatoes, with a side of mixed vegetables. Shannon chose to make a few veggie-heavy tacos at the taco-bar station. We found an empty table.

I soon noticed Flipper the Swimmer lurching toward our table. "Duuuude!" he said.

"Flip," I said. I sensed something strange with him, something I'd never seen before. His eyes were bloodshot, and while he normally smelled faintly of chlorine, now he stank of—could it be?—whiskey?

"Duuuude," he said. He looked—quick and unfocused— at Shannon. "Thish...thish guy you're with? He da man!" He burped, loud.

"Oh yeah?" said Shannon. Her face was dripping with amusement at this spectacle of an endrunkened Flipper, a kid who was normally cleaner than clean.

"Flip," I said, "you been drinkin', man?"

"Yeah," he said. He shrugged. "Yeah, couple."

"I thought you didn't drink at all, dude," I said. "You're, like, Mister Clean, I thought."

"'Zackly what I wannid ta tell ya," he said. "I'm on Sham-myAde, dude. Look!" He pulled up the bottom of his New Paltz Hawks T-shirt, revealing a heavily muscled chest and an eight-pack. He looked bigger, thicker, wider. "That shtuff be golden, homey."

"What?" I said. "What's that got to do with drinking?"

"I'm sho jacked right now, I can drink all day, all night, whatev. And shtill kick ash in the pool. Sho, now it'sh da besht. Party hard and shtill come out on top. Like the eighty-shix Mesh."

"Mesh?" said Shannon.

"The Mets," I said.

"Right!" Flipper said. "Anywizz, you da man! Damn, I'm hungry."

While odd, this seemed to me like an unusual opportunity, so I decided to give something a try. I said, "So, listen, man. You wanna do some promos for SammyAde with me? I know Barry'd like both of us to, so why don't we do 'em together. Just some quick vids for YouTube or whatever."

He stood up, unsteadily, unstealthily. "Yesh! Hell yeah! Me and you, bro!" he said.

We slapped five.

"Tell Barry I'm'a ride for whatevah," he said. "I'm down."

"Got it."

"A'ight, later, dawg," he said. "Barry be da man, too." He stumbled away in the direction of the cereal bar.

"Wow!" Shannon said. "There's a headline for *The Oracle*: Golden Boy Phillip Donpiseo Stumble-Drunk in Hasbrouck Dining Hall. How 'bout that?" She laughed.

"Yeah," I said. "Bizarre."

"Hey, but don't you drink that stuff?" Shannon said. "That SammyAde stuff?"

"Yeah, but you have to do it in a certain way," I said. "Barry told me that, too. You gotta do it properly, follow these procedures and all this stuff. Barry always tells everyone, and it says it on the label, too."

"Yeah?"

"Yeah," I said. "Seems like Flip is overdoing it. Big time. Or he's on some other shit, too. Who knows?"

"So, you're saying I don't have *that* to look forward to?" Shannon said. "You stumbling around drunk and showing off your solar plexus to random women in dining facilities?"

"Nah, ain't m'style, kiddo," I said. "If anything, I'm an elbow exhibitionist."

She laughed. "That's good," she said. "But tomorrow night? Tomorrow night, you're taking me out to a nice restaurant. When I'm eating with you, I don't want to be running into random drunks. Y'know?"

I felt that feeling I used to get in middle school, and in high school whenever the teacher would ask for an answer— any answer, even one I knew for locked-and-loaded sure. "Hey," I said, "that reminds me. Uhh, tomorrow. Barry was saying that if you wanted, he could set up that photo shoot for tomorrow."

"And, you want me to go because...?" she said.

"I think it's something you should try, that's all," I said. "See if you like it. You might as well find out if it's something you might be interested in. No regrets in life, that's all I'm saying."

"And this isn't just to get out of a nice dinner?" she said.

"Absolutely not," I said. "In fact, tell you what. We can go to dinner after. *If* you go."

"Deal!" she said, huge smile on her face. "But do *you* really wanna be on-camera with that psycho, Drunk Flipper, promoting some product?" Shannon said.

"Fetch me an *Oracle*, will you?" I said.

She made a dour face, but got up and retrieved a paper from the rack.

"Look at this, though," I said, finding the sports page I needed to make my point. "Since that one loss Flipper had, he's won his last three matches. And by pretty large margins, it looks like." I squinted. "I dunno, makes me think of someone like Jose Canseco. All juiced up, setting all kinds of records, and yet, you know he was partying like a rock star every night, right?"

Shannon shrugged. "If you say so, Enzo," she said.

Flipper plopped down inside our booth from behind me. It

scared the hell outta me. He had a tray with a bowl of dry cereal on it. "'Ey, lemme tell ya shomething," he said to Shannon. "Dis guy? Hang on tight to thish guy. That..." He burped, loud. "'Scuse me. That fastball he got now? Goooolden ticket, trush' me. Thish kid? Thish kid's goin all the downtown, baby. Belie' me. I sheen it happen before, previously. Like, for sure. Don' let the Gunks fool ya."

I bit my bottom lip and shrugged at Shannon.

On the way back to Bevier, I excused myself and called Barry on my cell. I got his voicemail, and said, "Operation Pledge Push is a go, repeat, Operation Pledge Push is a go. Also, Operation Flipper the Shiller may be a go, repeat, Operation Flipper the Shiller is in motion. Also, we may need to come up with better names for these crazy plans of yours. Hit me back, chief."

Prinziatta

"**D**on't worry about it, really," I said as we walked to the building. We were meeting Barry there, on the fifth floor, where there was supposed to be some kind of a loft for the photo shoot.

"How can I not?" Shannon said.

"Just trust me," I said. "It's no big deal."

She exhaled, letting her lips flap intentionally. In protest. "Well, I wanted to talk to you about something else, anyway," she said.

I felt that feeling I used to get in middle school, and in high school whenever the teacher would ask for an answer— any answer, even one I knew for locked-and-loaded sure. It was an all-over tremor of nervousness borne from the fear of public humiliation. I would be sweating, shaking, praying in my seat that she wouldn't call on me. Just the possibility of being called on and having it be revealed that I was wrong, the harrowing shame of being strip-naked exposed in front of everybody, was a devastating enough possibility to keep my unraised hand forever glued in my pocket. The Unbearable Darkness of Public Exposure. On a baseball field, yeah, I knew I could do no wrong. (Preinjury, anyway.) But the anxiety I felt when that teacher started looking around the classroom for answer, when she might, just might, horror of horrors, call on me? That's the level of anxiety I felt when Shannon started to dance around the idea of how serious this relationship was. I knew that path, where it led, and how disastrous it would be. "I think you're really gonna be a natural at this, I really do," I said. "Are you feeling confident about it?" I looked at her, dressed in a thick white sweater and white jeans, at Barry's request. I couldn't help saying, "You're beautiful."

She blushed. "Stop it," she said. She playfully slapped my shoulder. "Listen, En. I want to tell you about something, something that happened."

"Yeah, sure," I said.

"You know Professor Lawrence?" she said.

"Not really," I said. "What's he? English Department?"

"Yes, and I'm taking his Intro to Poetry class, and, uhh. Something happened," she said.

"What?" I said.

"I went to see him during his office hour, and... he was really creeping me out, Enzo."

"Creeping you out?" I said. "How? What happened, exactly?"

"I dunno," she said. "It was all so icky. He was, like, uhh. I don't know. He was being very suggestive and stuff."

I shrugged. "Maybe he was just being poetical."

"Enzo!" she said. She pouted her lips and stomped her foot.

"What?" I said, laughing.

"This is serious, Enzo!"

"Why, because some Professor creeped you out?" I said. "I don't think we need to alert the authorities on this."

She exaggerated a frown on her face, making herself look overly sad.

"Aww, c'mon," I said. "C'mere." I gave her a big, sloppy hug.

She giggled. "Mmn," she said, mock-disappointment in her voice.

"Now, we gotta get you focused. Let's just get you ready for this photo shoot, okay?"

"Mmkay," she said.

We got in the elevator, then walked into the reception area of the fifth-floor loft-space.

Barry stood up from a chair beside the receptionist's desk. There was no receptionist present, however.

"Okay guys," Barry said. "Thanks for coming. And on time, too. *That* is *mucho appreciado*, I can tell you that. Welcome welcome welcome."

We walked toward the back, and into the loft. It was blinding. Big lights reflected off the white landscape, which reflected off the lights, which reflected back again. It was like a whitewashed hall of mirrors. I shielded my eyes with my hand.

Shannon did the same.

I said, "Barry, what the fuck? She's not Nanook of the North."

He said, "Just let your eyes adjust for a sec. It's a theme. Shannon, Dmitri's got some shoes for you to try on."

"You know me," she said. "I will not say no to a free pair of shoes."

We laughed politely.

Barry pointed. He said, "It's just, uhh, down this hallway here, and then make a left, and he's in there."

"Got it," she said.

She walked off.

"So?" he said.

I shrugged. "She seems open to it," I said. "She's not *super*-excited about it. It's not like it's her life's passion or anything. But she's open to the idea of it. So, you should probably take it slow with her, or whatever."

"Well, what *is* her life's passion, then?" Barry said.

"Huh?" I said.

"What's her life's passion? Her mission?" he said.

"Uhh, how should I know?" I said.

"Enzo, Enzo, Enzo," Barry said. "Do I have to teach you *every*thing?"

"I guess," I said.

"I guess so," he said. "Look, that's something you should find out about someone as soon as you can."

"Why?" I said. "Who cares?"

"*You* should care. Because then, then you can design your war plans around that intel," Barry said. "See?"

"That's another thing, Barry." I said. "I mean, all this war plans this and Operation that and the other. Uh, we're not a black ops team trying to take down a fascist regime in a third-world country here."

"No?" he said, grinning like a psychotic maniac with a devious but brilliant plan brewing. "That's a matter of opinion, bro."

"Can't we just cool it with the military jargon?" I said.

"What you call jargon, *mi hermano*, I call a reminder of the constancy of the battlefield," Barry said.

"Whatever, dude," I said. "But what if Shannon's passion is to raise a family? Not everyone wants to run a Fortune five-hundred company, you know."

"Fortune one-hundred," he said.

"Whatev," I said.

"But so what?" he said. "Then you use that. Doesn't matter *what* it is, just that you *know* what it is. See?"

"Yeah, but that's precisely the problem," I said. "She wants to make sure this relationship is, like, serious or something. Like, see if it's going places. Raise-a-family places, y'know? I can feel it, I just know that's on her mind. She keeps talking about romantic dinners, and all this stuff. And I, uhh, I..."

"You what?" he said. "Your intentions are?"

"She started telling me about some Professor that creeped her out earlier, and she, I think, was, like, looking for me to protect her, or want to protect her, or some shit. I dunno, it's so confusing..."

Shannon walked in, all in white, including the new shoes, which turned out to be a pair of white Keds, adorned with "girlie" drawings and accents, flowers and rainbows and such. It was clear why Barry was so excited about representing her. Brooke Burke had nothing on Shannon Hestian.

After the initial shoot, we decided to hit a nearby Taco Bell for lunch. While Shannon was in the bathroom, Barry opened the top of her soda and poured in something from a vial.

"Dude!" I said. "What the fuck?"

"Don't worry," he said. "Completely harmless. Something we have in development. Got the idea from a Seinfeld episode. Remember the one where Kramer drinks some vodka, but you can't smell it on his breath?"

"Yeah," I said.

"And he goes on and on with these fake commercial pitches about being able to get boozed up without anyone knowing?"

"Yeah?" I said.

"Well, I thought, why not?" Barry said.

"Oh my God," I said. "You're the fucking devil, Barry, you really are."

"Chill out, chill out," he said. "She's just gonna be a little tipsy, and maybe we can convince her to do the bikini thing with the jeans shorts. She wasn't comfortable with it this morning, but we need her to be cool with that both for the Tucker Max thing, and also for representation. People need to see what a great body she has. And it's just a bikini."

"Barry, this is over the line, man," I said. "This is date-rape stuff."

"No, look, it's just the same as alcohol, without having your breath stink like rot."

"I dunno, man," I said. "If you slip something in someone's drink, it's not just a prank. And I know about it, so now that makes me an accomplice to your criminal madness. Unless I tell her. Like, right away."

His face became very serious, life-and-death serious, all of a sudden. "Look, you gotta decide if you're with me," he said. "And keep in mind, it'll just make her a little uninhibited for a few hours, and then she'll crash later on. She'll be exhausted. Plus, you'll be with her the whole time. And you're Mister Good Intentions, right?"

"So, no romantic dinner later?" I said.

He shrugged. "The target demographic is high-functioning but painfully shy alcoholics. It's the classic definition of a micro-niche. Anyway. So, you in?"

I felt a severe pain in my stomach, like a tiny Tasmanian devil was whirling a diabolical dervish of pain and angst. My brain started to throb. I couldn't let him do this, consequences be damned. This guy was crazy. God only knew what was really inside that vile vial. Probably P.C.P. or some crap that didn't even have a street name yet. "No," I said. "I have to warn her. This is too much, Barry. You've taken it too far. I'm sorry."

I heard a straw-sucking-liquid sound. "Ahhh," Shannon

said, at the table seemingly out of nowhere. "Hey guys," she said. "That bathroom is *gross*, don't go in there. Yuck. Needed to wash my mouth out with soda just to feel half-way clean."

Barry looked at me with victorious glory in his eyes.

"Me too," I said. I grabbed Shannon's cup out of her hand, removed the lid and chugged down the rest of her soda.

"Hey!" Shannon said.

Barry shook his head, disbelief in his eyes.

I burped at him.

37

Budski

Something freaky happened in the moments after Enzo tossed back the tainted cola. A kind of transformation occurred first on his face, and then throughout his whole body. I'm not saying it was Hulk-like, with muscles rippling through clothes or anything like that. It was subtler. Subtler, and yet no less stunning—a metamorphosis unlike anything I'd ever seen. I'd never *seen* anything infused with so much crimson-radiant joy in my entire life. I thought it both remarkable and disturbing. Watch him closely, I thought.

Once we hit the sidewalk outside Taco Hell, he jabbed—gently, playfully, masterfully—at Shannon, lightly touching her arm, her hair, her stomach. His smile was wide and devious. "See, you gotsta work on your speed, Hesty," he said. "Bap-bap-bap." (Three more jab-taps to the body.)

The lady giggled. "Enzo!" she said in mock-reprimand. "What the hell? Cut it out!"

"See, cuz, if you don't put up a quick defense," said the

boxer, bap-bap-bap, "I can get right into your body, see?" Bap-bap. "And if I can get into your body early, just like Pacquao says, then you're gonna fall by the middle rounds." Bap-bap-bap. "Latest."

Shannon awkwardly defended her body somewhat, but mostly smiled and giggled, seeming to enjoy the fake physical onslaught.

Enzo bounded up and down on his toes and winged his arms in the air, Rocky-style. He danced around, saying, "I'm the champ! I'm champ-een of the world!"

"Yeah, chump, maybe," I said. "More like it."

"Aww," said Shannon, "he's no chump. He's a champ to me." She snaked her thin arms around Enzo's waist, smotherly.

He broke free, throwing her arms off of him. He resumed his bouncing and shadowboxing. "See, thing about a champ-een is," he said, "you can't tie a good champ-een down. No sir. No way. No how. Notorious E.N.Z. in the hizzy!" He laughed, and then half-hugged Shannon.

Her eyes brightened with a special light: The light of enticement, of enrapture, of enchantment. It was the kind of look we needed to capture *in pictures.* And here she was wasting it on Enzo and his silly, schoolyard antics.

I monitored his histrionics closely, however. They were out of character, so I wasn't sure where they would lead. With Jenny Drama, such nonsense was simply a part, a big part, of her personality, her persona. It was who she was. With Enzo, it was novel, and therefore required close supervision.

"Did you know, for example," said the champ-een, "that any of the four big cats—lions, tigers, jaguars, and, uhh, leopards, yeah!—ahh, they can interbreed with any other kind of big cat?"

"What?" said Shannon, speaking for both of us.

"It's true," Enzo said. "Lions can breed with leopards, tigers with jaguars, and so on like that."

"That's not true," I said. Shannon and I shared a look of skepticism.

"It is," Champ-een said, "actually. So, you wind up with these really strange animals, like ligers and tiguars, like, tiger-stripes *and* a lion's mane on one creature, man. It's awesome! You can look it up. It's totally true."

I read Shannon's face again, and it said: I'm intrigued, I'm confused, I am in total and complete lust with this boy!

"I don't understand," she said in high, jocular pitch. "Why are you bringing this up?"

"Because it's awesome," said Enzo. "And why not? And also, plus, too..." He ran over to Shannon and snatched her cell phone from her hand.

"Hey, gimme that!" she said.

"Keep away!" he said, sinister-smiling. "Yo, Budski, go long, man!"

"Nah, I'm good right here," I said.

He threw me the phone.

I caught it.

"Back!" Enzo said. "Back up top!"

I handed the phone to Shannon.

"Aw man, you're no fun," Enzo said.

"Hmph," said Shannon.

"Kill the girl with the ball!" he said. He ran at and tackled Shannon in a patch of browning grass to the left of the entrance to the photo-shoot building. They rolled around, hugging, kissing, playing, falling madly into the inebriation of love.

I went inside, felt my head spinning like a kaleidoscope, and then blacked out.

(Afterward, I learned that the session went smoothly, the shots looked amazing, and, most importantly, Shannon felt comfortable with being captured on-camera in a bikini and jeans shorts.)

Prinziatta

As the spring sun crested over the Mohonk mountains, SUNYAC baseball returned to campus, lightning-bolt fastballs returned to my right arm, and a love-lock returned to my heart. Well, like Mr. Meatloaf says, two outta three ain't bad.

Semzy and I had also reconciled to the point where we could be non-combative teammates. I felt good about that. Beyond the necessity for the team, I also needed Semzy as my catcher. He made me a better pitcher.

"Yo, Prinzy!" a male voice, sportily jocular, full of jock-joy enthusiasm, trotted toward us from across the quad. Shannon and I were walking through campus toward the gym, goofy racquetball goggles around our necks, the rest of the gear in my black, shoulder-slung backpack.

I pointed at the dude. I had no clue who he was, but he was rapidly approaching us anyway. "What up, man?" I said. I held up my right hand.

He slapped it. "Yo, man. Great game Friday, man. You were really dealing."

"Thanks, bro," I said.

"Yo, but why they callin' you Zeus in *The Oracle*?" he said.

"Beats me," I said.

"Ain'tchou Italian, though?" he said.

"Yeah," I said.

"But Zeus is a *Greek* God," he said. "Italians, well, the Romans, really, called him Jupiter. Same dude, though."

"If you say so," I said. I shrugged. "But I like Zeus better. Sounds better. Y'know?"

"Yeah," he said. "I was thinkin', maybe I'd go see Chex about it and tell him to change it. But if you like it, I won't."

"Nah, I'm cool with it," I said. "But thanks for lookin' out, bro. 'Preciate that."

"A'ight, take it easy, Zeus-Man," he said.

"Be good, bro," I said.

We shook hands and he left.

"Dayy-umm," Shannon said. "Ain't *you* the big man on campus?"

I felt proud, but it was a familiar pride. The Return of the Prince to the Kingdom of the Arena. I smiled. "He's just a guy," I said. "Not a gaggle of paparazzi."

Shannon snuggle-hugged me. "It's ex*cit*ing, though, right? Isn't it ex*cit*ing?"

"Yeah," I said. "It's exciting."

"Who's Chex?" she said.

"Oh," I said. "He's the sports guy at the paper."

"They only have one sports guy?" she said.

I shrugged. "Small school," I said. "Sports is, like, eighty-fifth on the list of priorities around this place. They take care of the flower boxes more than they do the athletes."

"Yeah, I guess," said Shannon,

Cutting through the McArdle Theater building on our way to the gym, Jenny Drama, in a nude-colored body stocking and bubble-dress, appeared in the double-doorway, on her way out. She seemed taller, and upon investigation I saw that she was elevated on six-inch, clear stilettos.

"Hey," she said.

"Hey," I said. "You know Shannon, right?"

"Yeah," Jenny said. "'Sup?"

"'Sup?" said Shannon.

"What's, uhh, with the outfit?" I said.

"Lady Gaga," she said. "We're doing a version of *Plato's Apology of Socrates*, but—get this, it's so cool!—instead of Socrates, Lady Gaga's on trial for corrupting *America's* youth."

"Of course," I said.

"Of course indeed," she said, one-shoulder shrugging. She winked at Shannon. "Such a crafty and clever speaker am I."

"Yeah, well, it was nice to see you, Jennifer," I said. "We gotta get going..."

"Hey!" she said. "You playing racquetball?"

"Yeah, why?" I said.

Jennifer looked at Shannon, her bubbles bobbing and flittering in the breeze. "That's better than I could do with him," Jennifer said. "He totally flaked on *me* when I tried to get him to play."

I felt some tension in the air between the gentlegirls, but it seemed tempered by uncertainty. I needed to cleave them. "Hey, since I got you here, lemme holler atchou for a minute, Miss Bubblicious," I said to Jennifer. "Be right back, Shan."

Shannon squinted, hard. She clamped her lips shut, and mash-smushed them over to the left side of her face. She made a small "Mmnn" sound.

I walked Jenny—holding her by the bubbled forearm—
about fifteen feet away.

"So, you guys together now?" she said.

"Listen," I said. "Barry and me, we got something cooking
with this Tucker Max appearance—"

"Is it serious?" she said.

"Yeah, it's a pretty sweet plan, I gotta say," I said. "Wait till
you hear it. You're gonna—"

"No, I mean, you and Shannon," she said. "Is *that* serious?"

"Oh," I said. "Yeah. No. Kinda. I don't know. Why?"

"No reason," she said, with a half-smile. "Tucker Max?"

"Yeah, listen." I told her the plan. She loved it. She was
down with it immediately. Just give her an audience. She walked
away, bubbles bobbling all over the place.

I sauntered back to Shannon.

"And what was all that about?" she said, arms crossed,
sabre-like, across her chest.

"Aw, what?" I said. "No, 'I missed you, En'? No 'You've been
gone too long, Enzo!'? What kinda lurve you servin' me?"

"Shut up," she said. She pouted her lips like a melodramatic
little girl.

"All right, listen, missy," I said. "We're gonna hafta huddle
up on something, and I hate to inform you of this, but we're
gonna hafta also team up with Jenny Drama on it."

"Wait, why didn't you say our relationship was serious?" she
said.

"Say what now?" I said.

"When you were talking to Bubble-Brain over there," she
said. "Why didn't you tell her we were serious?"

I felt the timid tremors of nervousness in my gut. "Uhhh,
well, y'know," I said. "That's not really, I mean, we were talking about something else. The Tucker Max thing. And it wasn't

really about that. You, you shouldn't be so self-centered. Not everything is about you, you know."

"Uh-huh," she said, not believing. "I think it's time to get good ol' Chex on the phone and let him know that we're officially a couple. That way, he could get it in the paper."

"I really don't think that's something we need to alert the media about."

"I disagree," she said.

"And anyway, *The Oracle* doesn't really have a Society column or whatever," I said.

"Heyyyy!" she said, her face enlightening like the sky after a dark storm. "What a great idea! That's exactly the kind of thing this campus needs! Hey! And I need a project for my Modern Media class anyway! Yeah! A celebrity-style magazine! It could be like a color insert that goes within the paper, like, right inside it! And the first story could be about us! Zeus Confirms Hestian as Official Girlfriend! I am so *excited* right now!"

I hung my head in shame, praying that this would turn out to be a passing fancy that wouldn't last beyond the blue-balled racquetball game. That spring sun troughed back behind those mountains, cave-hid, and left everything in its faded wake blank, bleak, and black.

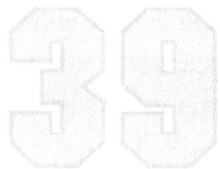

Budski

A wallet? Yeeees, of course. A discarded or disregarded wallet, black and cracked, with a metallic chain attached. After watching Enzo and Shannon's love-roll, I stepped inside the office, and—I'm told—blacked out and fell, hard. That metallic chain—or some extra-sharp kink in it—struck me, perforated me, chinked me, left its mark, its bloody mark, on my chest, on my pec flesh. A discarded wallet, black and pock-marked, hardly worthy of remark, save for its accidental transformation into a wounding-weapon. A harpooned, sharpened spoon of destiny.

After I regained consciousness, I had red-stained gauze covering the wound. I went back to the house to more properly dress it. (I knew Dmitri, the photographer, could get what I needed from Shannon without me.) But when I got home, I couldn't find any Band-Aids, so I just let the pec-wound fester and scar over of its own, air-free accord. As time marched forward, my pec-wound would spring up—shoot up—occasionally, as if the

scar were leaping from my skin to remind me, for some mysterious reason, of its presence. It seemed to say, "Don't forget about
me, Bucko. Don't you ever forget about me." Who in hell wants
to remember a scarring? Who in hell wants to recall a debilitating fall? Who in hell loves the haunt of hurt, the hunt of the
heartsick? It was a mystery to me.

L.O.V.E. If ever there was a four-lettered curse word, that
was it. A phony conception invented by ugly poets to dip their
quills in otherwise inaccessible ink wells. Besides that philosophical fact, the practical side of the matter was that nothing ever posed so great a threat to my flex-purpose business as
"Enzo-N-Shannon." I had plans for both of those two love-
doves, big plans. Enzo was my pitchman, my campus-popular
carnival barker, and Shannon was my Double B launching pad.
But now look at them. If they were going to be spending all
their time love-locked in each other's arms, then how the hell
was I supposed to execute any of my plans? People in love—in
the budding stages of love—can't possibly focus on blooming
business concerns. Not when they're college-aged and not when
they're not money-dependent yet. No, this love business would
not do because any threat to my business was not only a threat
to my future wealth, but also a threat to my business's charity:
The Fatherhood Foundation U.S.A. And that was a threat I
could not and would not allow to survive.

I wondered, over and over, grooves in a record, if working
with *all* beautiful, popular people was this debilitating, muti-
lating, cash-flow killing. I needed guidance, I needed council, I
needed acumen. I padded over to my Donald J. Trump Shrine
and lit a few candles on the table below His Imminence's framed
picture. I kneeled. Hands clasped, I prayed: "Oh my Lord, Donald J. Trump, please divine to me the solutions to my beguil-

ing business concerns. I submit to your hallowed, board-room highness the following facts of the case:

I need to increase my cash-flow and build up one part of my business which relies on scoring one particular new client. That client is now in a serious relationship with one of my "campus-celebrity" spokespersons. Because of this nonsense, their time and attention have become scarce to me. I could increase my marketing efforts without them, however, marketing to *establish* a brand is risky at best, and could result in sunk costs I can't afford to jeopardize right now. I could seek out other models on campus, or in the surrounding area, but Jenny and Shannon are two needles in a very large and homely haystack. The other long-term strategies are for the baseball team to win the SUNY-ACs, and to capitalize on the Tucker Max appearance, neither of which are actionable right now.

I submit these facts to the honorable Mr. Trump, and trust in his wisdom and guidance. In the name of health, wealth, and happiness, but most especially wealth, I shall go in peace and pray for The Donald to be with me."

I stood up, made the sign of the Trump, and then passed out on my bed.

I had a dream: *Donald Trump says, "Y'know, I've done a lotta great things in my life. I've built a city's worth of buildings with my name on them, I've written best-selling books, one of which,* The Art of the Deal, *is the best-selling business book of all time. I've given lectures to millions of people, and even founded Trump University, to help spread my knowledge and wisdom to as many people as possible. I'm a mega-watt television star, with my shows consistently winning the highest ratings on NBC. I'm also a great humanitarian and philanthropist, having given millions of dollars to a wide variety of charitable causes.*

Thank you."

I watch him turn around as if he's moving away from a Presidential-Seal lectern. "Uh, Mr. Trump?" I say. "Sir?"

He turns around. "Yes?" he says. "Would you like me to repeat what I said?"

"Um, no, sir," I say. "I was just wondering if maybe you could answer the question I had asked you."

"And what was that again, exactly?"

"About my business?"

"Ah, yes," he says. "I wanted you to remind me. To see if it was important enough to you to remind me about."

"Yes sir," I say.

"But it's clear to me exactly what you must do. Make a pilgrimage and forge or strengthen your strategic alliances."

"Ah," I say.

"Like with Meckal or whatever," he says.

"Mecca?" I say.

"Right," he says. "Now go, my child, and network your ass off."

I awoke. Strategic alliances, I thought. My pec-wound pounded a pulse of pain through me. It rattled my brain. Like all great advice, it was truer than true but congested with dangerous complications.

Prinziatta

Shannon's overflowing-with-excitement word-stream, her pipe dream to create a campus-gossip rag, halted me. I felt a cyclone of confusion storm over me. I felt that crushed-down feeling again, that oppressive, atmospheric weight bearing down on me. My mind felt like a torrent, a tortured, tormented hurricane of cascading thoughts all surf-crashing into one another on the beach of my being. And I felt naked, like I had no shield.

Images, flash-photo shots of a paparazzi culture being created on campus flowed through my wind-whiplashed mind. I couldn't speak, even, at first, because the storm had such a strangle-hold on me. But soon the words did come, in a tattered torrent all their own.

"Uhh," I said. "Y'know? Are you sure you want to do that? I mean, really, cuz that's like a ton of effort, and if you're not into it, you may be biting off more than you can chew." I bent down to re-tie my sneaker-lace in front of a tan bench.

"Yes!" she said, stopping. "It's gonna be *so* awesome! I'm super-excited!"

"Yeahhh, but don't you think, uhh, maybe, that's kind of, y'know, been done?" I said. "I don't know about you, but me, I think that whole thing is kinda like played out. It's like that whole zine-scene thing in the nineties. That stuff died, like, a slow, painful death. It's played."

"No," she said. "I don't know."

"I think, too, you might be underestimating how hard it is to run something like that," I said. "It's really, really hard, Shan." I stood back up, but stayed, strategically, in front of the bench.

"Maybe," she said. "But, but so what? It's for class. It's just a project. This is so exciting!"

Those storm waves crashed down again against the beach of my mind, washing over my shieldless body in a mind-scrambling rumble. I couldn't hear anything but the watery waste. The smell of the salt water poured through my nostrils.

I kicked my right heel backward, at the bottom of the bench, striking my Achilles tendon against it. The Achilles tendon immediately protested the move in the form of waves of pain. "Ow!" I said. "Shit." I hopped around on my left foot.

Shannon's face compressed into caretaker mode. "Ohmygod!" she said. "Are you okay, Enzo? Here, sit down. Over here."

She guided me toward the bench, and we sat down. "I'm fine," I said. The pain pulsed and rocked through me.

As we were benched, tending to my self-inflicted wound, Jared Besto ran toward us. "Duuude!" he said. "What the hell? What's wrong with you?"

"Nothing serious," I said.

"Hey," Jared said to Shannon.

"Hi," she said.

"I think I'm gonna hafta miss my start tomorrow, though," I said.

"Wait. What?" he said. "Against Binghamton? C'mon, man!"

"Yeah, I fucked up my Achilles."

"Aw, shit," he said.

"We need to get you to the Health Center," Shannon said.

"Yeah, in a sec, babe," I said. I turned to Jared. "Do me a favor, dude?"

"Sure," he said.

"Let Coach Hicks know I'm out for tomorrow and have him get Patroki ready," I said.

"Patroki?" he said. "Shit, man. Binghamton's gonna light his ass up."

"Nah," I said, "he's okay."

"He's just a freshman, dude," Jared said. "He gonna get killed."

"I'm sure he'll be fine," I said.

"Hey, why don't you give him your toe guard?"

"What? Why?" I said.

"Maybe it'll give him some confidence," he said. "To know he's got your guard on."

"Fine, whatever," I said.

"Cool," Jared said.

"But tell Coach to tell him to stay on the corners," I said. "And I'll remind him too, later. But we gotta make sure he's not too aggressive in the strike zone. Especially with their big guys. What're they called? Uhh, Euphorbin and Priamma, Hector Priamma, the big dude. Them dudes is beasts. Otherwise, they *will* kill him."

"Got it," Jared said. "Lemme run to the gym and get with Coach."

"Fly, Marathon, fly!" I said.

He smiled awkwardly, then took off.

Budski

"Well, if it isn't Mister Wet T-Shirt," Deborah said.

"Hey, Deborah," I said. "Is that any way to treat a man who's madly in love with you?"

"I can smell your insincerity from here, Budski," she said. "Whaddaya really want?"

"I'm serious, Deborah," I said. "I'm so hot for you, I think I might spontaneously combust."

"Okay, fine," she said. "I'll play along. What brings His Supreme Holiness to the lowly offices of the National Association of Girls?"

"Well, it just so happens that I have a business proposition for you," I said.

"Oh, good," she said. "Here I was thinking you were gonna make a different kind of proposal."

"Maybe some day, sweetheart," I said. "But certainly not today."

"Yeah, right," she said.

"But it's funny you should mention that whole wet T-shirt thingie," I said.

"Barry," she said. "Don't make light of that. Chardine was involved, don't forget."

"I know, Deborah. Please," I said. "I know. I mean, I know. Later today, I might be—"

"Whatever," she said.

"Well, I was thinking that maybe we could collaborate on something that would help us get past that, a little bit."

"Barry, you've already given us enough money," she said. "We understand you're remorseful. But you're also still an asshole."

"Why must you break my heart so, baby?" I said.

She exhaled as if the entire burden of overcoming cosmic oppression was awaiting her heroic, redemptive journey, and my presence was delaying her from taking up the sword to begin the fight.

I said, "Well, nonetheless, I think I've come up with something that will be a tremendous publicity *coup* for your Association. And as we all know, if your organization becomes irrelevant, you lose your admittedly awesome and radiant Goddess-power."

"I'm listening," she said. "But this *better* be good."

I heard the ring tone for my cell phone go off. "Oh, uhh, 'scuse me a sec," I said. I flipped it open and said "Hello?" into it.

*

I sped—sixty-five in a thirty sped—to Mr. Wilkins's trailer. When he let me inside the double-wide, I said, "Mr. Wilkins, I really want to thank you for finally agreeing to see me. I know it must have been hard for you to do, to... agree to do this."

He looked like saxophonist Clarence Clemons, both facially and in heft. "Son, I prayed very hard and very long on it, you can believe me," he said.

"Yes, sir," I said. My pec-wound itched.

"And it's only because so *many* people at the Foundation vouched for you that I eventually agreed," he said. "But it made me wonder, all these people volunteering to vouch for you, just how much money *have* you donated to the Fatherhood Foundation?"

"Well, I do believe in the cause, sir," I said. "So, it's really my pleasure to donate. You may not know about these new kinds of corporate structures we have today, where charities are part of the by-laws of..."

"Mm-hmm," he said, full of disdain and thinly-veiled disgust.

I felt a ticking nervousness as I stood there, a niggling sense of discomfort. "But anyway," I said, "I'm really grateful that you did, sir. Uhh, I've wanted to talk to you since the, umm, incident happened. I wanted to tell you that I had the pleasure of inter-acting with Chardine on a number of occasions, and she was always—"

"Interacting," he said, *soto voce*. "I heard you were the one got her on the news that time, with that wet T-shirt nonsense when they were opening up that gentlemen's club down there."

"Well, yes, sir, that was ours and Chardine did willingly participate—"

Mr. Wilkins snorted dismissively.

I said, "A-a-and she was amply compensated, I might add. I mean, I'm always about a win-win. I want to always provide a win for whomever we're working with—"

"And how's wetting my girl's body down while she wears a Sigma Alpha Mu T-shirt, how's that a win for Chardine, exactly?" he said.

That jangle of nervousness increased in volume. "Well sir, as I said, she did participate willingly," I said, "was of adult age, and was paid quite well, for doing something that a lotta girls think of as fun and would do perhaps for free or for some beads, like they do at Mardi Gras."

"You *would* say that," Mr. Wilkins said.

"Look, sir, the last thing that I wanted to do is come here, and somehow get you upset. I don't know why Chardine ended up dancing at Rolando's, but—"

"That's right," Mr. Wilkins said. "You don't know anything about it. Chardine was a good girl, always was. My oldest. Her mom died in a car accident when she was seven. *Seven.* Two younger brothers in diapers, pretty much. And back then, I had to work a lot, so I wasn't around much. She had grandparents and neighbors and babysitters helping us out, y'know, but you can't replace absent parents. Not really."

That nervousness began to fade, but a sense of deep shame crept in to take its place. "Yes, sir," I said.

"So, when I got hurt on the job, construction, by the way, where we build shit with our hands?"

"Yes, sir," I said.

"Well, something you may not know with your fancy new corporate structures is that disability don't pay shit in this state. And I got Chardine and Milton and Martin, the twins. So, when she was of age, and she had the, umm, ability, she made the decision to dance because we didn't have the money to send her to school, and she wanted to go. Rich college kids..." He coughed, but in a way that made it clear he was indicating me. "They got a lotta money to spend on girls taking their clothes off and dancing, I guess."

I felt ashamed, embarrassed. I felt like I hadn't honored Chardine enough on the night she died, or in the aftermath. I was busy making sure my business could survive, and she was busy dying. It felt like a massive maturity regression, honestly.

And that hurt like hell—and my pec-wound was killing me. "Mr. Wilkins," I said. "I'm very touched by your story and I honor you for sharing it with me. I can understand how much it hurts, being disabled. The other day, I was injured myself, and while it was minor, I started thinking about how much it would suck if it was more severe, and prevented me from doing all of the things I love to do."

"Thank you, Son," he said.

"If it's okay, I'd like to share a story with you."

He nodded.

I looked down at the trailer floor. I felt the need to run, to escape, to find some excuse to leave and just split, lickety-split-quick. But I couldn't. My body, instead, trembled, filled with an intense heat, and sweated as if I were about to address a thousand people about quantum physics. "Uhh, I can tell you that I know, uhh, what it's like to be waiting, y'know, waiting on an absentee father," I said, my voice unsteady and soft. "And I know that sometimes it's not bad intentions. It's not that he was being neglectful, although, I dunno. See, for us, me and my little brother, what *my* father would do is, he'd make all these promises in the morning before he went to work. Like, 'Of course we can go to the batting cage tonight after work, guys, I promise,' stuff like that. And so, around five, six o'clock, we'd be sitting there, on this little window-ledge thing we had, just watching the street, waiting for his car to come down the block, and it never did. It just never came. Full of empty promises. We found out later that he'd forgotten the promises he'd made to us boys in the morning, and after work he'd go for beers with the guys and drink his head off. So, y'know, I know what it means to have an absentee dad. Sometimes I would even wonder if it would have been better if he died. Then at least I'd have known it wasn't intentional neglect on his part."

I felt a huge, cathartic relief. I didn't generally talk much about my dad, especially not our relationship when I was young. It was a difficult thing to talk about, strangely difficult, but relating the story to Mr. Wilkins, a stranger no less, it felt—somehow, magically—therapeutic.

"Thank you for sharing that," Mr. Wilkins said. "It must have been hard."

I heard a car pulling up outside the double-wide. "Must be Gene," I said.

"Yup," Mr. Wilkins said. He opened the door, and a few minutes later, Gene Stentman from the Foundation walked in.

He then took over his role for the day, which was to provide Mr. Wilkins with a bit of a culinary education. How to cook healthy meals using fresh food, the importance of eliminating poison (fast food, junk food, soda, dairy, fruit, and the like) from the diet, and how quick, easy, and fun it could be to cook at home, instead of getting drive-through poison in a sack. I was just as much of a student as Mr. Wilkins. I thought about how these kinds of things had real-world impact, and that they would be felt generationally, by Mr. Wilkins's sons. A cycle that could go either positive or negative, based on how much access you had to vital information. By the end of the day, my cheeks hurt from smiling so much.

As we walked out the trailer door, Mr. Wilkins said to me, "Barry, do me a favor, please. Promise me you won't do any more promotional stunts that involve the objectifying of women."

My pec-wound itched like an intense surgery-stitch. "Okay," I said. "I promise. *No problemo.*"

My heart, beneath the itchy pec-wound, nearly gave up and collapsed.

Prinziatta

W arm-up jacketed with my ailing Achilles on the bench (our dugout was literally a wooden bench), I stole occasional glances behind me at Shannon in the stands. Brown-winged hawks cawed high above the newly-renovated Bartholomew Budski, Senior Field, home of the mighty New Paltz College Hawks baseball squad. In squeaky-clean white Keds, blue jeans, and a white V-neck with light blue buttons on the neckline, and a seemingly make-up-free face, Shannon seemed—upon upward, benched glances—the very epitome of the girl next door, the goodie-two-shoes kind that everyone in the neighborhood outwardly loves to pieces but inwardly hates like hell for making them feel ashamed for having any flaws at all.

In the top half of the sixth inning, Jenny Drama entered, stage right. Her own costume was rather simple for a change: white button-fly jeans, light blue V-neck with white buttons on the neckline, and white Keds blaring colorful, hand-crafted "girlie"

drawings on them. Throughout the next few innings, I espied
the two girls talking, laughing, giggling, scootching, smiling,
cheering, watching, consorting, conspiring, cajoling, cahooting,
rekindling some kind of lost, high school-era cohortish compan-
ionship.

As I leered at them throughout the game, I grew more and
more anxious. If the two former rivals became chummy, I knew it
would be impossible to *ever* be with Jenny Drama. A part of my
brain—the logical, just-the-facts-ma'am part—wondered why I
couldn't be happy with Shannon. She'd certainly make most men
happy. But the deeper, darker, more passionate, more mysterious
parts of myself drowned out such logical horseshit. When you
know you know, and logic has not a thing to do with it. When
your heart dances, in other words, it doesn't move by the power of
logic. It just *moves*. But I decided not to intervene in their behind-
the-bench revelry. It would have been far too awkward.

Patroki pitched well, dancing through the arrow-storm,
and the game stood knotted, 2-2, as our club trotted off the field
between frames of the eighth inning. Our team rallied, and eventually, Barry hit a grand slam, giving us a 6-2 lead. As he crossed
the plate with the sixth run, I first heard from behind me, then
turned and saw the girls doing a two-lassie cheer:

"Gimme a B!"

"B!"

"Gimme an A!"

"A!"

"Gimme an R!"

"R!"

"Gimme an R!"

"R!"

"Gimme a Y!"

"Y!"

"Because! What's that spell?"

"Barry! Barry, he's our man! If he can't do it, no one can!"

The rest of the fans went nuts at this spontaneous outburst of cheerleaderosity. All of the guys were laughing about it, too, and Barry had a massive fucking grin on his stupid face.

White-hot jealousy-rage exploded within me. Externally, though, I had to play it cool. Barry and I *were* teammates, after all, and we were now beating a conference opponent as the game's end drew near, so I couldn't exactly display my madness. Instead, I channeled it into a request. I went to Coach Hicks and said, "Hey Coach, I can give you three outs if you need 'em."

"'Ey," he said. "If you're hurtin', we don't need to push it."

"No," I said, stern as oak wood. "It's feeling better and I'm telling you, if Patroki gets into trouble in the ninth, I can save it for you."

He looked me in my eyes, wondering if he could trust me. "Fine," he said, after a short deliberation. "Let's hope it's smooth sailing, though."

"Yep," I said.

"You don't need your toe-guard?" Coach said. "I know you let Patroki use yours. You need to switch it on if I yank him, or what?"

"Nah," I said. "I don't need it just for one inning of work."

"Okay," said Coach.

Sure enough, Patroki started to get hit in the ninth. His motion consistency staggered. He looked cooked.

With a Conference game on the line, Coach barely hesitated. "Get ready," he told me as Binghamton's rally percolated.

I ripped off my warm-up jacket. I and our back-up backstop ran down the leftfield line so I could get my arm ready for battle. The Achilles was barking a little bit, but the pain was tolerable. When I started throwing, the prospect of ninth-inning pressure pumped the flow of sweet adrenaline through my body, reducing the pain even more.

Binghamton's rally continued quickly: two seeing-eye singles and a four-pitch walk locked-and-loaded their bases. No one out.

I was ready in the bullpen, adrenaline-amped.

Coach called time, and marched out to the mound. He took the ball from Patroki, and patted his ass. He pointed toward me.

I jogged in from the bullpen, and took the ball from Coach once I was on the mound. "Let's go," he said to me before departing the mound. "Get 'em," Semzy said.

I struck out the first two batters on six straight high fastballs, six swing-throughs. They couldn't catch up. I felt my velocity was down some, though, and I was worried that their best hitter, Hector Priamma, would be able to get out ahead of one. Just so happened, the six-four, two-forty lefty behemoth was up next.

I brushed dirt from the rubber with my cleat, mulling over pitch options. Priamma was a dead-red sitter, but I still wanted to see if I could beat him with the heater—even a sub-par one. I perched on the rubber and stared in for Semzy's sign.

He called for another fastball, my seventh straight. I wound up and threw it, uppish and innish.

Priamma fouled it straight back, the ball crashing—loud and ominous—into the chain-link backstop behind Semzy. He was right on it.

I looked in again, thinking we needed something off-speed. Semzy agreed, and called for the curve. I nodded.

I threw one, but hung it up and out, and Priamma, on his front foot just enough, crushed it far and deep and foul down the rightfield line.

I called Semzy out to the mound. He de-masked. "This guy's on my fastball," I said. "Just missed that last one."

"Another deuce then?" he said. "You just hung one. He just missed *that* shit, too."

"I know," I said. "I couldn't get the torque right. Something, I dunno, my Achilles is all right, but I still can't get enough leverage to break off my curve, my regular curve."

"So, what then?" he said. "Straight change?"

"Yeah, but a *real* change," I said.

"Like what?" he said.

"You ever see a Folly Floater? Or, the uhh, Eefus Pitch, sometimes it's called?"

"No."

"It's like a lollipop pitch," I said. "Real, real slow."

"Uhh."

I said, "He'll either be completely fooled and miss it, or it won't fool him, and he'll hit it nine miles. Make sure you're ready to block it, it could hit the ground before you can grab it, even if he misses it."

Semzy shrugged. "If that's what you feel comfortable with. I'll roll with it. Worst thing that happens is it's a tie game. And you blow Patroki's win for him." He looked at me with a warning in his eyes, re-masked, and jogged back behind the plate. He crouched but gave no signal. We didn't have one for "trick pitch never before thrown by pitcher in real game."

I went into my normal wind-up, but when my left foot landed at the front of the mound, I halted the motion and guided—sludge-slow—the pitch out of my hand, a looping, Bugs-Bunny-ish lob, toward the plate. Priamma hesitated his swing, then tried to re-gauge it, slipped a bit in the dirt, recalibrated, swung, and missed. Semzy caught it on the fly. Game over. Win saved. War won.

I smiled, then laughed at Priamma, pretzel-twisted in the dirt.

Semzy ran out to the mound, and the guys ran in, cheerful high-fives all around.

Priamma's meathead face bled anguished embarrassment. "Pussy pitch!" he said. "Pussy pitch, man! That's a fucking pussy pitch, Prinziatta! Throw me a man's pitch next time, instead of that pussy shit. This ain't softball, man! This is hardball."

My teammates closed ranks around me as the Binghamton guys dripped off our field.

"No big deal," Semzy said to me. "Don't sweat that shit. He's just blowing off some steam cuz they lost. Ain't no thang, dawg."

"Yeah," I said. "Ain't no thang."

The teams lined up to shake hands, only because NCAA rules stipulated that we had to. Semzy was right behind me, and Barry was in front of me. Bodyguards, I thought.

When Priamma got to me, he pointed in my face and said, "That was a pussy pitch, Prinziatta, and you know it. You ain't nothin' but a motherfucking coward."

A right-cross later, he was on the ground. The raucous cacophony of gang war exploded all around me. I kneeled on Priamma's chest and slugged his smug mug a few more times. Then I pulled my cup out of my jock strap and shoved it onto his mouth and nose, pressing it down, hard. "How's *this* for a pussy pitch, bitch! Don't you *ever* talk to me again, you fucking bitch. Just sit your ass down like the rest of 'em, bitch!"

Eventually everyone was pulled off of everyone else, we all calmed the hell down, and Binghamton's punk-ass bus pulled away for points west.

In the training room afterward, Barry said to me, "League suspensions, you think?"

I said, icing my bloody chin, "Gee, ya think?"

"If we're lucky," he said, "that's all it'll be."

Budski

I shook my head. "Why you always gotta be startin' shit, Enzo?" I said.

We were in the training room, post-scuffle, icing our wounds. Someone had landed a punch near my original pec-wound, giving it a purplish aura. Enzo treated some chin-wounds.

"You heard what he said," Enzo said. "You can't let someone call you a coward. A man's gotta have principles."

"Yeah, I guess," I said. "So listen, we got a little *problemo* with the Tucker Max Plan."

"Oh yeah?" Enzo said. He shook his melted-ice baggy, and tossed it into a large metallic sink. He stood up, found some Band-Aids, and mended his chin-wounds.

"You remember Chardine Wilkins?" I said.

"That stripper that died?" he said.

"Yeah," I said.

"Of course I do," he said. "Sad shit."

"I went to go see her dad the other day," I said.

"You did?" Enzo said. His eyebrows banged upward, and his eyes widened. "He, uhh, was cool with that?"

"Took a lot of convincing, a lot of negotiating, but yeah," I said.

"Wow," he said. "Uhh, okay?"

"And I sorta promised him that I wouldn't, like, use women's sexuality or whatever to help promote my businesses."

"Huh," he said. "Well, that's kind of a problem for us, isn't it?"

"Yeah," I said.

"If you care about keeping your word."

"Yeah," I said. "It's one of those whatchamacallits. Moral quandries."

How could I betray the Fatherhood Foundation by betraying Chardine's father, Mr. Wilkins? I felt an overburdening crush of realization that a betrayal on that level was really a betrayal of myself. It was beyond confusing. It made my head hurt. It seemed like there was no safe refuge for businessmen—that once you engage in the fight, the fight never ended. No timeouts, no tag outs, no "outs" of any kind, no way out of the octagon ring.

"But NAG's on board, though?" Enzo said.

"Yeah, I spoke to Deborah," I said. "They're down."

"And Jenny's got her little troupe ready?"

"Yep."

"Well, if the only problem for this is Chardine's dad, then I think you better march your ass over there, and get his blessing on it," Enzo said.

"Easy for you to say," I said.

"But you know I'm right," he said.

"Look at your hand, dude," I said. "Pay attention to that, dumbass."

"Just some swelling." He looked at his bulging paw. "No biggie. Later," he said, and left.

"Yeah," I said. I knew he was right. I had to go back to the double-wide.

*

In Mr. Wilkins's living room, I said, "Look, I just wanted you to know. We're doing a campaign in conjunction with this Tucker Max appearance and I—"

"Tucker Max?" Mr. Wilkins said. "That scumbag?"

"Uhh," I said.

"I sincerely hope, after our previous discussion, that you'll reconsider."

"Well, sir, we're not glorifying Mr. Max's exploits or anything like that..."

"I should hope not," he said.

"But sir, what I wanted to tell you is that we're working in conjunction with NAG on this," I said.

"What's NAG?" he said.

"Oh, uh, the National Association of Girls?" I said. "They're, like, a subsidiary or whatever, of NOW, the National Organization of Women."

"I see," he said.

"But, the thing is, they're on board with this, and they're, y'know, a super-pro-women-and-girls group, or whatever, so," I said, "even though a part of the promotion, a small part, but the part you may see on the news, may *seem* like it's disrespectful to women, it's actually part of a larger thing that is very respectful to women and all that."

He grimaced like he was experiencing some kind of existential pain. "Son, let me give you a nickel's worth of free advice," Mr. Wilkins said.

A skittish anxiety bumbled up from my gut. I realized, also, that I really had to pee. "Okay," I said.

"You never went through basic training, did you?" he said.

"No sir," I said.

"Yeah, that doesn't surprise me," he said.

"I've never exactly been the *Semper Fi* type," I said. As soon as the words left me, I regretted issuing them. I worried that they implied, tonally, that military service was a ridiculous concept.

They didn't seem to phase Mr. Wilkins, though. "Yeah, doesn't surprise me," he said. "But the thing to keep in mind is this. The boy must die for the man to live. Stop thinking about things like a boy, and start thinking about things like a man. Once you make that shift, everything falls into place."

"I'll take that under advisement, sir," I said.

"Promise that you will," he said.

"I promise," I said.

"Because if you do that, all the nonsense goes away automatically. It makes things easier."

"Yes, sir," I said. "Would it be too much trouble for me to use your bathroom?"

Releasing my anxiety into Mr. Wilkins's toilet, I decided that I had just received consent, and we could therefore move forward with the plan. As for the *Semper Fi* stuff, it sounded good, but I couldn't focus too much on it at the moment. Too much to get done to sit around and be all philosophical.

Game on.

Budski

"**L**et's go! Let's go! Let's go! Wake up! Wake up! Wake up!"

I ran through the house like my head was ablaze with hellfire. I felt alive, super-excited. It seemed like a smile was etched permanently on my face.

Once all the brothers were up and on their way to campus to enact their parts of the Plan, I drove to campus with Enzo, Jenny, and Shannon. Enzo's mighty right hand was taped-up, gauzed, and useless.

When I parked the car, I noticed that Channel Two, "Fairly Balanced News," already had a van on-site. We walked from the gravelly parking lot to the open area between McArdle Theater and the Student Union Building. The spot was bustling with hyper-frenetic activity. The sky was tranquil, the air full of rustic, upstate New York aromas. Birds chirped, crickets cricked, and a light breeze blew through every now and then to make the atmosphere just a little closer to perfect.

Deborah had one set of her people faux-studying, and other NAG protestors carrying signs that read, "Stop Raping Women!" while they walked in a femi-circle near the theater. Jennifer had her mini-troupes sprinkled throughout the area. The newspeople were setting up their equipment.

I had the brothers working as well, of course. The "main" camera guy was Tanjeeb, and he and two other brothers operated the high-end camera and microphone. Some of the other brothers operated less-expensive cameras from various points, both as a risk-control measure, and to increase editing options.

A human line snaked around itself outside of McArdle Theatre, where the sold-out Tucker Max speech would be taking place in about twenty minutes or so. Most of the kids on line watched the protestors' antics with amusement on their faces.

I smiled, and said to Jenny Drama, "This is gonna be great. If you guys just do what you're supposed to, this is gonna be awesome, trust me. Awe. Some."

"Yeah, it'll be fun, no doubt," Jenny said. "You know me. Gimme an audience, I'll eat 'em up."

"Right on," I said. "All right," I told the girls, "go get a sign and join in with the protestors. If you need anything, go see Deborah Cacaoux over there in the brown shirt. She's kinda like the leader, or whatever. She knows the plan. And you know what to do from there. Have fun!"

"Okay," they said, and walked away giggling and talking happily, the best of frenemies.

I noticed, too, a few members of the Administration lurking around, including Professor Gembull. This worried me. If they stepped in before the Plan unfolded, that could be disastrous.

Enzo, sunglass shaded, looked at me. "So, you still want me

to just mix in with them, too?" he said. "Or you want me doing something else?"

"I think we should stick with the plan." I pulled a FlipCam out of my pocket and gave it to him. "If you get bored, shoot whatever you want with this."

"Cool," he said.

"Yeah."

"How do you want me to act with the NAG people?" he said.

"Just be a really cool, athletic guy with them, joining in their ranks," I said. "I mean, all they got now is some dweebs and dorks, guys who'll never get laid in their lives, plus the NAG girls or whatever. So, you just go there, carry a sign, and pretend like you're protesting the appearance. Support the granoloids. Gives them more legitimacy, I think. And a better visual for Channel Two."

"Got it," he said. "Oh, uhh, one more thing."

"Yes?" I said, annoyance creeping into my voice.

"How, uhh, vocal do you want me to be, exactly?" he said. "I mean, do you want me to get all up into it, or just kinda lug around a sign, or what?"

"Your choice, dude," I said. "If you wanna fire 'em up, then fire 'em up. I don't care. Long as you're there, I feel good about it. The more legitimacy the protestors seem to have, the better. Better for the news coverage, which we need. That's what matters for the plan to work."

"Right," he said, and walked off toward the protestors.

I sat on a bench nearby where I could watch all the action, where I could supervise everything as it unfolded. I wanted to be able to step in immediately in order to fix anything that needed fixing. I felt a swelling sort of pride as I sat there, observing. It was tempered with a sense of relief that the Big Day was finally here after so much planning and so much hard work, but mostly I felt a big, bad sense of pride pumping against my chest. I had a flash of imagination that this must be akin to what parents feel about their kids when they achieve anything—just this overwhelming sense of grateful pride. A sense of *look at that!* with a touch of wonder and amazement peppered in, like an overwhelming feeling of innocent, pure exaltation and being awestruck at the sight of it. It felt like a reawakening, an emergence from black-white-grey half-death, jumping up into live, vivid, color. It shocked and humbled me all at once, hit me from an unexpected angle. So, I sat there, devastated yet alert, and watched:

The middle-aged newswoman from Channel Two, her straight black hair coming down to the shoulders of her grey pants-suit, performed her typical, faux-concerned stand-up piece about ten feet away from the protestors, occasionally making a hand gesture toward them. The cameraman panned over to them once, and then came back to the reporter.

Two of my Sammy guys were on either side of her, about twenty feet away, filming the filming, getting the context down.

After about a minute or so, one take, the newsers had what they wanted from the stand-up. Then I saw the journalist talking to the camera guy, and it was clear from her body language that she was explaining whom from the protestors she wanted to interview. The reporter stuck her microphone in front of a few NAG girls, did the give-and-take for a while. Then she came to our girls, Jenny Drama and Shannon Hestian.

I saw Professor Gembull and two other members of the Administration move toward the reporter. It seemed like they wanted to be able to hear what was being said.

I quickly stood up and jogged to within earshot.

Shannon had her left arm draped around Jenny's right

shoulder, to make sure the cameraman captured them in a beautiful two-shot, just like we had rehearsed.

Prinziatta was standing about ten feet away, holding his NAG sign by his side, and filming, lefty, with his FlipCam. Jenny started the dialogue into the news camera: "Yeah, we're against Tucker Max because, umm, because he goes around having all kinds of sex with women and not caring about them at all!"

Shannon said, in mock-solidarity, "Yeah, and the other thing about it, and this is what *really* matters, is this..."

Shannon jerked her arm from Jen's shoulders. The two girls simultaneously grabbed the bottoms of their T-shirts and yanked them clean and free over their heads, revealing their bikini-clad breasts. Each of their chests had "PLEDGE SIGMA ALPHA MU TODAY!!!" written in large friendly red letters on them.

On cue, the NAG girls ran over, did a mock-puking gesture, and took off their raincoats, revealing clothes with mock-suits of armor on them. The shirts also said, "Support NAG! We support girls!" They crossed their arms and legs, resulting in a metallic, pretzellized look.

On cue, Jenny's theater troupe emerged, eight girls in cheerleader outfits and pompons, who took their places, four each on each side of the Suits of Armor. They cheered three times: "Rah! Rah! Sis Boom Bah! Goooooooooo Sexuality!!!! Yay!!!"

On cue, more NAG girls wearing all brown mock-punched-out the cheerleaders, who pretended to fall down, injured. The brown-clad NAG girls shouted, three times, "Stop Rape! Rape Ain't Great!" They then did some kind of anti-rape dance, which is impossible to describe in words.

On cue, Jen and Shan, still bikini-top clad, went up to Channel Two's and Tanjeeb's cameras, which were side-by-side at that point, and said, big-smiling in unison, "The preceding street theatrics were brought to you by Sigma Alphu Mu. Pledge Sammy today, because it's *always* just. This. Exciting! Yaaaaayy!"

They turned around, and walked off, arms-over-shoulders, giggling in extreme merriment.

The newser was stunned at first, not sure of what to do. Then the cameraman cracked up laughing, and she did, too. They talked for a few seconds, then walked toward their van, apparently satisfied with what they captured on film.

The rest of the NAG protestors, the ones not in on the Plan, stood silent and motionless, seeming stunned.

I looked at my own camera guys and they gave me a thumbs-up. I looked at the area near the parking lot and saw someone who looked like Mr. Wilkins walking rapidly toward me.

I felt a great sense of relieved joy. I exhaled, internally. I thought of that great George Peppard line from the A-Team: "I love it when a plan comes together."

Professor Gembull quick-walked up to me, agitation on his face and in his voice, and said, "Barry, we need to talk. I did not pre-authorize this."

Then I heard Mr. Wilkins's voice from behind me: "Barry, I need to get with you, as well. This was not what we discussed."

I mashed my lips together, then said, "Jesus H. Christmas."

Prinziatta

I waded through the crowd-throng at the back of the stand-
ing-room-only theater until I reached Shannon and Jenny.
"How's it going?" I asked Shannon.

"Weird," she said.

"How so?" I said.

"He's being... normal."

"Normal? How dare he be *normal*?"

Shannon let out a mini-sigh of mock-disgust. "No, I mean,
it's not very, uhh, controversial. Or very Tucker Max-y."

"Well, what's he doing then?" I said.

"Selling hope."

"Uhh, saywhatnow?" I said.

Shannon said, "He's talking about, y'know, following your
dreams, and pursuing your passion, and all that stuff. Like a foul-
mouthed Deepak Chopra. With Wilt Chamberlain's love life."

"Huh," I said.

"Yeah."

"Like Eminem on *Lose Yourself*? You can do anything you set your mind to, man? That kinda shit?" I said.

"Yup, pretty much," she said.

"Wow," I said.

"Where's the mojo?" Shannon said. She sashayed her hips into mine with a little giggle added at the end for emphasis.

"Beats me," I said. I stood there and watched the speech. Shan was right. It did kind of suck. I guess debauchery only gets you so far, I thought.

Toward the end of the talk, Barry came in and maneuvered his way toward the stage. When Max's speech ended, and everyone was filing out of the theater, I stayed and watched Barry network with Tucker on stage. I could also hear what they were saying because Max's mic was still open.

I said good-bye to Jenny and Shannon, and told them we'd get together later for a potential nightcap on the town.

Barry said, "Hey, man, I'm Barry Budski, President of Sammy."

"Oh, uhh. Okay, dude," Tucker said. They shook hands.

"Cool talk," I said.

"Thanks," he said. "Yeah, they told me that you did a lot of work to make sure this happened, so I wanted to thank you for that. Sometimes we run into issues and stuff, so thanks."

"Oh, *no problemo*, dude," Barry said. "Wait'll you see what we did outside."

"What?"

Barry explained the publicity stunt to him.

"Ohh, that's so cool, dude," he said. "Sounds like something me and my crew would do."

"I just hope they put it on the news," Barry said. "It might be too out-there for them. I'm trying to increase the house's membership, y'know?"

"Were the chicks hot?" Tucker said.

"Yeah, dude," Barry said. "We got some video of our own, too. I'll show you at some point."

"Yeah, send me that, or lemme know when you put it on YouTube or wherever," Tucker said.

"*No problemo*," Barry said.

"You have my email?" he said.

"Yeah," Barry said. "So, are you doing a tour now, or—I forget what you said on your blog."

"Yeah, man, we just came from doing some book signings down in the city. Y'know, I noticed something strange. I really couldn't believe how many pregnant women there are taking the subway down there," Tucker said.

"Right," Barry said.

"I mean, that shit's dangerous. How can you endanger your child like that?" said Tucker.

"Whaddaya mean? What should they do?" Barry said.

"Just fuckin' stay home and incubate that shit," he said. They laughed.

"Like an incubator?" Barry said.

"Yeah, like a nine-month incubator," he said. "Just stay home, eat bonbons, and stop making people feel uncomfortable on public transportation. And then, but the thing is, the worst part is, like, okay. They expect you to get up for them and give them your seat! You're exhausted, it's hot as hell, and some fucking breeder expects you to stand up? Just because she allowed some drunk dickhead to ejaculate in her birth canal? Like that's some sort of an accomplishment? I mean, my buddy Jeff, he gets even more pissed off about this than I do, because he's a disabled vet, y'know. He served. And so, he's like, sooooo I'm disabled cuz I was injured on an airborne operation while me and my buddies were busy weaving the blanket of freedom you sleep under every night, and *you* want *me* to give up *my* seat just because some idiot shot his beer-soaked load into you and you're too fucking stupid to have that guy be rich enough so you can take a fucking cab around Manhattan? Uhh, no, I don't think so."

"Yeah," Barry said.

I could tell from his body language that Barry was uncomfortable, like he wasn't sure what to do next.

I myself felt really uncomfortable with what Max was saying, too. It's one thing to be against political correctness, but this? This was ridiculous. The uncomfortable feeling I had started to morph into indignant anger—but with my right-cross hand wounded, I wondered what the hell I could do about it. For the moment, my feet stayed planted.

Max continued: "I mean, we've been made to believe all this bullshit about how being a mother is the hardest job in the world and all this bullshit, all this femiNazi horseshit. Like raising children in any way compares to having a good, lucrative career. Total bullshit, y'know? You think about everything you have to go through, everything you have to do to keep a good salary and benefits going, y'know, climbing the corporate ladder, and you're comparing *that* to making sure a child doesn't drown in the pool, or whatever? Uhh, no, sorry."

With brute-strength violence not possible, I wondered what else I could do about this verbal abomination. Then I remembered that Barry had requested that Max's performance be taped on audio, for some other scheme he had concocted, one of the six million he had going at any given time. I snipersighted the sound system, and walked, slow and sly, toward it.

"I mean, here's life for the modern American woman: be relatively attractive, don't be obese, manipulate some dumb moron into marrying you without a pre-nup, have the same moron impregnate you a couple of times, *care* for the kids, and really, that's all you have to do is *care*, which comes naturally anyway—wait till the kids are like eight, nine, ten years old, divorce the moron, take his house, a car, and half his money plus child support until the little tax deductions are eighteen, and live happily ever after, eating bonbons and watching soap operas. That's it. It's the biggest scam ever. And I'm someone who's dealt with sleazy Hollywood producers. So that's really saying a lot!"

One of the tech guys who had been running the A/V system for the speech ran up to them and said, "Uhh, guys? Tucker's lavalier mic is still live. You just broadcast out what he was saying to the room."

The room had been emptying out, so besides me, not too many people heard the sexist rant. I couldn't tell, just looking at his square-jawed face, if Tucker was excited or worried. Or disappointed. With this guy, who knew?

My right hand, in tape and gauze, was more like a club than a hand. No good for a snatch-and-grab operation. I knew if I tried to snatch the DAT-tape lefty, I probably wouldn't be able to make a clean snatch. If I couldn't snatch it clean, the A/V guy might step in and prevent me from taking it. I had a tiny window of opportunity and I knew I had to take action. So, I ripped off the gauze and the tape. I flexed my fingers in and out, seeing if I could handle the pain. I could.

When the A/V guy stepped away from the console, I made my furtive move. I snuck up the stage to the system, and grabbed the DAT-tape. My right hand ached with pain as I did so, but I was able to snatch it out of its tight cradle.

I looked over at Budski and Max, waved the tape at them, and yelled, "Property of Sigma Alpha Mu!" with a crazy smile on my face.

Tucker said to Barry, "Dude, you gotta get me that tape, dude."

"Don't worry," Barry said. "I run the house. I'll let him calm down and I'll get you the tape. *No problemo.*"

"All right, thanks, dude," Tucker said. "Oh, and the two girls who flashed the cameras? What were their names again?"

Budski

Of the "Big Three" bars in New Paltz—Murphy's, McGillicuddy's, and P&G's—"Cuddy's" was the new kid on Main. It was the most expansive of the three, as well as the most expensive. It gave you a lot of room to breathe, whereas with the other two, you constantly felt packed into a compact space. The bar, situated in the middle of the space, was also the largest and squarest in town. Enzo and I had arranged to meet Jenny and Shannon there for a pre-party party after the Tucker Max Day festivities. Ghostface Killah's album "The Big Doe Rehab" played overhead.

Jenny and Shannon—changed out of their bikinis and into more conservative garb—were already there, seated in one of the booths to the right of the entrance. Enzo and I went up to the bar and ordered two beers (his an O'Doul's), and then slid into the booth with them.

I said, "This is a great day, guys, a great day! Let's toast to flawless execution of the plan! Cheers!" I raised my beer bottle.

The rest of the crew reciprocated, then we clinked them together. We drank down some of the sweet nectar of victory.

"Okay, listen," I said. "We're gonna have a little get-together later tonight—invited guests only—and I, of course, wanted to invite you guys, since you did such an *amaz*ing job today!"

"Woo-hoo!" Jenny said. "Par-tay!" She held up her left hand and Shannon right-high-fived it. "Wait wait wait!" she said. "What was, like, your favorite part?"

Shannon, her face illuminated with joy, said, "Rah! Rah! Sis boom bah!"

Jenny, similarly joy-infused, said, "Yeah, yeah, exactly! Goooooo sexuality!"

We all gut-laughed like a tsunami of ecstasy, carefree and pure and liberated. That freedom-laughter made me feel like it was the last day of chainy, dreary, droney, boring, phony, heavy-lidded school before the sweet release of summer vacation—a sense that screamed, "Let's get the fuck outta here and run yawping into the sun, the wind, the sand, the sanctified, green-and-brown diamonds of high-jinked baseball death-defiance, our veritable Valhalla for little boys and their baseball (g)loves!"

Jenny, I thought, with a reverent head shake. The girl's just got that *magic*, whatever that may be.

Post-laughter-tsunami, Shannon said, "So, what kinds of mysterious goodness await us at this intimate *soiree*?"

Enzo started talking about what we had planned, but his voice faded from my attention when I noticed through the Cuddy's glass-front Tucker Max and his crew of two other large, thickly-muscled dudes in Nike basketball shorts and tops crossing Main, toward the bar. I hadn't counted on him and his crew staying in town after his talk, especially since New Paltz wasn't a massive-campus school, which, from his writings, he seemed to favor.

My pec-wound, faded but still persistent, itched. An uncertain anxiety inflamed my breast. The freedom-laughter was lost forever as the moment shifted from carefree joy to a hardened awareness of the potential for combative conflict.

The Max Crew glided into the place as if cloud-walking, shoulders thrown back, heads rebar straight.

I noticed an atmospheric shift from the normal, fractured attention of a public space to a communal focus—sharp and laser-like—on them.

The Crew headed straight to the square bar. They were handed short glasses of whiskey by the cute, perky bartendress.

I wrinkled my brow at this, as Tucker was pretty famously a beer man. Confirmation of my suspicion that something strangely sinister was about to happen, I felt.

After peering around the place like a predator hunting his mark, Tucker spotted us and he and the Crew walked over to our booth.

"Barry Budski!" he said. "President of Sigma Alpha Mu! Controversial, news-getting frat kickin' ass and takin' names, right bro?"

I slid out and up, the better to deal with the force of nature known as Tucker Max. We shook hands. "You know it, bro," I said. I turned to the booth and held out my hand. "Guys, Tucker Max, Tucker, these are the guys. Enzo Prinziatta you've met, kinda, and this is, uhh, Shannon and that's Jennifer over there." They all hand-shook.

Tucker half-turned his back to the girls and said to Enzo, "You're the one I read about in *The Oracle*, right? The guy they call Zeus?"

"Yeah," he said. "And I'm not even Greek." He half-smiled. His face looked insecure—a look I'd never before seen on Enzo "Zeus" Prinziatta's face.

"So, what the fuck are you doin' pitchin' for No Place?" Tucker said.

Enzo shrugged.

"Well, listen," Tucker said. "My buddy Cardi here, he played for Cortland, what, like five, six years ago?"

"Yeah," Cardi said. At about six-four, two-forty, he fit the prototype of Cortland ballplayers. They were the perennial SUNYAC champs for a reason.

"He doesn't talk about it much, but he got drafted by the Pirates, played a few years in the minors, then blew out his fuckin' knee," Tucker said.

"Is that right?" Enzo said.

Cardi said, "Yeah, I was taking out the shortstop on a double play, same as I'd done a million other times, and I heard, like a pop in my knee. Torn A.C.L. After rehab, I just wasn't really the same player, and eventually they let me go." He shrugged. "Can't hardly blame 'em. But Coach Landsman, he still owes me a favor or two."

"Um, okay?" Enzo said. That insecure look had not faded, had not retreated to whatever safe-haven it came from.

"And, of course," Tucker said, "Landsman's still got those scouting connects. So, if you really throw as hard as they were saying in the paper, I'll be happy to have Cardi make a few calls for you."

"Hey, thanks," Enzo said.

"*If*," Max said.

"If?" Enzo said.

"*If* you do a little something for me," Max said.

"What's that?" Prinziatta said.

"Nothing too hard," Tucker said. "Just hand over that tape from after my talk, and we're all good." He sipped his whiskey with a confident grin that made it clear he was in charge of whatever he was doing, and whomever he was doing it to.

Enzo looked at me. For guidance, his insecure eyes said.

I just shrugged at him with a look on my face that said, "Couldn't hurt, dude."

Enzo dug into his pocket, fished out the tape, and flipped it to Tucker.

I felt happy that Tucker would probably see this as a major favor, for which he would feel an instinctive need to reciprocate. I had him! For what, exactly, I would figure out later.

"Thanks, bro," Tucker said, tucking the tape into his shorts pocket. "We'll make sure Coach Landsman understands the fact that you may be lookin' to kick it up a few notches from your current station."

"Sounds good," Enzo said.

"And you may want to make sure you pitch well against them next time, too," Max said.

"Right," Enzo said. His eyes, his face, his voice, everything about him screamed "Insecure!" It was beyond strange.

"And speaking of connections," Tucker said. He finally turned to face the ladies in the booth. "If either of *you* fine young ladies here are looking to do some modeling, some acting, any-thing in the entertainment industry really, you give me a call." He made a gesture to the non-Cardi guy in the Max Crew, the one who hadn't said anything yet.

Silent Guy found two business cards in his wallet and handed them to the girls. He then went back to his duty station, which apparently was standing two feet from Tucker, muscley arms crossed, face scowl-scarred.

Tucker said, "Even though I hate it out there, I have a lotta contacts still from selling a T.V. show, and this whole thing we're going through right now with seeing if we want to sell this movie script we've been shopping around the City of Angels. So, anyway, if you're interested, next time I'm out there, I can bring you along, introduce you to some people, and see where it goes from there."

The girls' faces looked stunned, star-struck. I had never met anyone who could paralyze Jenny Drama's tongue. It was turning out to be one of those other-worldly, life-changing nights.

"Okay?" Tucker said.

"Uhh, y-yeah, th-thanks," the girls stutter-mumbled.

"Okay," Tucker said. He turned back to me. "We gotta run, Barry. It was great seeing you, pal. Let's keep in touch, okay?" He motioned to Silent Guy, and he handed me a business card. The card was plain-white with blue lettering: "Tucker Max. tucker@ tuckermax.com," as if any other information would be a ridiculous, useless waste of ink.

"Yeah, *no problemo*," I said.

"Okay, have a good one," Max said.

I shook hands with Tucker, Cardi, and Silent Guy, they left their glasses on our booth's table, and split. I sat back down at the booth. "Wow," I said. "See, now. That's the awesome power of teamwork leverage. That's exactly what we need more of Enzo!"

I felt high from the joy of the day. I completely dismissed the niggling feeling in my gut that Tucker Max had just dealt me a death blow. I drank down the rest of my beer and headed to the bar for another one. The glorious night was just beginning.

Prinziatta

A few weeks later, with my hand and my Achilles
healed, and our SUNYAC suspensions over, Barry
and I were in the visiting-team locker room dressing
for battle with the big, bad Cortland Dragons.

"Barry," I said. "I gotta tell you something."

"Yeah?" he said.

"Yeah," I said. "I'm glad the promotion with Tucker Max
Day went great and everything, and I'm glad Sammy's doing
well, but I think I want, I think I need something different."

"What do you mean?" Barry said.

"Barry, dude," I said. "I'm breaking up with you. It's not
you, it's me, and where I want to go, and what I want to do."

Barry laughed his high-horse, President-of-a-Kick-Ass-
Frat, King-of-the-Assholes laugh. "All right, bro," he said.

"Look," I said, "I dunno why you're laughing. But I also
wanted to tell you that I want to annul my brotherhood with
Sammy."

"Annul it?" he said. "What, you think this was a marriage or something?"

"Well, kinda," I said. "I mean—"

"Look, man, lemme explain something to you, Prinziatta," he said. "See, technically, you *never were* a brother anyway."

"What?"

"Yeah, see, according to the by-laws, you can't be a brother without going through an initiation process," he said. "It's not some magical thing, where I can just say *poof*, you're a brother! Doesn't work like that. No life-threatening initiation, no brotherhood."

I felt confused, dizzy. I stopped tying my cleat-lace. "B-but, you, I mean, you said—"

"Whoopsie!" he said. He shrugged his Kingly shoulders. "Broke m'own rules. Bad President."

My mind recovered, and searched for a vengeance tactic. "You're just an asshole, plain and simple," I said. "You know that?"

"I've heard that before, yeah," he said. "Usually from losers, though, so it don't bug me none."

"Y'know, I've still got that T-shirt," I said. "The one Chardine was wearing that night. Her father just might be interested in knowing his daughter didn't just randomly show up at the party that night. That you and her were a *litt-le* more acquainted than that."

"A T-shirt?" he said. "Enzo, how stupid are you? I know all about your T-shirt. Why do you think I worked so hard to get the Fatherhood Foundation to broker a meeting with Mr. Wilkins? I told you I spoke to him a while back. You think I didn't explain everything? You think he'd be cool with me if I was shady with him? Jeez. He's cool with everything about that night, believe me. He *was* a little disappointed by the Tucker

Max Day thing, yeah, but after I slapped five g's into his palm,
he got over it. Professor Gembull, too. See, and this is what you
never really got through your thick skull, Enzo. This world?
It runs on dollars. We're living in a *capitalistic* society. Got no
capital? Then you ain't shit. Sure, it's gonna hurt my cash flow,
temporarily, that Jenny's going to Cali with Tucker, but I'll
recover, long-term. There's Shannon, and she's a start and then
we build—"

"Wait. What?" I said.

"What what?" he said.

"Jenny," I said. "She's leaving?"

"Yeah," he said. "Didn't she tell you?"

"No."

"Oh," he said. "Well, I'm sure she just forgot or something.
Or maybe she's saving you for last cuz you're, like, the most special or something." He laughed.

"Yeah," I said.

"But don't worry," he said. "I'll give you a good deal on
Econ One-Oh-One when I open up Budski University. We'll
smarten you up real quick. I think I'll call it the Ignoramus
Special..."

Barry's voice faded as the realization of Jenny's absence,
her permanent absence from my life, hit me like a boulder to
the gut. I felt voided, drained, blackened. I felt like a great and
wonderful dream, the kind that had the possibility of actually
coming true once you awakened, was lost into the ether of jet
exhaust, dark clouds, and Los Angeles casting couches forever.

I knew, too, feeling that depth of melancholic emotion
upon learning of Jenny's departure, that I would have to break
up with Shannon. I couldn't possibly sustain a heart wound
over Jenny, and then turn around and fully give my heart to
Shannon. What girl wants to receive a wounded heart as a

suitor-gift? It wasn't right. It wasn't fair. And it wasn't what I wanted. I needed a clean break. From everything.

"Fuck it," I said to Barry. "Let's go kill the Dragons. I'll kick your ass after."

"Okay," he said.

"Yo, check it. Chex said he's gonna record the game," I said.

"Chex?" said Barry.

"Yeah, Charles Excena? From *The Oracle*? I call him Chex."

"Oh, right," he said. "He made the trip?"

"Yeah. He said he's gonna kinda broadcast the game into this digital doo-hickey thing he's got. A Zoon recorder, or something like that. And then, after, he's gonna put the file up on his website."

"Zoom," Barry said.

"Whatever."

"Charlie's Barley?" he said.

"Yeah, okay," I said. "Stupid name for a website, but still."

"Yeah," Barry said. "That's cool if you do good. But what if you get lit up?"

"Ha," I said. "Not likely."

"This is Cortland, dude," he said. "SUNYAC champs seven years running? I don't care what you did against Vassar, man. This is Cortland right here. Not to mention Shannon's here, too. You don't wanna be embarrassed in front of your girlfriend."

"Fuck Cortland," I said. "Fuck seven years. Fuck running. Fuck the Dragons. Fuck everything."

"Yeah," Barry said. "And don't worry about Jenny Drama, man. You—and I—just couldn't give her as big an audience as Tucker Max could. No use worrying about it."

"Yeah," I said. "I guess."

We click-clacked our spiked way out of the locker room, and onto the running track that led to the baseball field. The sun beamed down on The Dragon's Lair, the clouds whisped white and light in the sky, and hawks swooped and glided overhead. The smell of the grass and dirt and the spring air turning summery made me realize that *this* was exactly where I belonged. It was a glorious day for anything, including SUN-YAC baseball.

Chex

"So, here we go in the bottom of the ninth, folks. This is your faithful broadcaster, Charles Excena from *The Oracle*. Your New Paltz Hawks lead the Cortland Dragons, one to nothing. Yes, you heard right, folks, little ol' New Paltz leads big, bad Cortland, in the ninth inning. The Dragons have won the SUNYACs seven years running, remember, and last year in four head-to-head match-ups with New Paltz, won all four games by a combined score of fifty-two to three. So, this game has been nothing short of a spectacular performance, and it's been because of the efforts of two players: Barry Budski and Enzo Prinziatta. Budski led off the fifth inning with a long fly ball to leftfield, which barely cleared the fence. And that's been it for the scoring. And *that's* been thanks to the mighty right arm of Enzo 'Zeus' Prinziatta. He's pitched a masterful game so far, shutting out the formerly indestructible, fire-breathing Dragons on only two hits and two walks. Four baserunners, that's it. And he's struck out an incredible seventeen men so far, with three little ol' outs to go for the win.

"Okay, warm-ups are over, and we're ready to begin the bottom of the ninth. First up is the number two batter for

Cortland, second baseman Luis Ortega. Ortega's one for three so far this afternoon.

"Ortega is striding to the batter's box with an absurd smile on his face. He steps in, and he's... wait a minute. He's pointing his bat out toward centerfield, like he's calling his shot, Babe Ruth-style! Oh, that's not gonna sit well with Prinziatta. As you know, he sometimes has trouble controlling his emotions.

"Semend puts up his hands and calls time. He's running out to talk with Prinziatta now. Probably a good idea for the catcher to go out and have a chat with Enzo before he does anything hot-headed to ruin this gem he's working on. They're having an animated chat out there... Okay, Semend now jogs back to his position. But Prinziatta is stomping around out there. It looks like the talk with his catcher just made him madder. Wow.

"Okay, Ortega gets into his stance. Semend gives his target low and outside, pounding his mitt. Prinzy's in his motion and here's the pitch... and it's over Ortega's head! Ortega hits the dirt as the ball hits the backstop! And now Ortega is getting up and looking out at Enzo. Zeus is yelling at him! He's yelling right back at him! The umpire comes out from behind Semend and is, it looks like, warning Enzo. He flips a new ball to Prinzy, and it looks like Enzo is trying to make his case with the umpire... He seems to be calming down some now.

"The Cortland bench is starting to get animated now, and the crowd is getting riled up as well. Ortega gets into his stance, no calling his shot this time. Semend sets up low and away again and flexes his glove for emphasis. Prinzy winds and here's the pitch. Oh! It nails Ortega in the back! Prinziatta nailed him! The Cortland bench is in an uproar! Ortega...is...a little wobbly and slow in getting up off the dirt, but he makes it up to his feet. And he...*smiles*! He's smiling out at Prinziatta, like that's exactly what he wanted to happen! And now he's merrily jogging down to first base! Wow!

"Zeus snaps at the throw from Semend with his glove. No sign of umpire intervention so far. But that is not the way Prinziatta wanted to start this ninth inning, that's for sure. Now, how will he handle the rest of the inning? Can he regain his composure? Coach Hicks is walking up and down the bench and now, it looks like, yes, Nick Patroki is heading out to the bullpen area down the third base line to warm up in back of Prinziatta.

"Coming up for Cortland is their best hitter, Tim 'The Mountain' Montane. As his nickname implies, he's one huge dude. He's a left-handed-hitting first baseman, with tremendous power. Last year, he connected for twenty-seven homeruns in just sixteen games played. So, this guy can win this game with one swing from his mountainous bat very quickly.

"Here's the first pitch... And Montane smacks a hard grounder to second, and oh! Budski boots it! It was an easy double-play grounder, Montane runs like a catcher, but Budski booted it, and by the time he recovered, it was too late. Everybody's safe.

"Budski flips Prinzy the ball and Prinzy's talking to Budski now. Looks like he's telling him not to sweat it, that he'll pick him up. A very level-headed gesture. And kind of surprising coming from the normally very hot-headed Prinziatta. Patroki is getting ready in a hurry out there in the bullpen for New Paltz.

"So now Cortland has a rally going, their first real threat of the game. Runners on first and second, and *nobody* out. Stepping up to the plate now is the shortstop, Freddie McCartry. He's oh for two on the day, with a walk. Last year, McCartry, in his sophomore season, hit three-sixty-two for Cortland, with twelve homers and twenty-six RBI. So, this guy can rake. He's probably the best all-around athlete Cortland has.

"Right-hand batter. Here's the pitch... Striiike. Curveball floated right over the plate. Looked like McCartry was taking all the way there. With one strike on him now, he won't be. Prinzy to the wind, here's the pitch... Swing, and a miss, oh and two. Zeus reared back and gunned a high fastball right by him on that one. Let's see if he goes back to that nasty curve or maybe his slow change now.

"Prinziatta looks out, checking the runners. Into his wind, and here's the pitch... Struck him out! High cheese! Zeus blew him away that time! He gets the ball back from Semend and he looks out toward Budski. He's kind of giving him a look, like, 'Hey I got your back. Don't worry about that error, man.'

"Coming up now for Cortand is the centerfielder, Dakoty Greene. Greene's oh for three so far today. Left-handed batter, with good speed. Here's Enzo's first pitch... and it's a strike, fastball. Prinziatta is really bearing down now, trying to nail down this crazy, improbable win for New Paltz. He gets the ball back from Semend, and gets right back on the rubber. Working very quickly, even here in the ninth inning. Not showing any fatigue whatsoever. He checks the runners, and delivers. Greene swings and misses, and now the ball gets away from Semend, rolling toward the backstop! The runners are on the move, and they move up to second and third. Now the tying run is only ninety feet away! Oh! Cortland is set up now. The pitch was a change-up or a splitter, couldn't tell which, but it dropped right out of the zone and Greene chased it. But it dropped *so* fast, it fooled the catcher, and he couldn't corral it.

"Enzo calls time, huddles up with Semend. Seems to be a more level-headed meeting this time. Could we be seeing the maturation of Enzo Prinziatta right before our eyes? Maybe, folks, maybe. The kid's been unbelievable today, but now the Dragons are breathing fire right down his neck. Second and third, only one out, but he does have an oh and two count on the hitter. The infield for New Paltz comes up now. They wanna cut off the run at the plate on a ground ball, trying to preserve the win. They know their bullpen can't match Cortland's, so they do not want extra innings, if they can help it. Outfielders are moving in a few steps as well to cut down the runner at the plate if they can.

"Prinziatta's ready on the rubber. Here's the pitch... Swing and a miss, strike three! Another high heater from the Zeus Man, and Greene could not catch up! Strikeout number nineteen for Prinziatta on the day! And now there are two outs in the inning, and Cortland will need a hit to score the runs. That is a *big* out for New Paltz. Now the infield can go back to normal depth, and the outfield can play at their normal positions as well, not having to worry about trying to cut down the runner on a potential sac fly.

"Enzo will go back to the wind-up, which should help him maintain velocity. We've got two outs in the bottom of the ninth, New Paltz leads Cortland one to nothing, but Cortland is threatening with runners on second and third. Coming up is the leftfielder, Robbie Sodality. Sodality is oh for three in the game. Right-handed batter. Enzo winds and here's the pitch. Sodality waaaay out in front of a slow change, oh and one. Prinziatta fooled him badly on that one. He was all geared up for the express and he got the local. Way out in front. Prinzy from the wind-up, glances at the runner on third, and delivers. Swing and a miss, he blew that one by him. Fastball on the outside corner, and Sodality couldn't catch up. Wow, Zeus is still smokin' those lightning bolts in there, and here we are in the bottom of the ninth inning. Incredible!

"So, New Paltz is one little ol'strike away, one little ol' out away from this *huge* upset, which would be one of the greatest wins in school history. Just one more out, one more strike, to bring this win home!

"Prinziatta steps off the rubber and goes to the back of the mound. He is...taking something out of his jersey, looks like a pendant of some kind, shiny, and he's rubbing it with two fingers while looking up at the sky. His lips are moving, and it's almost like he's saying some kind of a prayer. Weird. He puts the pendant back under his jersey, turns around, and walks back on top of the mound. He's on the rubber now and getting the sign from Semend.

"Prinziatta into the wind and here's the pitch... Sodality swings and hits a ground ball past the mound, toward the middle... Budski to his right, he's got it! He comes up, he—he double-clutches! He throws to first, and... it's over his head, the ball rolls away, toward the fence... here comes the runner from second to score! That's gonna do it! Cortland wins! New Paltz loses! I can't believe it! I can't believe it! Budski had 'im! He had plenty of time, but he double-clutched and he threw it away! He threw it away! He threw it away! New Paltz loses! Budski threw it away!"

Prinziatta

The sun trekked westward, as we sat there, Barry and I, still stunned by what had happened, still in uniform, still in our God-damned cleats. The rest of the team had just begun the long trek up to the gym, to shower and change before hitting the road to home.

"Fucking Dragons," Barry said.

"We had 'em," I said. "We fuckin' had 'em."

On his way to the gym, Cortland's coach, Coach Landsman, stopped in front of us.

I looked up at his goatee'd, sunburnt face.

"Tough one there, fellas," he said.

I half-nodded.

"Listen, Prinziatta," he said. "One of my former players, Cardi, he put in a good word for ya, so I was anxious to see if what he was telling me was true. And, boy, the way you were throwing...y'know, you're better than New Paltz, you really are. No offense to the program Coach Hicks has put together. But I remember reading about you, when you were at Xaverian, down there on Shore Road in the city. Was gonna recruit you, before. Before you got hurt. But obviously, you've done a great job of rehabbin' yourself. So, if you're interested, gimme a call."

He held out a business card.

I snatched it.

"If you're thinkin' about transferrin', gimme a call, let's see what I can do for you. Past five years, we've had six guys get drafted. As you know, New Paltz's never had anyone. I think with the right coaching and connections to guide ya, ya got a helluva shot, Son."

"I'll think about it," I said. "Thanks, Coach."

"Okay, fellas," he said. "Good game today." He walked away, toward the gym.

"Pretty cool," Barry said.

"Yeah, maybe I can start over here. Put all this New Paltz crap behind me. Start out fresh, new, free. Try and forget her. Try and get myself free," I said.

"Cool," he said. "See what I did for ya? Who's lookin' out for you, kiddo?" He wrapped his slimy arm around my shoulders. "Know what you should do? You should retain me as your unofficial agent and financial manager. Couple good years here at Cortland, then I'll get you a killer deal in the pros. And, y'know, that would be an even better SammyAde endorsement, if you were up at Cortland..."

"What *you* did?" I said. "You blew the whole game, you—"

I was going to say more but there was someone else casting a shadow down on us. Shannon Hestian.

"Hey Shan, great news," Barry said, looking up at her. "Got a call from an agency in the city—"

"Hey Shan," I said. "We need to talk."

She said, "I'm pregnant."

THE END

About the Author

Frank Marcopolos is a former U.S. paratrooper with the 82nd Airborne Division and NCAA baseball player. His written work has appeared in *Broken Pencil*, *The Urban Bizarre*, *The Whirligig*, *Oracle*, *Scowlzine*, and many other places. He lives in central Texas without a pet. He can be found online at FrankMarcopolos.com, Twitter (@frankmarcopolos), Instagram (@frankzmarcopolos), or YouTube.com/BrooklynFrank.

Other works by Frank Marcopolos

Infinite Ending: Ten Stories

A Car Crash of Sorts

The Whirligig Literary Magazine: 2000 – 2006

www.ingramcontent.com/pod-product-compliance
Lightning Source LLC
Chambersburg PA
CBHW020240180626
46810CB00006B/2281